PAUL SAWYIE
305 WAF
FRANKFORT,

CW01150648

F   841162
   West, Pamela.
     Madeleine.

PAUL SAWYIER PUBLIC LIBRARY
305 WAPPING STREET
FRANKFORT, KENTUCKY 40601

MADELEINE

MADELEINE

PAMELA ELIZABETH WEST

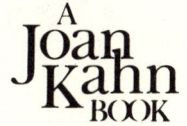

A Joan Kahn Book
St. Martin's Press
New York

Grateful acknowledgment is made to The Pennsylvania State University Libraries for permission to reprint the almanac pages preceding the title page.

MADELEINE. Copyright © 1983 by Pamela West Katkin and S. Leonard Rubinstein. All rights reserved. Printed in the United States of America. No part of this book may be used or reproduced in any manner whatsoever without written permission except in the case of brief quotations embodied in critical articles or reviews. For information, address St. Martin's Press, 175 Fifth Avenue, New York, N.Y. 10010.

Library of Congress Cataloging in Publication Data

West, Pamela.
   Madeleine.

   "A Joan Kahn book."
   I. Title.
PS3573.E8246M3   1983   813'.54   83-9600
ISBN 0-312-50355-5

Design by Lee Wade

Copy editor: Renée Cafiero

First Edition

10 9 8 7 6 5 4 3 2 1

For Andy and Becky

The characters in this story
come, in name and spirit, from the
true story of the trial of
Madeleine Hamilton Smith
Scotland, 1857

SECOND MONTH.] **FEBRUARY, 1857.** [XXVIII DAYS.

The Moon's Changes.

FIRST QUARTER.
1st Day, at 20 m. past 8 afternoon.
FULL MOON.
8th Day, at 53 m. past 11 afternoon.
LAST QUARTER.
17th Day, at 19 m. past 2 morning.
NEW MOON.
24th Day, at 58 m. past 11 morning.

Length of Days.

M.D.	Equation of time. Add to time shown by sun-dial.	L. of Day.	Day's incr.	Day brk.	Twil. ends.
1	14m.	9 4	1 20	5 44	6 45
6	14	9 22	1 38	5 37	6 52
11	15	9 40	1 56	5 31	7 1
16	14	9 58	2 14	5 21	7 9
21	14	10 17	2 33	5 13	7 17
26	13	10 37	2 53	5 2	7 25

D of M	D of W	Remarkable Days. Mean Periodic Phenomena in Cambridgeshire (Rev. J. Jenyns' Obs. Nat. Hist.)—(see ante, p. 4.)	SUN. Rises. h. m.	Sets. h. m.	MOON. Rises. h. m.	Sets. h. m.	D of Y
1	S	4 Sunday after Epiphany	7 41	4 47	10 4	0 15	32
2	M	Candlemas	7 40	4 49	10 23	1 43	33
3	T	Pied wagtail first seen	7 38	4 51	10 54	3 8	34
4	W	Field Speedwell fl.	7 37	4 53	11 37	4 29	35
5	T	Spurge Laurel fl.	7 35	4 54	0 36	5 39	36
6	F	The Water Eft seen	7 33	4 56	1 45	6 36	37
7	S	Blackbird s. c.	7 32	4 58	3 2	7 17	38
8	S	Septuagesima Sunday.	7 30	5 0	4 22	7 45	39
9	M	Pigeon lays; Primrose fl.	7 28	5 2	5 43	8 2	40
10	T	Gold-crested Wren s. c.	7 26	5 4	6 59	8 14	41
11	W	Partridges pair ; Elder l.	7 25	5 5	8 9	8 25	42
12	T	Red dead Nettle fl.	7 23	5 7	9 21	8 35	43
13	F	Yellow Hammer s. c. [fl.	7 21	5 9	10 31	8 43	44
14	S	Honeysuckle l.; Dandelion	7 19	5 11	11 41	8 52	45
15	S	Sexagesima Sunday.	7 17	5 13	morn.	9 4	46
16	M	Spring Crocus fl.	7 15	5 14	0 54	9 20	47
17	T	Greenfinch s. c.	7 13	5 16	2 8	9 42	48
18	W	White Alysson fl. (Forster)	7 11	5 18	3 16	10 16	49
19	T	Daisy fl. (Forster)	7 9	5 20	4 24	11 2	50
20	F	Lesser Periwinkle fl.	7 7	5 22	5 21	0 2	51
21	S	Ring-Dove coos	7 5	5 24	6 7	1 14	52
22	S	Quinquagesima or Sh. Sun.	7 3	5 25	6 42	2 36	53
23	M	Brittle Willow fl.	7 1	5 27	7 4	4 6	54
24	T	Shrove Tuesday	6 59	5 29	7 19	5 34	55
25	W	Ash Wed.	6 57	5 31	7 32	7 1	56
26	T	S.-scented Coltsfoot fl.	6 55	5 33	7 46	8 29	57
27	F	Hare Hunting ends	6 53	5 34	7 57	9 58	58
28	S	Alder and Yew fl.	6 51	5 46	8 11	11 25	59

MEAN TEMPERATURE OF THE MONTH, at Greenwich.— (See ante p. 4)—
Of the month 38.80
Lowest at night 33.76
Highest daily 44.01
Daily variation 10.25
Highest mean 43.98
Lowest mean 32.33

FOREIGN FARMING.
S Caroli.—Potato plantd. N. Zealand—Potato crop harvested ; cucumbers ready ; plums ripe; pruning time.
Jersey—Parsnip crop sow. China—Earliest tea pick. Bengal—Sug. canes plnt.

MEAN TEMPERATURE—FEB.
England 39.6
Toronto 23.71
Philadelphia .. 29.4
Bahamas 73.0
New Zealand .. 67.0
Paris 39.54
Berlin 31.66
St. Petersburg 18.68
Vienna 33.53
Sebastopol ... 36.52
Cairo 56.12
Messina 54.21
Turin 36.3
Madrid 44.42
Lisbon 53.6
Jerusalem 53.73

THIRD MONTH.] MARCH, 1857. [XXXI DAYS.

The Moon's Changes.

FIRST QUARTER.
3rd Day, at 30 m. past 4 morning.
FULL MOON.
10th Day, at 17 m. past 4 afternoon.
LAST QUARTER.
18th Day, at 3 m. past 9 afternoon.
NEW MOON.
25th Day, at 23 m. past 10 afternoon.

Length of Days.

M.D.	Equation of time. Add to time shown by sun-dial.	L. of Day.	Day's incr.	Day brk.	Twil. ends.
1	13m.	10 48	3 4	4 56	7 32
6	11	11 8	3 24	4 45	7 40
11	10	11 28	3 44	4 33	7 49
16	9	11 47	4 3	4 21	7 58
21	7	12 8	4 24	4 8	8 8
26	6	12 27	4 43	4 55	8 18

D of M	D of W	Remarkable Days. Mean Periodic Phenomena in Cambridgeshire (Rev. J. Jenyns' Obs. Nat. Hist.)	SUN Rises. h. m.	SUN Sets. h. m.	MOON Rises. h. m.	MOON Sets. h. m.	D of Y
1	S	1st Sun. in Lent. St. David	6 46	5 50	8 25	morn.	60
2	M	The Pilewort fl.	6 44	5 42	8 54	0 59	61
3	T	Wild Goose departs	6 42	5 43	9 33	2 20	62
4	W	Mistletoe fl. Lady-birds ap.	6 40	5 45	10 28	3 34	63
5	T	Stock Dove n. c.	6 37	5 47	11 35	4 34	64
6	F	The Dor Beetle ap.	6 35	5 48	0 47	5 29	65
7	S	Pigeons hatch; Violet fl.	6 33	5 50	2 7	5 51	66
8	S	2nd Sunday in Lent.	6 31	5 52	3 26	6 11	67
9	M	Gossamer floats	6 29	5 54	4 42	6 23	68
10	T	The Apricot fl.	6 26	5 55	5 55	6 32	69
11	W	The Ivy-leaved Speedwell	6 24	5 57	7 6	6 43	70
12	T	The Peach and Daffodil fl.	6 22	5 59	8 16	6 52	71
13	F	Coltsfoot fl.	6 20	6 0	9 26	7 0	72
14	S	Gnat and Red Ant ap.	6 17	6 2	10 38	7 11	73
15	S	3rd Sunday in Lent	6 15	6 4	11 53	7 24	74
16	M	Woodcock last seen.	6 13	6 6	morn.	7 43	75
17	T	St. Patrick's Day	6 10	6 7	1 4	8 18	76
18	W	Dog Rose and Lilac l.	6 8	6 9	2 13	8 52	77
19	T	Black Currant l.	6 6	6 11	3 9	9 45	78
20	F	Humble Bee & Banded Snail	6 4	6 12	4 0	10 50	79
21	S	Elm fl.; Sweet Briar l. [ap.	6 1	6 14	4 40	0 6	80
22	S	4th Sunday in Lent.	5 59	6 16	5 7	1 30	81
23	M	Creeping Crowfoot fl.	5 57	6 17	5 24	2 59	82
24	T	Hyacinth fl.	5 55	6 19	5 46	4 27	83
25	W	LADY DAY	5 52	6 21	5 50	5 56	84
26	T	White Poplar fl.	5 50	6 22	6 2	7 26	85
27	F	Geese hatch; Almond fl.	5 48	6 24	6 17	8 57	86
28	S	Gooseberry fl.; Hazel l.	5 45	6 26	6 32	10 31	87
29	S	5th Sunday in Lent	5 43	6 27	6 55	morn.	88
30	M	Lampern fishing ends	5 41	6 29	7 31	0 2	89
31	T	Cowslip fl. Horse Chestnut l.	5 39	6 31	8 21	1 22	90

MEAN TEMPERATURE OF THE MONTH, at Greenwich.—
(See ante p. 4)—
Of the month 42.04
Lowest at night............ 35.73
Highest daily.............. 48.52
Daily variation............ 12.79
Highest mean............... 47.10
Lowest mean................ 35.37

FOREIGN FARMING.
S. Caroli.—Cotton plntd.
Calcutta — Hot season commences; apples and pears ripe
Milan — Sewage water meads—2nd cutting
Borneo—Hot season com.
New Zealand — Autumn

MEAN TEMPERATURE-MARC.
England........ 42.0   Vienna 40.8
Toronto .... 30.37   Sebastopol 42.37
Philadelphia .. 38.78   Cairo 64.58
Bahamas .... 73.0   Messina .. 56.66
New Zealand . 65.0   Turin 44.56
Paris .... 43.99   Madrid ... 48.2
Berlin .... 38.17   Lisbon.... 56.3
St. Petersb.... 25.5   Jerusalem. 60.01

MADELEINE

ONE

Inside the carriage, Madeleine sat erect across from the blue-coated officer. He sat stiffly, his stovepipe hat held on his knee.

Madeleine closed her eyes and let her body sway with the movement of the horses. Their hooves clacked through the night. Soon the horses would reach the crossroads.

She sighed, just a breath, and opened her eyes, smoothed her grey skirt. Tomorrow, of course, they would let her put on fine silk, but for the passage, she was dressed in prison muslin.

Her hands fell to cover the rough seam. She smiled, remembering the seamstress, years ago, kneeling beside the stool on which Madeleine was standing, talking between pins of the Princess Royal. And afterwards, when she was behind the green davenport playing dolls, talk of a man and woman, an Albert and a Victoria, talk of their marriage bed. And the seamstress confiding, as she ripped out a seam, that she was a cross-eyed seamstress: that she couldn't even "mend straight." And Mama laughing that sudden laugh.

Would they laugh like that—the people in the court—when her letters were read? Would she, even if she were let go, all her life be followed by snickers?

It would be better perhaps to hang her. Would they do it in Glasgow or in Edinburgh? Would the watchers be strangers or friends? She could see herself, head swaddled in black, her hands behind her. . . . No, she wouldn't think of it. Not unless she had to.

She listened to the horses' hooves, strike against strike upon the worn road.

The horses slowed. In the faint glow of the carriage lantern she saw ahead, parked by the side of the crossroads, the tall van and the double team of four black horses.

The carriage stopped.

The officer opened the door, climbed out, and offered his hand.

She lifted her skirt and stepped down.

A tall man, not young, erect and graceful, with salt-and-pepper hair framing a noble face, stepped forward. He was dressed in black—like a minister—with a white collar and dark tie.

"Miss Smith?" he said, his voice clear without being sharp. "I am John Inglis, the barrister your father engaged. I thought perhaps it would ease the situation if I were to accompany you on this latter part of your journey."

She offered her gloved hand.

He walked beside her to the waiting van, helped her in as if it were a liveried coach. He seated himself across from her. She looked once through the window, at the lights of her carriage, which had already begun its circle in the middle of the road, then out the other window, towards the Edinburgh road.

The sun came up as they rode. The shadows fell off from around their faces.

Inglis yawned.

She rubbed her eyes, blinked.

He was looking at her intently.

She met his gaze.

"An infinity of reflecting mirrors, that's what you and I are, *chérie*," Emile had said to her once. What was she now?

The eyes she met did not scold her, did not fall away. They were not Glasgow eyes. They were impartial.

Inglis smiled.

"I think you shall wear a light veil tomorrow," he said.

She nodded, looked down.

2

TWO

There was already a long line when the doors opened at eight that Tuesday. Policemen in blue stovepipe hats stood on either side of the massive doors. They had had strict orders from the Sheriff of Lanarkshire not to accept money; still, it seemed it was the rich who passed into the courtroom.

The less fortunate who found places in the square across the street traded theories.

"Suicide," said a gentleman in a grey top hat.

"Hah," one in a blue redingote said. "Involuntary."

"Hear!" said a third, stroking his muttonchop whiskers.

The first said, "Have you seen her?"

The others shook their heads.

"Well, wait till you see her, fools, then let me hear you call it murder."

"Well, I'll give you they won't hang her. It'll be a Scots verdict, and I'm willing to wager on it."

"A Scots verdict?" a man carrying a portmanteau asked his companion.

"Not proven," the companion said.

As the three men in the circle made their wagers, the two onlookers turned away, made their way across the square towards St. Giles' Cathedral.

The companion held out his hand.

"'Not proven' means that the prisoner is not guilty, and"—he slapped his hand—"please don't do it again."

The High Court of Judiciary began at ten. The courtroom was packed. In the pit below the judges' stand, lawyers were bowed over thick, leather-bound briefs.

A murmur ran from floor to gallery; the room hushed as the prisoner was led in. The scratchings of the reporters' quills fell silent.

Madeleine wore a rich chocolate-brown silk dress, lavender gloves, a narrow scoop bonnet with the veil gathered above, a sprig of white heather at the crown. White heather, the symbol of good luck, did not go unnoticed by the reporters.

The police matron in grey beside Madeleine was mannish, hatchet-faced. The two women took their places before the bar.

"Silence!" the court officer called. The massive doors opened and the judges entered, taking their places beyond the austere curved arch.

"Court is in session," the court officer intoned.

The Lord Justice-Clerk Hope cleared his throat.

Lord Hope was sixty-three, a handsome man with an aristocratic, aquiline face.

The audience looked at him, admired his scarlet silks and ermine tippet.

The reporters looked at Madeleine. Young Don Campbell of the *Scotch Thistle* wrote: "Face full of character and breeding: good bones, nice skin, dark grey eyes."

"Court is in session," Lord Hope said, his voice a polished bass.

The prosecutor, Lord Advocate Moncreiff, stood now, nodded once at the audience, walked before the bench, looked up.

Lord Hope smiled down at him, then looked over at the Dean of Faculty. John Inglis nodded and stacked his papers on the table.

Moncreiff raised the parchment sheet. Forty-five years old, son of Sir James Wellwood Moncreiff, ninth baron of Tullibole, he had been raised amongst lawyers, weaned on talk of the trial of the famous body snatchers, Burke and Hare.

The matron's hand emerged from beneath her black Spanish lace shawl, clutching a vial of smelling salts. Moncreiff nodded to the judge and adjusted his sausage-curl wig.

"Place the prisoner before the bar," Lord Hope said. Two policemen led her forwards. Her step was light.

"Madeleine Hamilton Smith," Moncreiff began, "You are charged with two counts of attempted murder and one count of murder, in that: one, on February 19th or 20th, of the year 1857, anno Domini, you did administer arsenic or other poison to Pierre Emile L'Angelier; two, on February 22nd or 23rd, you did again administer arsenic or other poison to the same; three, on the third occasion, on or about Sunday, March 22nd, you did, by means of arsenic, murder the aforesaid Pierre Emile L'Angelier."

Moncreiff turned to the second page of parchment.

He read the indictment he had drawn up: "Madeleine Smith or Madeleine Hamilton Smith, now or lately prisoner in the prison of Glasgow, you are indicted and accused, at the instance of James Moncreiff, Esquire, Her Majesty's Advocate for Her Majesty's interest; that albeit. . . ."

Madeleine met the charge levelly, her shoulders erect. Only when Moncreiff looked away from her, towards the jury, did her glance shift. She looked over at the table for the defence, at John Inglis.

Inglis was almost smiling

". . . by the laws of this and every other well-governed realm, you did wickedly and feloniously, administer, or cause to be taken, arsenic, with intent to murder the deceased, Pierre Emile L'Angelier. . . ."

Oh, Moncreiff, Inglis was thinking, "wicked and felonious"! For this pretty head?

As Moncreiff finished reading, Inglis shifted in his seat, looked over at Madeleine.

". . . ought to be punished with the pains of law; to deter others from committing the like crime in all time coming."

Lord Hope leaned forward. "And now," he said, "the accused may step forward."

Madeleine Hamilton Smith lifted her skirt a fraction of an inch and stepped to the bar.

"How does the prisoner plead to the indictment?"

Madeleine lifted her chin and said in a distinct and unshaken voice:

"Not guilty."

THREE

The jury was empanelled. On the whole, Inglis thought, he had done quite well.

He surveyed the men as they filed into the three rows of raised seats: Charles Scott King, a writer from Shakespeare Square; Alexander Momson, currier; a merchant from York named Combe; a farmer named Kilpunt; Hugh Hunter, cabinetmaker from NW Circus; Robert Andrew, cow feeder; William Moffat, teacher from Duke Street; David Forbes from Scotland Street; Mr. Alexander from Torphichen; a Sharp; a Weir; a Parkside clerk; two more farmers; and a Glover Street shoemaker.

He was satisfied. The fifteen men were of all ages, trades, and whiskers, but they were of one decided cast: gentlemen all . . . and all with an eye, as far as he could discern, for the ladies.

The jury in place, Moncreiff called the first witness to the stand: Archibald Smith, Esquire, Sheriff Substitute of Lanarkshire, Glasgow. No relation to the prisoner.

Moncreiff held a parchment before the witness.

"Do you recognize this document?"

"Yes," Smith said. "It is the prisoner's declaration of Tuesday, March 31st."

"It is signed by the prisoner?"

"Yes," Smith said. "In my presence."

Moncreiff turned to Lord Hope.

"Your Honor, it if please the court, I would now like to read the prisoner's declaration into the record."*

Lord Hope nodded.

Moncreiff cleared his throat and held the paper on high:

My name is Madeleine Smith. I am a native of Glasgow, twenty-one years of age; and I reside with my father, James Smith, architect, at No. 7 Blythswood Square, Glasgow. For about the last two years I have been acquainted with P. Emile L'Angelier, who was in the employment of W. B. Huggins and Company, and who lodged at 11 Franklin Place. He recently paid his addresses to me, and I have met with him on a variety of occasions. I had not seen M. L'Angelier for about three weeks before his death, and the last time I saw him was on a night about half-past ten. On that occasion, he tapped at my bedroom window, which is on the ground floor, and fronts Mains Street. I talked to him from the window, which is stanchioned outside, and I did not go out to him, nor did he come in to me. This occasion was the last time I saw him. He was in the habit of writing notes to me, and I was in the habit of replying to him by notes. The last note I wrote to him was on the Friday before his death, viz., Friday, the 20th March current. In consequence of that note, I expected him to visit me on Saturday night, the 21st current, at my bedroom window, but he did not come, and sent no notice. There was no tapping at my window on said Saturday night, or on the following night, being Sunday.

In the course of my meetings with L'Angelier, he and I had arranged to get married, and we had, at one time, proposed September last as the time the marriage was to take

---

*At this time, a defendant was not permitted to take the stand.

7

place, and subsequently, the month of March was spoken of. It was proposed that we should reside in furnished lodgings. He was very unwell for some time, and had gone to Bridge of Allan for his health; and he complained of sickness, but I have no idea what was the cause of it. I remember giving him some cocoa from my window one night some time ago, but I cannot specify the time. He took the cup in his hand, and barely tasted the contents; and I gave him no bread to it. I was taking some cocoa myself at the time, and had prepared it myself. As I attributed his sickness to want of food, I proposed to give him a loaf of bread, but I said that merely in a joke, and, in point of fact, I never gave him any bread. I have bought arsenic on various occasions. The last I bought was sixpence worth, which I bought in Currie, the apothecary's, in Sauchiehall Street, and prior to that, I bought two quantities of arsenic—one of these in Currie's, and the other in Murdoch's. I used it all as a cosmetic, and applied it to my face, neck, and arms, diluted with water. The arsenic I got in Currie's shop I got there on Wednesday, the 18th March, and I used it all on one occasion, having put it all in the basin where I was to wash myself. I had been advised to the use of the arsenic by a young lady, the daughter of an actress, and I had also seen the use of it recommended in the newspapers. The young lady's name was Guibilei, and I had met her at school at Clapton, near London. I did not wish any of my father's family to be aware that I was using the arsenic and, therefore, never mentioned it to any of them; and I don't suppose they or any of the servants ever noticed any of it in the basin. When I bought the arsenic in Murdoch's I am not sure whether I was asked or not what it was for, but I think I said it was for a gardener to kill rats or destroy vermin around flowers, and I only said this because I did not wish them to know that I was going to use it as a cosmetic. On all the three occasions, as required in the shop, I signed my name to a book in which the sales were entered. For several years past Mr. Minnoch, of the firm of William Houldsworth & Co., has been coming a good deal about my father's house, and about a month ago, Mr. Minnoch made a proposal of marriage to me, and I gave him my hand in token of acceptance, but no time for the marriage has yet been fixed, and my object in writing the note before mentioned was to have a meeting with M. L'Angelier to tell him that I was engaged to Mr. Minnoch.

I never administered to Monsieur L'Angelier arsenic or anything injurious. And this I declare to be the truth.

Madeleine Smith

There was a stillness in the courtroom. The name hung for a moment in the hush. Someone coughed.

Faces turned toward the defence table. Moncreiff laid the paper on the clerk's desk, nodded to Inglis.

Inglis rose and walked slowly to the witness stand.

"Mr. Smith, what cause did you have to examine the defendant?"

"Suspicion of murder."

"On what grounds?"

"The sudden death of a young man is unusual. The reports of a series of attacks and the apprehensions of the young man's friends made exhumation of the body seem advisable."

"You questioned her yourself?"

"I and the constable. The greater part of the questions were put by me."

"And her statement was in answer to your questions?"

"Yes." Smith stood erectly, the badge bright against his dark coat.

"And how were the answers given by Miss Smith? Reluctantly? Hesitantly?"

"No, not at all."

"How then?"

"The answers were given clearly and distinctly."

"No appearances of nervousness—or hesitation or reserve?"

"No." Smith looked at the jury box. "None."

"How would you characterize her appearance during your examination?"

"One of frankness and candour."

"Thank you, that is all." Inglis took his seat, smiling.

FOUR

At eleven, the prosecution called Mrs. Anna Jenkins to the stand.

Mrs. Jenkins, a slight but healthy-looking middle-aged woman, was led to the stand and sworn in.

"Mrs. Jenkins," Moncreiff said, "would you tell us the occurrences on the eve and day of L'Angelier's death?"

Mrs. Jenkins gripped the brass rail of the witness stand and recited the story.

"Well, I was surprised to see him come home that Sunday. It was about eight when he came in and I asked him why he came home. He said that the letter I had forwarded to him had brought him home, and he asked when it had arrived. I told him on Saturday afternoon. Then, about nine, he came and said, 'If you please, give me the passkey, I am not sure but I may be late tonight.'

"I was to wake him early so he could catch the train back to Bridge of Allan, but at half past two, I heard a violent ringing of the outer bell. I rose and called, 'Who's there?' and he said, 'It is I, Mrs. Jenkins, please open the door.' So I did."

She closed her eyes; her gloved hands tightened on the gleaming brass.

He had been standing there, his arms closed across his stomach. "Mrs. Jenkins," he had said. "Mrs. Jenkins, I am very bad; I am going to be sick."

His knees were trembling. She had helped him up the stairs and down the carpeted hall to his room. He had lain on the bed.

"Mrs. Jenkins," he said thickly. "I'm cold. Could you bring me a hot water bottle?"

She ran and got four blankets and two horsehair mats. She took the simmering kettle from the stove and poured water into two bladders. When she returned, the chamber pot was full of green bile; it was thick stuff like gruel. Like the other times.

She put the mats under him and the blankets above, and he seemed to get a little better. Then around four, he seemed worse.

"I am going to get Doctor Thompson," she said.

"No, please, it's too early, it's all the way to Dundas Street."

"No, I shall go."

"Please don't go. I am feeling a little better."

"Truly?"

"Yes."

At five he began to vomit again, and his bowels got very bad. It was still dark, though the sky was beginning to lighten.

Mrs. Jenkins rose. "I shall fetch Doctor Stevens then. He is only in the next block."

"What kind of doctor is he?"

"Don't you worry, he is a good one. He treated my warts just last month."

"Well, if you think it not too much trouble."

She went at once. She heard him purging as she went down the stairs. Outside, the March air was sharp. Over on the ridge, the cocks were beginning to crow.

She was back in ten minutes. "Oh, I am sorry but the doctor himself is badly. He says to take twenty-five drops of laudanum and lots of hot water and to put a mustard blister on the stomach and to call again later if you aren't better."

"I cannot take laudanum," Emile said. He held his arm out stiffly, looked at it blankly. "It disagrees with me."

She brought the water and the blister.

"Not the blister." He drank the hot water, began to vomit, choking.

11

She sat with him till the light brightened. He was dark around the eyes.

"My throat is bad," he said.

She took the pitcher from the marble stand and poured cool water into the cup. She lifted his head and brought the cup to his lips. He drank a few sips, then began to vomit again, his head turned to the pail beside the bed.

"I think I shall go for Doctor Stevens now."

"Yes, if he will come." He suddenly seemed eager, anxious.

"I shall make him."

"Tell him . . ."

"What?"

He choked a little. "Just tell him to hurry."

Dr. Stevens was a large man with a square wiry mustache. He filled the doorway when he entered.

"Where is the mustard plaster I ordered, woman?"

"He . . ."

"Go and fetch it at once."

She brought it back, set it on the table, then brought over the slop pail to show the doctor.

"Take it away, woman, can't you see it is making him faintish? Throw it out!"

Emile lay silent while the doctor applied the mustard.

"Doctor, what do you think?" Emile's voice was a whisper.

"I think we should wait to see the effect, and give you, I think, a little morphia."

Emile shook his head. Stevens opened his black bag, took out a syringe, filled it, injected the needle.

"Doctor," Emile said, as the syringe was withdrawn. He pointed to his forehead. "Here . . . I feel something here."

"Yes," the doctor said. "That will subside."

"Can you do anything?"

"Time and quietness will help. We shall see."

"Oh, my poor mother," he said.

The doctor stood, looked down at the flushed face. Mrs. Jenkins went to the door, motioned to the doctor to follow her.

She led him partway down the landing.

"What's wrong, Doctor?"

"Tell me, Mrs. Jenkins, is Mr. L'Angelier a man who tipples?"

"Tipples? Heavens no. He hardly ever takes a drop."

"Hmmm, it is curious."

"You know, it *is* strange. This is the third time he has gone out well and returned ill. I must speak to him and ask him why."

"That avails us little now. I'll get a little breakfast and come back between ten and eleven."

"Do you think . . . ?"

"We shall see."

Mrs. Jenkins hurried up the stairs. L'Angelier was pale, shivering, bright red spots on his cheeks, and his fingers shrunken, as if he had been a long time in water.

"If only I could get some sleep, I think I would be better."

"Well, I'll draw the curtains, and you shall sleep."

She sat on the chair by the window in the darkened room, listened to his raspy breathing, his tossing and turning.

After a while, he began to struggle to sit up. She helped him. His appearance scared her. He looked so badly, so gray, and his features were pinched and drawn.

"Is there anyone you would like to see, sir?"

He thought a moment. "Yes, a Miss Perry, at 44 Renfrew. Could you send for her?"

"Of course." She fitted the blanket around him and walked to the door.

"Mrs. Jenkins?" His voice was weak.

She turned.

"I am . . . You are good."

She smiled, went downstairs, and dispatched the kitchen maid to Miss Perry's. When she came back, carrying more hot water, he seemed about to fall off.

"... five minutes' rest," he muttered.

She tiptoed out. When she came back to check him five minutes later, he was asleep, breathing noisily, curled like a baby. The sun had come out and dust motes swirled in the shaft of light touching the bed. She had gone downstairs to wait for the doctor.

"And this was the last time you saw him alive?" Moncreiff said gently.

She nodded, rubbed a tear on her cheek. "I received the doctor downstairs and we went up together. He went to the bed and lifted L'Angelier's head. Then he told me he was dead."

"What time did Miss Perry arrive?"

"About midday."

"What did you tell her?"

"I said, 'Are you the intended, ma'am?' and she said, 'Oh, no! I am only a friend.'"

"You thought she was the intended?"

"I had supposed that, when L'Angelier asked to see her."

"Yes, go on."

"I told her that L'Angelier was dead."

"And what was her reaction?"

"She was very sorry, very strikingly so—very much overwhelmed; she cried a great deal."

"You said 'very strikingly so'—why were you so struck by her reaction?"

"I . . . I was surprised, that's all—as she was not the intended."

"Did you and Miss Perry discuss the intended?"

"Well, when she said that she was not that person, I said I heard as he was going to be married, and how sorry the lady would be."

"And?" Moncreiff said.

"She told me not to say much about the intended, and to leave the matter alone."

"And then you showed her the body?"

"Yes, after it was laid out. I took her up and she kissed the forehead several times. She cried and said how sorry she was for his mother."

"Was it violent grief, Mrs. Jenkins?"

"No, I wouldn't call it violent. But she was very sorry."

"Thank you, Mrs. Jenkins, no further questions."

Moncreiff turned to Inglis.

"No questions," Inglis said.

Just past midday the court adjourned for refreshments. The judges retired to chambers for wine and cake. In the courtroom, everyone was astir, discussing the evidence, sharing biscuits and sandwiches. A matron approached the prisoner with a glass of water. She shook her head.

"At two, Thomas Fleming Kennedy, cashier to Huggins and Company, was called to the stand.

Moncreiff clasped his hands behind his back and began the examination.

"Tell us, Mr. Kennedy, were you aquainted with the deceased?"

"Intimately. He was in the habit of coming frequently to my house."

Moncreiff walked to the exhibit table and picked up a photograph in a gold frame. It showed a handsome young man with a mustache. The eyes had been painted blue and the curls and mustache blond.

"Can you identify this likeness?" Moncreiff said, showing the picture to Kennedy.

"It is L'Angelier."

"Thank you. Now, please tell us, how would you describe L'Angelier's character?"

"He was a well-behaved, well-principled, religious young man. I had great regard for him."

"You feel you had ample means of judging his character and conduct?"

"Yes."

"Was he in good general health?"

"Yes, while in our warehouse. He was not much off duty from bad health till latterly. I never thought him very strong, though."

"Did he ever speak to you of Miss Smith?" said Moncreiff.

"Once or twice. Till shortly before his death, I knew only that they corresponded."

"But shortly before, you learned something else?"

"He came to me one morning in February, and said, with tears in his eyes, that he had received a letter demanding back all of the correspondence."

"And what was your reaction?"

"I advised him strongly to give back the letters."

"And did he?"

"He did not."

"Did he say why she wanted the letters back?"

"He said that she wrote that a coolness had arisen."

"A coolness—on his part or hers?"

"I understood she felt there was a coolness on the part of both," Kennedy said.

"What, precisely, did he say in reaction?"

"He said he would never allow her to marry another man as long as he lived."

Moncreiff stepped back and looked at the jury. Then he spoke again to Kennedy.

"What was your reaction to that statement?"

"I said I thought it foolish. He said that he knew it was."

"He knew it was foolish?"

"Yes."

"Thank you, I have no further questions."

Inglis rose and approached the stand. Kennedy brushed a hand through his sandy-coloured hair, swallowed.

"The deceased said to you that he would never let Miss Smith marry another as long as he lived?" Inglis said.

"Yes."

"Do you think he meant it?"

"Well . . . he certainly meant it at that moment."

"And what was his state at that moment?"

"He was exceedingly excited."

Inglis looked over at the jury box. At least seven of the fifteen men were taking notes. Inglis turned to the letters on the center table.

"Were you present when the letters were taken from L'Angelier's desk at the warehouse?"

"Yes, I saw Stevenson take the letters and put them in a large paper box."

"Did you read them?"

"Yes."

"Why?"

"To discover his mother's address."

A guffaw came from the gallery. Lord Hope scowled.

"Did you find it?" Inglis said.

"No, it was got otherwise."

"Were the letters of further interest to you?"

"Pardon me?"

"How much of the letters did you have to read to discover that Mr. L'Angelier's mother had not written them?"

"Pardon me?"

"No further questions."

The next witness was called: William A. Stevenson. Moncreiff conferred with his assistant, then rose and approached the witness.

"What is your occupation, Mr. Stevenson?" Moncreiff said.

"I am warehouseman with Huggins and Company, Bothwell Street."

"So you knew the deceased?"

"Yes. Mr. L'Angelier worked in our warehouse under me."

Moncreiff turned to the bench. "If it please the court, I would now like to read a letter—a letter sent from Bridge of Allan on the Friday before his death." He raised a paper, read:

17

Dear William,

    I am happy to say I feel much better, though I fear I slept in a damp bed, for my limbs are all sore, and scarcely able to bear me. This place is dull as a chimney. Are you very busy? Am I wanted? If so, I am ready to come home at any time. Just drop me a line at P.O. If any letters come, please send them to me here. I intend to be home not later than Thursday morning.

                              Yours sincerely,
                              P. Emile L'Angelier

"Is this letter in L'Angelier's handwriting?" Moncreiff said.

"It is," Stevenson said.

"Did you expect L'Angelier to be in Glasgow on Sunday night?"

"No," Stevenson said. "The letter suggested he would stay part of the week."

"Tell us, when you went to his lodgings on the Monday of his death, did you examine his effects?"

"I saw his clothes lying on his bedroom sofa. I examined them."

"Could you identify these items as his effects?" Moncreiff said, indicating exhibits 37–48 on the exhibit table.

"Yes, those are his effects."

"This letter," Moncreiff said, picking up a slim envelope. "Where was it found?"

"In his vest pocket."

"Would you please read the postmark on the envelope?"

"It was posted at Glasgow Friday morning, March 20th, 1857, and again at Bridge of Allan on March 22nd."

"Thank you. And now, if you please, would you read the letter aloud?"

Stevenson held the letter before him. He looked once at the defendant. Madeleine's face was composed, listening.

"It reads as follows," he said.

Why, my beloved, did you not come to me? Oh, beloved, are you ill? Come to me, sweet one. I waited and waited for you, but you did not come. I shall wait again tomorrow night, same hour and arrangement. Do come, sweet love, my own dear love. Come, beloved, and clasp me to your heart. Come and we shall be happy.

Mimi

Stevenson lowered his hand.

"And how was the letter addressed?" Moncreiff said.

"To Monsieur E. L'Angelier, care of Mrs. Jenkins, 11 Franklin Place, Glasgow. And the envelope is marked: 'Deliver Immediately.'"

On the bench, Lord Hope leaned forward. "Mr. Stevenson, did you know then who *Mimi* was?"

"No."

"Could you explain to the court," Moncreiff said, "why you did not know?"

"My relationship with L'Angelier was in matters of business, not otherwise."

Moncreiff walked to the exhibit table, picked up a small red leather memorandum diary, held it towards the jurors. He walked back to the witness box.

"Can you identify this little book, Mr. Stevenson?"

"Yes, it is L'Angelier's memorandum book."

"The entries are all in his handwriting?"

"Yes, they are."

"What did you do with this book when it came into your hands?"

"I took the book to our office, sealed it up, and I later gave it up to the police, to Officer Murray."

"When was this?"

"On the 31st of March, after the exhumation and Miss Smith's arrest."

"Thank you, Mr. Stevenson. No further questions." Moncreiff turned and laid the small red book on the crowded exhibit table.

Inglis scooped up the small book and held it open before the witness.

"Look at that label: 'Glasgow, 30th March. Found in the desk of the deceased.' Is that your signature?"

"It is."

"You found the book in L'Angelier's lodgings?"

"Yes."

"Who was present when you found it?"

"Dr. Thompson, Monsieur Thuau, a fellow lodger, and perhaps Mrs. Jenkins, the landlady."

Inglis held the book open, walked three steps towards the jurors. "The entries are in pencil. Some of them are very faint, and it is difficult to identify such."

"I was accustomed to see L'Angelier write in pencil," Stevenson said. Inglis had his back to him, facing the exhibit table. Stevenson looked at the bench.

"Mr. Stevenson," Inglis said, turning and facing the witness. "Did you ever see L'Angelier write in this book?"

"No."

"No further questions." Inglis placed the book in the middle of the exhibit table, remained standing. Moncreiff was on his feet, his arm extended for the little book.

He grasped it and walked to the bench, held it aloft. "And now, if it please the court, I would like the witness to read the entries from the book."

"I object!" Inglis said.

"State your case," Lord Hope said.

"Your Honour, there is no evidence whatever of this book being a journal. If it is a memorandum book, it was irregularly kept, and there is no reason to believe that the entries were put under proper dates."

Moncreiff shook his head. "But the memoranda are in the deceased's handwriting and certain dates do tally with other events, as we will be able to prove. Whether all these entries were written on the dates they bear is another matter, but if we can prove that some were, it would go far to prove the other."

Lord Hope turned to Lord Ivory and Lord Handyside, exchanged a few words.

"The witness may step down," Lord Hope said. He rose and led the way to his chamber. In ten minutes, the three returned; the witness was recalled. Lord Hope gave their decision.

"Gentleman, we are of the opinion that insufficient ground has been laid for the admission of the memoranda. At present, we do not know the individuals by name in the entries, or by the blanks that occur in several of the entries. Perhaps later sufficient reason will be established, but at present we cannot allow these entries to be read."

Stevenson was then recalled and the examination resumed. It was half past five when Inglis ended his cross-examination. He ended it gently.

"The letters you found in his room and his desk at the office, did you read them?"

"Some of them, those in the travelling bag."

"And you put them back in their proper envelopes?"

"Yes."

"Might you have shifted some?"

"No. I was very careful."

"Thank you. That is all."

Stevenson stepped down from the stand at six o'clock. Stomachs were grumbling in the courtroom.

Lord Hope, closing the Bible in front of him, intoned the recession:

"It now being six o'clock in the evening, in respect of the impossibility, with due regard to the justice of the case, of bringing this trial to a speedy close, we continue the diet against the prisoner till tomorrow morning at ten o'clock, and ordain the hail parties, panels, and all concerned, then to attend, each under the pains of law; and the hail fifteen jurors now in the box to repair, under the charge of the macers of the Court, to the Regent Hotel, Waterloo Place, to remain till brought here tomorrow, being strictly secluded from all communication with any person whatever on the subject of this trial. Meantime, we ordain the prisoner to be carried to, and detained in, the prison of Edinburgh."

The bailiff bent, gripped at the countersunk iron ring in the floor, and pulled the trap door open. Madeleine and the matron rose, walked to the opening, and descended.

FIVE

It was past 8 P.M. and George Young, the assistant, had just left Inglis' apartment. The pouches under Inglis' eyes were deeper than usual. He plucked a pinewood stick from the box next to the fire, laid it atop a coal, struck a brimstone match. The pine caught instantly, the spark leapt from point to point, and soon there was a lively bituminous flame. As he watched it darting, his mind reframed the day's events. He picked up a cheroot, took a coal from the fire with his iron tongs, and lit it. Then, for the third time that evening, he read the phrenologist's report which the prosecution had commissioned.

MADELEINE SMITH: AGE 21
This young lady's head is of an English form, and of the usual size, but more than usual force of character, owing to large combativeness, self-esteem, love of approbation, and firmness, powerful affections. . . .

The report went on for three pages. It sounded more like a description for the society news than for a criminal trial.

He scanned the second page:

Reasoning powers are good. Apt to look on the bright side of things. On the whole, a very clever head.

On the whole, a very clever head. Clever enough to . . . ? Since Inglis had first stepped before the bench at twenty-five, he had not encountered such a case. The lady—she was a lady, despite the evidence—remained unabashed. Today, with all pointing a finger at her, she had remained . . . composed.

Inglis put down the report. His cigar had gone out and the fire in the box was low. The moon shone brightly on the polished hearth.

He picked up the copy of the memorandum book, read the poem that had been penned on the last page:

> Go! you may call it madness, folly;
> You shall not chase my gloom away!
> There's such a charm in melancholy
> I would not if I could be gay.

Below the poem was the clerk's notation: "Note: in original, a leafy vine has been drawn around the poem—a Union Jack adorns the bottom of the page."

Samuel Rogers, Inglis thought, if he remembered his literature. The poem would further the suicide defence, show L'Angelier's state, but of course he could not use it. The pencilled memoranda were too damaging. He scanned the list:

Mon. 16 Feb.—Wrote M.—saw Mr. Philpots
Tues. 17 Feb.—Dined at 44 Renfrew
Thur. 19 Feb.—Saw Mimi a few moments—was very ill during the night.
Fri. 20 Feb.—Passed two pleasant hours with M. in the Drawing Room
Sat. 21 Feb.—Don't feel well—went to T. Kennedy's
Sun. 22 Feb.—Saw Mimi in Drawing Room
                Promised me French Bible
                Taken very ill

February 19–22. She was accused of two counts of poisoning during this period. By the deceased's own account, he had seen her thrice in this span.

Inglis put the page under a paperweight, picked up the phrenologist's report, turned to the second page.

> She possesses both masculine and feminine qualities, more especially the former . . . should be good at mathematics . . . memory good for events, faces, places, and history . . . requires amusement and recreation . . . a great flirt; will at all times have a warm side towards gentlemen, and will prefer their society to that of her sex. They will be drawn to her, for she possesses a magnetism that will draw them round her like bees round a rose tree.

He rubbed his eyes, took his raincoat from the pine rack, put his low hat on his head. It was raining hard out. So much the better. There would be few walkers out.

He walked head down, the steps ingrained in his legs. The way to Greyfriars Parish was short. He came in the back gate, then turned down the side lane and approached his father's grave.

The stone marker was water streaked with green, the color of the ledger in his father's vestry:

THE REVEREND JOHN INGLIS
REST WITH OUR LORD

Inglis stopped before the stone, the rain pelting like heartbeats against the marble.

The stone seemed to glow. If his father had been alive, Inglis could never have come to him. He had been too proud a son, too sure that he must stand on his own feet—apart from his illustrious father.

You are puzzled, son, he could hear the old man's burly voice saying.

"Aye."

Tell me. . . .

"I dinna ken whether to believe her or not."

If she killed a man, she must be punished.

"But Father, I am her guardian. It is my duty to defend her."

Even if she is guilty?

"That is for the law to determine."

Religion is easier than this law you practice.

"It is my religion, father."

How well do you know her?

"I did ride with her in the prison van. At a special request sent by the mother."

Have you visited her in gaol, where, perhaps, she most needs someone to talk to?

"It is not my practice to visit prisoners in gaol. It is against the code. *Prisoners are consulted in chambers.*"

Does it break the ten words?

"No. But . . ."

But?

The rain had stopped and Inglis looked with dry eyes at the marble scrolled before him.

He had never visited a prisoner in gaol before.

SIX

The women came down the dingy stone corridor that smelt of oil lamps, into the room where Inglis was seated on the low divan, black top coat over his knees, his hair wet from the rain. The matron took a seat in the corner, slumped almost immediately in sleep.

They talked softly.

Inglis was reminded of the child Victoria, receiving the news of her queenhood. The clothes brought the picture to mind: the soft grey muslin, the fresh face—Miss Smith seemed more of a child in this candlelight.

"Miss Smith. Did I waken you?"

Madeleine shook her head. "Not at all. And I am glad of the company."

He pulled the chair out, seated her at the oak table, went round to the other side.

"It was a good day, wasn't it?" she said.

"Yes."

"I thought you did well."

"Thank you." And curiously, he was flattered.

"It's true."

"I don't know exactly why I came. To ask about your childhood, I suppose."

"I have just been thinking on it. . . . Prison does that to you. I live over scenes, try to lodge out the forces that . . ."

Inglis waited.

"But that isn't why you came, Mr. Inglis."

"I don't know why I came."

"Why, to find out if I did it, of course."

"I thought of that on the way over."

"It is necessary that you know whether I did it?"

"No."

"You would try to have me found innocent though you knew me guilty?"

"The philosophy of law is that it is for the fully exercised process of the courts to determine whether you are guilty. Not even a confession could—or should—stop the process. No single person can usurp that system of justice."

Madeleine smiled. "You sound more like a minister than a lawyer."

Inglis laughed.

"Does guilt or innocence mean did I poison Emile or didn't I?"

Inglis looked at her calm face. "Fundamentally, yes."

"'Even to deny,'" Madeleine said, "'would be some stooping, and I choose ne'er to stoop.'"

"An attitude admirable in a poem," Inglis said, "but dangerous in court."

They watched each other for moments. Madeleine smiled faintly.

At last Inglis sighed and spoke. "Miss Madeleine, I wish to ask you something as a private person, not as your lawyer."

Madeleine brushed her dark hair back from her face. "Can you make that distinction?"

"I don't know."

She nodded. "Ask me anything, Mr. Inglis. But only if you want the truth. I am done with lying. No one can ever again make me lie."

"Shall I ask you whether . . ."

"Only if you want the truth."

Inglis looked into Madeleine's intense face. "In that case," he said, "what did they serve you for dinner this evening?"

Madeleine's face relaxed. She laughed.

Inglis opened his leather folio and drew out a corked jar and a quill. He spread a sheet before him.

"Miss Smith, do you remember the night of Sunday, March 22nd? Do you remember any details?"

"I can't even begin to see that night."

"Anything?"

She shook her head.

Inglis looked at her. "Miss Smith, it is important. We must know all there is to know. We must be ready to fight anything they bring up."

"I understand, but it is a blank. I remember his death, my arrest, my first night in Glasgow Prison. I remember court today. I remember when I met him, each letter, but I don't remember that night. I wasn't to see him that night."

"Yes, I know."

"You believe me?"

"Should I not?"

"It is the truth." Her eyes fixed on him.

"Then I shall defend you with the truth."

"Good."

Inglis leaned across the table. "Miss Smith, perhaps if we talked about something more distant—your childhood?"

27

"I don't know. What do you want to know?"

"Anything that might enable me to understand more about your relationship to your family"—he paused—"and to this young man."

Madeleine looked at him, her lips pursed.

"The prosecution will claim that the motive for the alleged murder lies in a desire to conceal a shameful liaison from strict and severe parents. Perhaps there is something in your past history that would illuminate things for me."

"I had a perfectly ordinary childhood," she said.

"Did you?"

"If only I knew what would be useful, Mr. Inglis."

"Aye, that is the problem."

"Or what Mr. Moncreiff might bring up."

"We must be prepared for anything."

"You know," Madeleine said, "I believe I have heard that name before. Moncreiff . . ."

"It is a reputable name. Where did you hear it, Miss Smith? Do you remember?"

Madeleine shrugged.

"Perhaps as a child?"

"Truly? Perhaps a friend of my father's?"

"Not likely."

"Perhaps you know more than I do."

"A Moncreiff helped to write the briefs in the Burke and Hare case."

"The body snatchers?"

"Yes."

"This Moncreiff?"

Inglis laughed. "No, this is the son. You thought perhaps he was a child prodigy?"

Madeleine touched her cheek. "You know, I think I do remember where I heard it."

Inglis opened his notebook. "Please, tell me."

"It was at Row. I don't know the year, but . . ."

"Yes?"

"A boy told me. Ben Campbell."

"We could begin there. Whatever you remember."

Madeleine nodded. "We were just children. He told me a story—about seeing Burke's tanned hide in the museum. That was all." She shrugged.

Inglis nodded. He put the paper back in his folio and rose. "It is late, Miss Smith. I'll come back tomorrow night if you'll permit me."

She smiled. "I'll try to remember all I can."

Inglis bowed, left her to the matron.

Back in her cell she tried to think about her childhood. Hadn't it been ordinary? Expected? Conventional—up to some point, anyhow? She tried to remember what she had heard them say about her as a girl. She drew a blank. She tried to picture Glasgow, her house. What was home now?

If a whole mirror faces a fragmented mirror, are not both cracked?

She could begin at the beginning. The year of her birth, March 29th, 1836. Had she been born a few months later, she would certainly have been named for the new child queen, Victoria. As it was, Papa and Mama had quarrelled for three days; in the end, Mama had won. She was named Madeleine Hamilton after her great-grandmother. Madeleine: "the demoniac healed." A family name.

Growing up in Glasgow, spending summers at Row.

Glasgow.

In 1836 Glasgow was the center of the new industry. Trade with the colonies began and ended on the River Clyde. Up the Clyde went sugar and tobacco, and down came foreign currency, raw materials, Napoleon-blue silks, and beribboned bonnets.

Like a sponge, Glasgow absorbed the people of the countryside. They came on foot and by stage and from the Clyde steamer, but always they came, the rawboned men, women, and children who filled the vats and spun the bobbins, stoked the furnaces and packed the tall-roofed grey rooming-house streets, grew solid and honest on barley and oatcakes and little else save dreams.

On the rooming-house side of Glasgow, in the red-flaring night, sweating grease-streaked workers spewed out of the factory gates, went home in the dark to stewed pears and oatcakes, then God-blissful sleep.

On the other side of Glasgow lived the professors and ministers and the men who had built schooners and become captains and their sons who now captained the steel and coal. The Hugginses and Smiths had joined the rolls of society, mingled with the McFirths, the Campbells; bought boxes next to them in the Music Hall; went "doon the watter" with them in summer.

On that side of Glasgow, the last century was closer. A quiet cathedral, the University. Scholars and cows roamed the dusty roads, ruminating. Frocked ministers, their long French noses in Books of Common Prayer, saluted them both.

Small Alberts and Victorias grew up on the society side without ever having connection with the small Alberts and Victorias of the working side.

Ways were changing. People were talking of a new age, a Golden Age. Men talked of Progress and Evolution, of Liberty and Equality. And they were not burned at the stake.

Some things changed more slowly than others.

Once Madeleine had gone with her father on an errand of mercy. It had been Gaudete Sunday, the third Sunday in Advent, and Madeleine had opened a door of her Advent calendar to reveal a goose. Which was what they were taking to Papa's clerk.

Madeleine, wearing her sleigh dress of swallow-blue velet, wadded throughout and edged with white lace, stared out of the carriage window at the smoke and steam belching from the stacks. The frosted air swirled down the street.

"Papa, is that Hell?"

"Almost, child, almost," he had answered, tousling the three-year-old's black curls and pulling the tartan wool blanket closer around her.

The night matron, Miss Aitken, had given her a bottle to help her sleep. She opened it now, took the drops with negus, dressed for bed, then lay for hours, one memory tumbling upon another.

She kept seeing a large white-framed picture from her Sunday-school classroom, the cherubim under glass against a sky of blue, overlooking the throne of God. And the minister, with his watery blue eyes, saying to the class:

"At last God will sit upon his white throne and open the book. He knows all you have done and thought. He will read out of his book all you have done. We must pray for mercy, not because we deserve it, but because His only Son, Jesus Christ, died for us."

There had been no pictures of the book, and Madeleine was curious.

"Is the book in Heaven?" she said.

The minister had looked down at her, his eyes kindly.

"Yes, Madeleine."

"What color is it, sir?"

"What color is it?"

"Yes."

"Child . . ." he said. "I don't know."

"But you are sure it is there?"

"Madeleine, to doubt the Lord is blasphemy."

"But . . ."

"Don't you believe the Lord knows all?"

"But can He know what I have not yet done?"

"Time is all-present to God. Nothing is beyond Him. Do not dare to doubt!"

She, stupid, innocent, asked yet again. "How can God know what has not yet happened?"

"Oh, Madeleine," he said, his voice kindly. "If you doubt,

you will be a little girl there in Hell, dressed in a suit of burning clothes, writhing in agony on the flaming floor. Forever! Oh, if you could hear the horrible screams of that girl!"

Madeleine decided then that there would be no more questions. But was it a white book or a black book? It was black, she had decided; it must be to contain sins.

Madeleine reached over to the small bedside table, took the bottle of laudanum and opened it, poured another dose, and drank it down. But still, she did not sleep.

She tried to do as Mr. Inglis had asked, to reveal rather than conceal. She thought again of the child in Sunday school. Was it all written in the book? Even then?

She forced the book from her mind, thought of pleasanter things.

There was the dress Miss Tweedle had made for her seventh birthday: a striped peau de soie with a basquine of dark taffeta, slashed at the sides and cross laced, the sleeves cut in a double rank of leaf-shaped lappets. Mama had given her a doll and Papa had given her a toy whip. And that summer, she had met Ben.

Papa had gone with Grandpapa that year to open up the house. A week later, Mama woke the children before dawn and they set off in the closed barouche to the steamer. She smelled the perfume of the earth, drew in the musty smell of worn leather, mingled the smells in her nostrils as the sleek horses moved through the darkness of the giant hemlocks, the paraffin side lamp giving off a smoky haze. At last they emerged from the woods into the morning air.

Madeleine had been the first up the gangplank. She ran her gloved hand over the rosewood fretted rail, stopped to inspect a gilt pineapple, rambled on down the deck till she found a window seat. Mama, large with child, followed with five-year-old Bessie, and the nurse brought up the rear with little Jack. Madeleine pressed her nose to the pane, straining for the moment when the grey would recede and they would emerge into a greening land of lakes and mountains penetrated by fingers of the sea. The steamer was fairylike to her. It was leaving home and arriving home all in one, the ride; for Rowaleyn, more than India Street, was home to her. As if the place itself were a person: the house—its body, stately and freshly whitewashed; and beyond, the gardens, hills, fields—the limbs.

Such a summer it would be. She had felt every inch the princess, dressed in tartan taffeta with *à revers* scallopped sleeves, her new straw bonnet banded with white satin and topped with wax cherries. She lifted her legs from the seat, her grey kid boots with patent leather toes peeping out like mice from beneath her embroidered pantalettes.

A man was singing somewhere off down the deck: "'Sailing up the Clyde wi' a lassie by your side.'"

They were closing in on the shore now, and Madeleine could see a cluster of white stone houses on the green velvet, some wee toe-rag children playing.

At Row, after supper, Madeleine went into the drawing room and read Virgil to Papa.

"Very fine, little pet," Papa said.

The next morning, Grandpapa cut her man-shaped garden plot, spread chicken manure through the soil. Madeleine set the tiny plants in six inches apart: brown pansies for the frock coat, pink sweet William for the waistcoat, and blue gentian for the eyes.

Then Grandpapa gave her sixpence and hitched the billy to the primrose-yellow two-wheeled cart. Madeleine, wearing a pink-checked poplin sack with white cuffs and embroidered cambric collar, hopped in. Grandpapa handed her the whip and told her to use it.

Bessie jumped up and down and screamed to go, too, but Grandpapa said no, she was still a baby. It was Madeleine who would ride to Mrs. Butterworth's, buy the paper for Grandpapa, and perhaps, if there was anything left over, a petticoat-tail cake.

Bessie was still crying, so to make it up to her, Madeleine

promised to stay with her in her cot that night till she fell asleep. At that, Bessie sniffled and rubbed her sleeve over her red eyes. Madeleine cracked the whip and the billy started off stiff-legged down the drive. She had to switch him twice to get him down the lane. From then on, all he did was grunt and trot.

At the end of the elm-lined lane, she turned east, down the cart-rutted road.

"Hey!" A redheaded, freckle-cheeked boy in a leghorn hat and buttoned gaiters said, his elbows on a neat stone wall. "Where you going?"

Madeleine lifted her head and looked at him, clucked at the goat to go on. The goat stopped.

"Nowhere, eh?"

"Come on, Billy, giddyup!" Billy proceeded to eat dandelion greens at the base of the stone wall.

"Can I have a ride?"

"No." She looked up at the boy. He was quite tall. At least eleven years, she thought, almost a man.

"That's a bonny cart," he said.

"Thank you," she said, lifting her chin and tugging on the reins.

"I'd give you sixpence."

She laughed.

"You don't believe me?"

"I've already sixpence." And she pulled harder, jerking the goat's head around. It started off down the lane.

"Stuck-up!"

Her cheeks flushed.

"Hey you!" He had climbed the wall and run up beside her. But she wasn't afraid.

"What?"

"You really got sixpence?"

"I never lie."

"What you gonna buy?"

"An *Edinburgh Review*."

34

"Ah, Papa reads that too. And the twopence left?"
She shrugged.
"For a ha'penny, I'd show you a wasps' nest."
She pulled up on the reins, weighed the offer against the prospect of petticoat tails. She was sorely tempted.
"Live wasps in it?"
"Word of honour."
"Where is it?"
"First the ha'penny."
"Well, I don't know. When could I see it?"
"Now, if you like."
"I can't now."
"Then after you get the paper."
"Maybe."
"Don't forget the ha'penny."

Ben, Madeleine decided that afternoon, was a bonny lad. She met him at the crossroads and together, with sticks, they thrust at flying wasps, pretending they were winged dragons. She took off her hat and left it on a fence post, and the sun brought the freckles popping out on her nose. Ben was from Edinburgh and he was going to be a major in the Queen's Army when he grew up and fight the bloody Russians.

"You ever hear of Burke and Hare?" he asked now.

She shrugged. "Of course I did," she lied.

"'Up the close and doun the stair. . . . But and ben wi' Burke and Hare. . . .'"

"But and ben wi' Burke and Hare?"

"'Burke's the butcher, Hare's the thief. . . . Knox the boy that buys the beef.'"

"Who's Knox?"

"Ah, I knew you dinna know. They was the body snatchers. I've seen Burke's tanned hide and skeleton in the museum."

"Truly?"

"If you ever come to Edinburgh, I'll show you."

She came home with flushed cheeks and freckles over the bridge of her nose. She stopped in front of the hall mirror, tried to rub them off.

In the drawing room, Mama and Grandpapa were on the sofa, listening to a man in the wing chair.

". . . singing in Russian and Portuguese, by two eminent exiled counts. At twelve, Madame lectures on the art of dress, with illustrations from nature. We lunch at one, and the marquis instructs the young ladies in the habits of refined eating as practised in Europe. At two, visitors—between you and me, sir, young men whom I engage by the month . . ."

He turned to Mama, or so it seemed by the tilt of his cigar on the side of the chair, by Mama's leaning forwards.

". . . in order that my young ladies may be perfect in the art of receiving company."

Mama nodded, her side curls bobbing.

"At half past three, Signor Buonaventura reads to the girls for a quarter of an hour a portion of an Italian romance . . ."

Grandpapa's eyebrows shifted.

". . . of most exceptional morality."

Mama nodded.

"At six, dress for dinner. We dine at seven, and the rest of the evening is devoted to light conversation, under the auspices of a poet, a divine, or an ex-foreign ambassador. So you see, our time is pretty well occupied, and we finish our pupils pretty thoroughly."

"Pretty thoroughly indeed," Grandpapa said, taking out his pipe.

"Well then, I shall speak to Mr. Smith when he returns," Mama said. "And you must meet Madeleine."

"Oh, but I had hoped to speak with Mr. Smith."

"He is away," she said, lowering her eyes. There was silence in the room, then Mama laughed and said who would care for tea, and Madeleine stole upstairs, not wanting a gentleman to see her freckles, wanting time to think. Were they talking about *her*?

She sat at Mama's skirted dressing table and looked in the mirror. She was a sight! She took the puff from the glass dish on the counter, dipped it in the powder, blotted at her face.

She squinted. More powder. Now her face was powdered white. Not a freckle in sight. She smiled. There were bottles and tubes on the table: She uncapped the rouge, dipped her finger in, and outlined her lips. With a cloth, she blotted her lips as she had seen Mama do. She picked up the cut-glass bottle and squeezed the rubber ball; the spray tickled her nose, but now she smelled like flowers.

She would surprise them. She walked down the stairs and slowly, deliberately, entered the smoke-filled room.

Mama's hand stopped halfway to her mouth. She gaped at Madeleine. "Madeleine, what have you . . . ?" She laughed, turned to Grandpapa. "Papa, look at our little angel."

Madeleine smiled, made a pirouette in front of her Grandpapa.

Madeleine lifted the hem of her skirt and curtsied to the gentleman in the wing chair. He was a big man with speckled skin and a broad face. He nodded his head.

"Well, this is our Madeleine," Mama said.

"And quite a little lady, she is, the noo," Grandpapa said. He rubbed his finger on her face, the powder rising in a cloud.

The man looked her up and down. Madeleine smiled at him and walked across the room to his chair.

"I am pleased," she said, "to—"

"Mrs. Smith," the man said, "the child is evidently eager to learn the art of cosmetics." He waved away the traces of powder in the air.

Her mother laughed. "Well, it's evident she needs to."

Grandpapa laughed. "Go oopstairs and wash yer face, darlin'."

Madeleine felt the tears welling up. She turned and ran out the door. She had been beautiful . . . but *now* . . . She ran down the path, hid behind the smoke shed, waiting for Mama to call her. But all was silent. She broke a branch off the willow and tried it out against the smoke shed door. She ran from behind the shed to the chicken house and from there through the field that bordered the main lane, hitting the ground with her willow, striking up a cadence, singing "A Mighty Fortress Is Our God" at the top of her lungs. That got her to the lane. She switched to "The Pied Piper of Hamlin."

> Rats!
> They fought the dogs and killed the cats
> And bit the babies in the cradles
> And ate the cheeses out of the vats
> And licked the soup from the cooks' own ladles. . . .
>
> With shrieking and squeaking
> In fifty different sharps and flats. . . .
>
> Rats!

At the end of the lane, she paused. She looked up at the rooks circling in the elms, then turned to the cowslips to search out a trace of fairy dust, feeling a tear well up and seeing it drop onto a leaf.

"What you looking for?" a voice said.

"Ben!"

"Did I scare you?"

She shook her head.

"What you looking for?"

"I was looking for fairy dust," she said.

He picked a dandelion, held it to his mouth, blew.

"Here now, count the seeds, Madeleine."

The floating wisps gathered into five groups, fell to earth.

"Five o'clock by the fairy clock," he said. "Am I right?"

They looked at the sun high above the horizon.

"Past teatime," she said.

"I saw a gigelorum once, or at least I think I did," Ben said.

"But they're too tiny to see."

"I know, but in a pond once, I think I saw one moving in the water . . . or an echo of him."

He reached out his hand towards the flower where her fingers were parting the petals, touched her fingers. She held her hand still.

A cow's nose appeared in the picture over the horizon and Ben turned towards the tinkling of the bell, called to her, his hand lifted now in a gesture to the cow.

"Prush, Madame," he called. He whispered down to Madeleine: "That is French, for she *is* a Jersey cow."

SEVEN

Wednesday was a bright and sunny day. Madeleine wore an ivory silk dress, light-blue kid gloves, a white straw hat trimmed with white ribbons. She sat calmly, almost detached, as the first witness, Jane Bayne, was called to the stand. She was a woman in her middle forties, dressed in Waterloo blue.

Moncreiff ushered her on to the stand, stood by as the clerk administered the oath. Mrs. Bayne swore to tell the whole truth.

"Mrs. Bayne, could you please tell the court how you came to make the acquaintance of the deceased?"

"I live at Bridge of Allan. Mr. L'Angelier came to my house on holiday on March 19th, 1857, between five and six in the evening. He lodged in my house till Sunday, March 22nd."

Moncreiff walked to the exhibit table, lifted a Moroccan leather bag.

"Can you identify this portmanteau?"

"It is like the one he had with him."

"How did he seem to you that Sunday, Mrs. Bayne?"

"He seemed in good health and spirits."

"Did he eat his meals well?"
"Yes."
"When did he depart from your house?"
"He left on Sunday, just as the churches met in the afternoon session."
"Did he tell you he was leaving?"
"No, I was surprised."
"Why?"
"He had said he was to stay longer."
"Thank you, Mrs. Bayne, no further questions."
Lord Hope turned to the defence table.
"No questions, Your Honour," Inglis said.

Dr. Hugh Thompson next ascended the stand. Moncreiff consulted a paper on his desk; then he approached the stand.
"Would you please introduce yourself to the court and tell how you knew the deceased?"
"I am a physician in Glasgow. I knew the late Monsieur L'Angelier for fully two years. He consulted me professionally; the first time in the spring of 1855."
"What was his complaint?"
"He had a bowel complaint. He soon got better of that."
"When was the next time he consulted you?"
Dr. Thompson pulled out a small memorandum book, opened it.
"On February 3rd of this year."
"What was his complaint?"
"He had a cold and cough, and a boil at the back of his neck. He was feverish, and the cough was rather dry."
"Did you prescribe for him?"
"I did. I saw him next about a week later. He was better of his cold, but another boil had made its appearance on his neck. I saw him again on Monday, the 23rd of February."
"At his place or yours?"
"He came to me. He was feverish; his tongue was furred and had a patchy appearance, from the fur being off in places;

he complained of nausea, and said he had been vomiting and purging the night before; he was prostrate; his pulse was quick."

"And you prescribed for him?"

"Yes, I took his complaint to be a bilious derangement and I prescribed an aperient draught. He was confined to the house for two or three days afterwards."

"Did you see him after that?"

Dr. Thompson wet his finger, turned the page of the small book.

"I saw him briefly on March 1st; then I saw him eight or ten days after. He called on me. He looked very dejected; his colour was dark and jaundiced, especially around the eyes."

"Did you prescribe for him on this occasion?"

"No, but I told him to give up smoking; I thought that was injurious to his stomach."

"When did you see him next?"

"I never saw him again in life."

"But you did see the deceased L'Angelier?"

Dr. Thompson nodded gravely.

"Could you describe that time?" Moncreiff said.

"On the morning of March 23rd, Mr. Stevenson and Monsieur Thuau called on me and mentioned that L'Angelier was dead, and they wished me to go and see the body, and see if I could give any opinion as to the cause of death."

"And you went?"

"I went to the house. The body was laid out on a stretcher, dressed in grave clothes, and lying on a table. The skin had a slightly jaundiced hue."

"Did you give them an opinion as to the cause of death?"

"I believe I said that the symptoms were compatible with a bilious derangement."

"But later you changed that opinion?"

"Yes, later I did."

"Now, tell us, you saw him again, eight days after death and five days after burial?"

"Yes."

"Could you describe the body?"

"It was remarkably well-preserved. Almost no deterioration."

"Is that a symptom of anything you know, Doctor Thompson?"

"Uh, no, not that I know of," Dr. Thompson answered.

"No further questions," Moncreiff said. He bowed to Inglis.

"I have no questions," Inglis said.

Dr. Penny was called then to the stand and sworn in.

Moncreiff smiled at the witness, then addressed him.

"Doctor Penny, could you please introduce yourself to the court?"

"I am Doctor F. Penny, Professor of Chemistry in the Andersonian Institute, Glasgow."

"Could you tell the court what transpired last March 31st?"

"Dr. Thompson came to the institute and delivered a bottle. It was securely closed and sealed."

"What did you do then, Doctor Penny?"

"I broke the seal and made an examination of the contents."

"And the contents?"

"They were a stomach and a reddish-coloured fluid."

"Tell us, why did you make this examination?"

"I was requested to examine the contents to ascertain if they contained poison."

"At whose request?"

"At the request of one of the clerks of the Fiscal."

"And what was your analysis, doctor?"

Penny opened a black portfolio, took out a stiff parchment. He read aloud:

The stomach contents, poured into a glass beaker, measured 8½ ounces. On being allowed to repose, the turbid, sanguinolent fluid, which contained much flocculent matter, deposited a white powder. The powder was a coarse, gritty, white shining crystalliform, which upon experimentation: sublimed at a gentle heat; condensed in sparkling octohedral crystals; was slowly soluble in boiled distilled water; gave a sulphur-yellow precipitate with sulphuretted hydrogen water; a lemon-yellow precipitate with ammoniacal nitrate of silver; an apple-green precipitate with ammoniacal sulphate of copper; and on being mixed with hydrochloric acid and boiled on copper gauze, yielded a dark greyish-black encrustation which, on being heated, became again bright copper red and at the same time yielded a ring of white sparkling crystals.

The powder was, therefore, oxide of arsenic.

Moncreiff looked over at Madeleine; his lip twitched. He turned back to Dr. Penny. "How much arsenic would destroy life?"

"It is not easy to answer that—four or six grains are generally sufficient."

"How much arsenic was there, doctor, in L'Angelier's stomach?"

"Its weight corresponded to a quantity of arsenic equal to eighty-two grains, or to nearly one-fifth of an ounce."

"Such a considerable amount?"

"Enough to kill several families—and their horses, sir."

The audience laughed. Even the judges smiled. Madeleine's expression did not change. She retained the same Mona Lisa look she had had during the reading.

"Now," Moncreiff said, "please tell us, to your knowledge, does arsenic prevent tissue decay?"

"I wouldn't say that it prevents it, but I have heard that it does retard the process of decay."

"By what authority, doctor?"

"I believe Orfilla, in his treatise *The Favourite Medical Receipt Book.*"

"Thank you. Now, tell us, you also examined the contents of all the bottles and vials in the deceased's room?"

"I did."

"Did you find any that contained arsenic—in any form?"

"None at all."

"Would you say that there might have been an even larger dose administered, perhaps as much as an ounce, some of which was vomited off during the course of the sickness?"

"There certainly might have been."

"Are there cases on record where you have observed such a large dose?"

"I know of them as a matter of reading."

"And the victims swallowed such doses unknowingly?"

"Well . . ." Dr. Penny hesitated.

The Lord Justice-Clerk Hope leaned down. "Go on, sir."

"Well, the cases in which a very large quantity of arsenic was found did not turn out to be cases of murder by a second party. In the cases to which I refer, the substance was taken by the parties voluntarily."

A whisper ran over the courtroom. Inglis suppressed a smile. Moncreiff moved quickly on.

Inglis, on his cross-examination, returned to the point.

Would not arsenic delivered on such a scale be impossible to dissolve adequately? Wouldn't the victim know?

Dr. Penny scratched his ear, "It would be very difficult to give a large dose in a liquid."

"Doctor Penny, tell me, have you ever heard of arsenic being used as a cosmetic?"

"It would be very dangerous to use it in *any* way."

"I believe you, sir. But the question was: Have you heard of cases where arsenic was used as a cosmetic?"

"There are cases in which it had been applied to the skin, and in which symptoms of poisoning were produced—vomiting, pain, but not death. In one case, it was rubbed on the head; I don't remember the details of the case."

Inglis bowed his head. "Thank you."

Moncreiff rose. "Doctor Penny, let me put another question to you: Could a large dose be suspended in cocoa or coffee?"

"It would be possible."

"Could a person drink the dose without detecting it?"

"Well . . ." He pulled at his earlobe. "There is a difference between suspicion and detection. If the liquid were stirred, a person might drink a large dose, but he would have to gulp it down not to suspect."

"Thank you."

Inglis was again on his feet, approaching the box. Dr. Penny suppressed a yawn.

"In case of chocolate being boiled and stirred, wouldn't some gritty material still persist?"

"Yes, there would be some gritty particles."

"Do you think a person drinking such poisonous chocolate would suspect something when the gritty particles came into his mouth?"

"He might."

"Thank you." Inglis took his seat again.

The Lord Justice-Clerk coughed, spoke: "Could you describe the period in which the arsenic produces its effect?"

"Well, it varies according to the mode of administration. It is a slow-acting poison. Death occurs, on the average, in about twenty-four hours. Burning pain in the stomach and excessive thirst come first; then vomiting, tightness of the throat, diarrhea, lethargy, palsy, and convulsions."

"And how many grains do *you* think might be dissolved in a cup of hot liquid?"

"Before saturation? Ten, fifteen, maybe twenty-grains."

"Thank you, Doctor Penny."

Dr. Penny bowed, stepped down.

The Prosecution then called Dr. Robert Christian to the stand.

"Doctor Christian," Moncreiff said, "you made a chemical analysis of portions of the deceased's body, did you not?"

"I did. On April 10th, Doctor Penny delivered samples to me, with the view of ascertaining if they contained poison."

Moncreiff handed Christian a parchment.

"Could you identify this for the court?"

"It is my report."

"And your findings?"

"That the samples contained arsenic."

"Now, tell me, you also made an examination of two packets of arsenic, purchased, respectively, at Currie's and Murdoch's?"

"I did. On May 6th, Doctor Penny put into my hands two small paper packets, duly sealed, one supposed to be arsenic mixed with soot; the other mixed with indigo, according to the Act for the sale of arsenic."

"Did they contain the due proportion of soot and indigo?"

"The one marked 'Murdoch's' I found to contain the due proportion. The other did not contain quite enough colouring matter. Also, the indigo was imperfectly mixed."

"Could it have been removed by someone wishing to?"

"Oh, yes, indigo could have been removed by flushing the powder with cold water, the colouring agent dissolving more quickly than the arsenic."

"Doctor, how much arsenic do you think could be dissolved entirely in eight ounces if a proper vehicle were used?"

"Perhaps half an ounce."

"Would chocolate or cocoa be such a vehicle?"

"I think either would make an excellent vehicle."

"Would active exercise hasten the onset of arsenical-poisoning symptoms?"

"It might. Exercise accelerates the actions of all poisons except narcotics."

"Do you think the colouring matter of the arsenic might have been in the articles you examined without your observing it?"

"It might have. My attention was not directed to the point."

"Thank you, doctor." Moncreiff walked back to the table.

Outside, the town clock struck the hour. The chimes died away.

"Your witness, Dean of Faculty," Lord Hope said.

Inglis drew a breath, rose, approached the stand.

"Did you detect any colouring matter in the samples of the dead body?"

"No, my attention was not directed to it."

"And you noticed none on your own?"

"I did not see it, and I did not search for it."

"If it were there, could it have been found by careful examination?"

"I can't say."

"In such huge quantities as reported, you can't say whether the colouring matter could be detected?"

"Perhaps it could, if a search were instituted."

"Is not soot insoluble?"

"Many of the component parts are; but it might have been partially removed by vomiting."

"If indigo had been mixed with the arsenic, would that have been removed by vomiting?"

"Not entirely. It would have been found more easily from the intensity of the colour and the sharp definition of chemical properties."

"Tell me, is it easy to remove soot from arsenic?"

"It is very difficult."

"Tell me, what is the ordinary time that elapses between the administration of arsenic and death?"

"Oh, from eighteen hours to two and a half days. But it could be shorter."

"Is the size of the dose a determinant of the time lapse?"

"No, not necessarily."

"In this case, where vomiting occurred, how much would you say the original dose was?"

47

"I think the dose must have been double, probably more than double, the quantity found in the stomach."

"Perhaps as much as two hundred grains?"

"Yes, perhaps."

"In the cases of suicide you have seen, was as large a dose swallowed?"

"I can't say precisely; but in suicide, the dose is generally found to be large."

"How do you account for that?"

Dr. Christian smiled. "Oh, obviously, by the desire of the unfortunate person to make certain of death."

"In a case of murder no such large quantity would be used, would it?"

"I can't say."

"Isn't it in cases of suicide that double-shotted pistols and large doses are used?"

"But murder, even by injuries, and also by poison, is very often detected by the excessive violence or doses. In almost all cases of poisoning by arsenic, more is used than is necessary."

"But do you know any case in which so great a dose as the present was administered?"

"I cannot recollect at the present."

"Well, let me put this question—did you ever know of any person murdered by arsenic having eighty-two grains of arsenic found in the stomach?"

"I don't recollect at present," Christian said, drawing his knees together.

"Or anything approaching it?" Inglis said, leaning towards the witness.

"I don't recollect. Evidently, the exact amounts in excess of fatal dosage have not impressed themselves on my memory."

"You are not, at all events, able to cite any specific case?"

"Not at present."

"If a person designed to poison another, the use of a large quantity of arsenic, greatly exceeding what is necessary, is a thing to be avoided?"

"It is a great error if the person wishes to avoid detection."

"No further questions." Inglis drew in a breath, walked rapidly back to the table.

Lord Hope looked at the clock. It was half past five.

"Lord Advocate," he said, addressing Moncreiff, "unless you feel you can finish within the next hour, I shall recess the court."

Moncreiff walked to the judges' bench, conferred with Lord Hope.

Lord Hope nodded, rapped his gavel. "Court dismissed until ten o'clock tomorrow morning."

EIGHT

Inglis arrived Wednesday night at half past eight, carrying a parcel wrapped in brown paper. He set it on the table, held Madeleine's chair for her.

He didn't know what to ask. He knew only that he needed to know more.

He asked her about her family.

"Oh," she said, "my family is a respectable, loving family."

"Your father is terribly concerned about you."

"Yes," she said. "My family is a highly respectable family."

"Respectable?"

"Do you see my father—or my mother—in the courtroom?"

"I understand they are both ill."

Madeleine twisted the ring on her finger. "Of course."

"Are you close to your sisters and brothers?"

"Of course."

"Have they been in the courtroom?"

Madeleine laughed. "No. They must be taking care of my parents."

Inglis rose and stood silent. "Miss Madeleine," he said, "I

am your lawyer and I must know all that you can tell me if I am to be effective. If you do not speak to me directly and fully, we waste valuable time."

Madeleine looked up at Inglis. She blushed.

"Mr. Inglis, it was childish of me. Please sit down. Ask of me what you will."

"Why did you keep your liaison with Mr. L'Angelier from your father and mother?"

"My parents are Church of Scotland, Mr. Inglis. They love me and are good to me—as long as I am obedient and a source of pride. My father approves only of what he initiates."

"And of what does he disapprove?"

"Of anything I initiate."

"You are accustomed to hiding your will from your father?"

"Thoroughly."

"How do you hide your will from your father?"

Madeleine looked up through her lashes and smiled.

"Mr. Inglis, are you married?"

"No, I regret to say."

"Mr. Inglis, every girl learns that skill."

Inglis began to laugh. "Madeleine, are you using that skill now?" He sobered quickly. "Remember, Miss Smith, you are charged with a capital offense. Please don't be so coy. Just give me direct answers."

She folded her hands in her lap. "I'm sorry," she said.

"I need to know all about you—all about the woman who was in love with that man."

"Please, then, go on, ask what you must."

"The statement. Is there anything in it that you wish to revise? That might be disproved?"

She looked him levelly in the eye. "No, Mr. Inglis, not a word."

He was silent a long time. At last, he sighed and pushed the wrapped parcel across the table. It was banded and secured with the court seal.

"What is it?" Madeleine said.

"The copies of the letters."

"Oh," she said.

"I don't know when they will get to them. But we should be prepared."

"You mean if there is anything in them that the little toad might use?" Madeleine said.

Inglis laughed. "That is exactly what I meant."

When Inglis left, he did not go home. The air was sharp tonight, crisp. More like September than July. He could almost smell the icy lakes doon watter.

The tip of a glacier. That was all he had touched. This girl, dressed in soft muslin, those luminous grey eyes. Was she a child, innocent? Or was she a cool, composed, jagged peak of a woman? Had she ever been a child?

His steps slowed as he neared the kirk. The ground in the yard was soft and spongy beneath his feet.

He knelt at the base of the moonlit stone.

"Father," he whispered.

Yes, son?

"I am confused, father."

Of course you are.

"Papa, I am sure she lied in her statement, and yet, I trust her absolutely."

Oh, yes indeed.

"Don't mock me, father. How can I believe that she is lying and trust her word absolutely at the same time?"

His father's voice was sombre. *I do not mock you, son. Women cannot lie. Men need, to survive in society, to depend on truth. Women can survive only by saying what is needed, not what is true. For a woman, necessity is the equivalent of truth.*

"Father, you are harsh."

My son, religion not too long ago denied that women had souls. It is not I who am harsh. We become what we need to be.

"Father, should I believe her?"

No.

"Then I should disbelieve her?"
No.
"Oh, father, what then?"
Trust her.

NINE

Madeleine sat before the table in her cell. On the wooden surface was the stack.

She peeled off the seal.

Inglis had said there were seventy-seven letters. Had she written so many?

She lifted the stack and read the familiar words in this unfamiliar hand:

> My dear Emile,
>
> I do not feel as if I were writing you for the first time. Though our intercourse has been very short, yet we have become as familiar friends. . . .

Madeleine made a slight snorting sound. That child, copying with elaborate brown-ink strokes onto white French paper those words of intimacy from *Godey's Lady's Book*, scenting the envelope, sealing it with the finest wafer of blue wax.

She turned the page over atop the stack, pushed the bundle to the corner of the table.

The ink showed, heavy and masculine, through the back of the rough parchment. The copier's quill needed recutting.

She got up from the table and pushed her chair in. Then, with a sigh, she took the bundle, leaving the band and seal upon the table, carrying the letters to the narrow cot, pulling the cotton blanket over her feet.

She had been schooled for such intercourse. At Mrs. Gorton's Academy, near London, she had been finished. She had not gone to boarding school at the age of ten, as Mama had desired. Papa had not subscribed to that school of thought. Though Aunt Tabitha and Mama wheedled him, he stood fast in his belief that during those "tender" years, a girl should be under the wing of her family.

But finally, when she was sixteen, he had relented. She could go to be finished if the proper place were found.

"I know the perfect one," Mama said.

Two years. She had boarded the train a child, burdened down with six layers of horsehair and starch, hobbled by doubts. She had returned a woman, her hope chest filled with heavy artillery; fine cambric chemises, embroidered with rushes of scallops; off-the-shoulder ball gowns edged at the décolletage with Valencia lace; long black net gloves.

On the train going home, she had worn a green-and-lilac-striped barege blouse and a hooded shawl wrapped burnous-style around her shoulders.

The skirt was a flounce of tiers atop a bobbing hoop of steel. With measured steps, she moved down the aisle, lifting her skirt artfully, first this way past a valise, then that way around a gentleman's cane, effortlessly effecting the passage.

She knew that she looked very much like a walking bell. And she felt like ringing.

She took her seat in the compartment, anchored the hoop with her ankles before lowering herself.

Be careful, she thought. A haughty spirit goeth before a fall. In the best regulated of families, mishaps occurred. Look at Aunt Rose. What if her own destiny were spinsterhood? What if *he* were dying now on the Crimean front? Or already dead? If so, what good would knowing the dates of the kings of England or the origin of guano do her?

Two verses competed for her future: "Be good, sweet maid, and let who will be clever," and "Where my heart lies, let my brain lie also."

She could serve mankind, like the saintly Miss Nightingale. She knew, as any wellborn lady did, a lady's duty. But she hadn't Miss Nightingale's passion for suffering.

She would serve in her own way and in her own time. Now she was needed at home, to help Mama. If her destiny had been to go to the front and put on a brass-buttoned uniform, she wouldn't have been born blanching at the sight of blood.

Her mind turned from the men at the front to the men at home. Mrs. Gorton had pronounced her finished. Her character was formed, made especially to please. There would be no mishap. Romance lay ahead.

Papa was at the station with Big Jed to drive her home. He hugged her gruffly, then hurried her into the carriage.

"A new dress?" he said, when they were seated.

She smiled. "The latest from Paris."

"Hmmmph," he said, and lapsed into silence.

Her lower lip protruded but she forced a smile. She would not let him spoil her coming home.

They rode in silence through the streets. Ice was melting in the yards, running in rivulets past the dried bracken, onto the cobblestones. There, by a cavity of ice, a crocus popped its acid-yellow head up from the black mulch.

She looked over at Papa. Dark hair, fair skin—in many ways they were so much alike. But in others—

A vague unease stirred her. As if she were pigment on a canvas an artist had left unfinished. Something simmered, wafted, chafed inside her . . . waiting to become. Was everyone like this? Was anyone? Had Papa ever had thoughts like hers?

Did only she worry and muse so? Was anyone else filled with this waiting to exist? Everyone her age was in love, or had been. She felt herself a terribly aged child.

Perhaps it was there, in that book, filed away on some celestial shelf: her fate. Perhaps she was not real at all but was just a dancing figure in God's camera obscura.

Poor crooked thoughts.

The stars came out in the royal-blue sky, and a crimson belt lingered over the horizon as they turned down India Street. Papa shifted in his seat.

Ahead, the lights of home shone butter yellow and warm.

There are two main streets in Glasgow. There is Argyle Street, next to the River Clyde, the center of commerce; and there is Sauchiehall, the beau monde, the center of fashion.

At 8 A.M., the shop shutters are taken down on Sauchiehall Street. The doors open all at once: sugared doughnuts, hats, sheet music, stays, blue silk hose, daguerreotypes, point-lace shawls, fine French kid gloves, engraved stationery.

The street has its own cycles, its own rhythms. On a Saturday afternoon, it is an anthill of fashion and flirtation. Clerks emerge from their offices, eat their finest meal of the week in the local chophouse, then go for a walk. The daughters of bank clerks, carrying their striped hatboxes, stop to admire the tableaux of *poses plastiques* in the wide glass windows, stop again to point at the lace, while émigré Parisiens—"Pierres" to the native Glaswegians—admire the daughters and speculate on dowries.

Children run past, rolling hoops of iron, while their matronly mothers, hair parted in the middle after the Queen, promenade them. Horsewomen canter along the road. On the upper-story jaw boxes, wide-breasted women hang laundry. They lean over the railing, pointing out costumes that strike their fancy.

It was Madeleine's birthright, as a Smith, to be part of that parade, to be selected out as fashionable. It was her nature to enjoy it.

Madeleine stood in front of the winged chiffonier, trying to decide between the steel-blue taffeta and the champagne silk. She finally decided on the silk, and its matching satin bonnet trimmed with marabout feathers. Bessie wore the box-pleated promenade costume of pink satin with the concealed yoke and small mother-of-pearl buttons. Both girls took parasols and cloaks.

"Good-bye, Mama," they called out as they passed the sitting room. Mama was bent over the Ouija board with Mrs. Ferguson. Just last week, when Mama had visited Mrs. Ferguson, the first visit since getting up from her sickbed, Mrs. Ferguson's and Mrs. MacDiarmid's fingers had flown to and fro over the board, spelling out "Emma." Now it seemed that the speaking spirit was the poor dead soul of a boy who had claimed Mama as his own "Mamma," and would only speak to her. It took a long time, as the poor dead boy made many spelling errors.

"Good-bye, Mama. Good afternoon, Mrs. Ferguson," Madeleine said again, louder. Mama looked up, nodded happily at the sight of the parasols.

"Use them, children, won't you?"

"Yes, Mama."

"And Madeleine, put on your gloves. It is not enough to carry them, you know."

"Yes, Mama."

"It is not enough to carry them, you know," Madeleine said, as soon as the door was closed. She took off her gloves and put them in her beaded bag. Bessie burst out laughing.

As soon as they reached the end of India Street, she put the gloves back on.

At Mr. Baird's emporium, Master Robert Baird was standing outside, talking with a gentleman. He waved at Bessie, started across the street, bringing his friend with him. Madeleine and Bessie were escorted across to the sidewalk.

Baird, his Adam's apple bobbing, said: "Miss Smith, Miss Smith, may I introduce to you a friend of mine, Mr. L'Angelier?"

L'Angelier bowed. His clothes were English: tight grey-striped white fustian trousers, a tight-waisted teal-blue redingote, a blue cravat that, Madeleine observed as she curtsied, matched his eyes.

Bessie bobbed a curtsy. L'Angelier tipped his light-grey top hat. He was wearing kid gloves and carrying a slender cane.

"Ladies," Baird said, "please tell my friend how wrong he is in his opinions before I have to do him violence."

Madeleine looked from Baird to L'Angelier. Both men were smiling.

"Splendid," L'Angelier said. "Let me put my case before these two undeniably fair judges. Baird says that what we call progress—our industrial production, our transport distribution—is accident and illusion; that our lives are the worse for it."

Madeleine held her parasol to her breast.

"Heresy!" she said. "And you, Monsieur L'Angelier?"

"I, Miss Smith"—he gripped his lapels and coughed slightly—"I say to all assembled that progress is *not* an accident, that progress is a necessity, without which society would wither and perish."

Bessie's mouth was open. Madeleine laughed. "You are not alone, Monsieur L'Angelier. You are in the company of Spencer, who says that progress is a part of nature."

"Then I win?"

"Yes, you—and Spencer—win."

He bowed soberly. When he straightened, he was smiling.

Bessie nudged an elbow into Madeleine's ribs.

"Well, gentlemen," Madeleine said, "you must excuse us—we have some cloth to buy."

Baird turned and opened the door, showing Bessie, as he ushered her in, a bolt of Napoleon-blue silk in the window.

Baird turned back. L'Angelier nodded. Baird went in.

L'Angelier turned to Madeleine, held out his hand.

"Miss Smith," he said, "please believe that I *do* have some original ideas."

"Are you from Paris?" she asked, pausing on the bottom step.

"Miss Smith, we are not *all* from Paris."
"I didn't mean . . ."
"I am from the island of Jersey . . ." he said, his hand outstretched.
"So you are English," she said, placing her hand in his.
". . . where the customs are French," he said. He lifted her hand, kissed it.

Sunday morning in the kirk, between services, Bessie gave Madeleine an envelope, slightly wrinkled. It was sealed with red wax.
"Robert said to give you this," she said.
Between the covers of her prayer book, atop Hymn No. 82, she read the note within:

Dear Miss Smith,

The progress I devoutly wish most has nothing to do with machines or commerce.

Having had the honour of meeting you—and hearing you—I understand, as never before, that progress is, as Spencer says, a part of nature.

May we discuss it at further length?

Avec les sentiments très honorables,

P. Emile L'Angelier

Monday, Madeleine and Bessie were, by chance, on Bothwell Street, at the ticket booth to the Botanical Gardens.
The town clock struck one. Clerks spilled out of nearby buildings, some carrying lunch pails, some entering nearby eating establishments.
"The Misses Smith!"
They turned. L'Angelier walked swiftly towards them.
"Ladies, what a pleasure!"
Bessie curtsied; Madeleine smiled, dipped her head.

And so matters progressed. If they did not talk of Spencer, it was not because Madeleine had exhausted the topic, though that was nearly so. They talked instead of Nature.

The pebbled path led to the white greenhouse. L'Angelier held open the door. He set his Balmoral cap upon a flower stand, led the way down the center aisle.

Madeleine inhaled the hot heavy air, the smell of moss and fungus and oxygen. She took off her gloves, ran her fingers lightly over the fleshy, speared leaf of a large plant.

"What is this?" she said.

L'Angelier came up beside her, examined the leaf. "It is a liliaceous plant, of the genus *Aloe*, a succulent. Certain species of it yield a drug. It has some medicinal properties."

"And what do you call this flower?" Bessie called.

L'Angelier let go the leaf, turned. "*Dianthus caryophyllus*, Miss Smith."

"It's beautiful," Bessie said, sniffing the blossom.

L'Angelier smiled, walked back to the caretaker, and after a few whispered words returned with a pair of enamel-handled shears to cut off a white flower and a pink one.

Madeleine watched as he attached the pink flower to Bessie's collar.

"How do I look, Madeleine?" Bessie said.

"A perfect picture," Madeleine said.

"You look like a Tintoretto, mam'selle," L'Angelier said.

Bessie blushed.

L'Angelier turned to Madeleine, the white flower in his hand.

She lowered her eyes. He touched her collar, lifted it. She stood still, aware of the dark, close circle of his fingers, the scent of soap and tobacco. He pulled the stem through the buttonhole.

He stepped back.

"What is *she*, Monsieur L'Angelier?" Bessie laughed.

"Ah, a Botticelli, there's no doubt about it," he said.

Madeleine smiled serenely.

The clock chimed. L'Angelier looked up.

"I'm sorry, ladies, I must be back at work."

"But you've missed your lunch," Madeleine said.

"I never eat lunch," he said.

"But you'll be sick."

"No, I'm never sick," he said, and rapped his knuckles against the white trellis. He took his cap from the flower stand. "I'm glad you are lovers of botany," he said, his cap held behind his back.

"I like flowers," Madeleine said.

"Papa encourages us to collect specimens," Bessie said. "It is a hobby of his, too."

"I should like to meet him." He bowed slightly. "Look at the hanging mosses before you go; they are a favorite of mine."

Madeleine moved down the narrow aisle to let him pass. He spoke to her in a low voice.

"The gardenias will be in bloom soon. I shall replace this carnation when it has faded."

"What is a gardenia?"

"A lovely white tropical flower—named after a Scottish naturalist."

She lowered her head, smelled her carnation. "I'm sorry, but we leave for Rowaleyn on Wednesday."

"You summer there?"

"Yes."

"You will be gone the entire summer?"

"We do come sometimes to town."

"If you let me know . . ." He broke off, looked at his feet.

"Well . . . Papa and Mama are coming in on Sunday. But I think we shall stay home."

"I have a good friend near Rowaleyn. If I were to come on Sunday?"

"Perhaps fate will be kind," Madeleine said.

"You have fate in your grasp, Miss Smith."

Madeleine smiled, shook her head.

"Mine," he said, settling his cap on his head.

That afternoon, on Sauchiehall, Madeleine bought a diary with a small key to lock its Moroccan leather cover. She had quills cut. Then, when Bessie was occupied, she bought brown ink and a good costly white French paper with gold edges, lightly scented. And fancy sealing wax that would leave the finest of thin wafers when pressed.

At home, she opened the diary and sat for a long time at her writing table, looking down at the blank page.

P. Emile L'Angelier: An angel with blue gentian eyes.

She wrote the date: *March 19, 1855*, and sat looking at the floral design on the wall. At last she redipped her pen and wrote in perfect, rounded letters:

> Blue is everlastingly appointed by the Diety
> To be a source of perpetual delight.

Madeleine had burned the diary, too, that day at Rowaleyn. It had burned more slowly than his letters. The leather had smelled like seared flesh.

She looked down at the letters on the cot, picked up the first page, looked down at the letter copied there.

The letter was dated April, 1855. She finished reading it:

> We feel it rather dull here after the excitement of a Town's life. But then we have much more time to devote to Study and Improvement. I often wish you were near us, we could take such charming walks.
>
> I wish I understood Botany for your sake as I might send you some specimens of moss. But, Alas, I know nothing of that study.
>
> We shall be in Town next week. We are going to the Ball on the 20th so we will be several times to Sauchiehall Street before that. Papa and Mama are *not* going to Town this Sunday. So of course you do *not* come to Row. We shall not expect you.

Bessie desires me to remember her to you.

Your flower is fading. . . . I must now say adieu. With kind love, believe me, your very sincere

Madeleine

She had been frightened after she had sent it, afraid he would think her too forward.

His answer had come by return mail. She knew it by heart:

Dearest Madeleine,

Your epistle reached me last night. I have thought of nothing but botany and long walks since then.

Your gardenia will be ready next week. Might I have the honor of pinning it on?

Believe me, your devoted
Emile

She had spent the entire evening copying his name next to hers in her old school notebook.

She sang as she dressed for riding—breeches under her saxon-cloth skirt, a leghorn hat, steam-coloured kid gloves. Her jacket was the latest from Paris, cut wide like a man's top coat. There had been a cartoon just this week in the *Review* poking fun at the mannish coats. Well, let them. She didn't care a whit. If Monsieur L'Angelier happened to see her, *he* would know her for a lady.

She rode out past the Army barracks, through the pasture, to the field's edge, then over a rude timber bridge and up over a hill to a curved stretch where the valley fanned out below. The sun hung red and wobbly in the tuck of hills.

Suddenly, her life seemed full of direction, purpose.

She would take over the running of the house, pay bills monthly, buy in quantity, keep the servants in their place, encourage high morals, ease the burden on Mama, comfort Papa by making the house a place of peace and grace. She would be the true "angel in the house."

When an offer of marriage arrived, she would be ready.

She rode home, visions of a vine-covered cottage in her head—and inside, a down-covered bed.

Papa was waiting in the courtyard, a scowl upon his face.

My Dear Emile,

    Many thanks for your kind epistle. We are to be in Town tomorrow. Bessie said I was not to let you know. But I must tell you why! Well, some friend was kind enough to tell Papa that you were in the habit of walking with us. Papa was very angry with me for walking with a gentleman unknown to him. I told him you had been introduced and saw no harm in it. Rest assured I shall not mention to anyone that you have written me. I know from experience that the world is not lenient in its observations. But I don't care for the world's remarks as long as my heart tells me I am doing nothing wrong.

    We are to be at McCall's at 12. If you should be there and say how surprised you are to see us . . . well . . . then we shall see what Bessie says. Only if the day is fine expect us. Bessie does not know I am writing you, so don't mention it.

    Adieu till we meet. Believe me, yours most sincerely,

                                       Madeleine

At McCall's on Saturday, Madeleine's face had lit up and she had put down the gloves she had been examining, turned to him.

Bessie said, "Mr. L'Angelier, how nice!"

L'Angelier bowed, inquired of Bessie after Baird. Madeleine turned back to the glove counter, picked up the blue kid gloves.

He came up the aisle and stood behind her.

"Which pair do you think?" she said softly, not turning.

"I am sorry if you are in trouble because of me, *chérie.*"

"I brought it upon myself," she said. She turned and held the gloves out.

"You have done nothing wrong," he said.

"No, but he thinks—Oh, it isn't fair!"

"It is my fault. I was too rash." He fingered the gloves and smiled.

"I'm afraid now Papa will never receive you."

"You don't know my will."

"You don't know my Papa's."

"Mine is indomitable."

She laughed.

"You will see, Mam'selle Smith."

"Madeleine," she said.

He looked at her with wide eyes. "Madeleine," he said, softly. He was smiling.

"Emile?" she said.

He nodded, his eyes even wider. "What, *chérie?*"

She smiled. "I just wanted to say it."

He lifted his hand as if to touch her cheek, stopped midway.

She had reached out, to the place where the vein lifted out of the skin and ran down the middle finger, touched it.

Bessie had come up behind them. "Are you ready, Madeleine?"

"Just a minute, Bessie," she said. She turned back to Emile, her face sad.

"What, *chérie?*" he said.

She shook her head. "Nothing."

April 5, 1855

Dear Emile,

    I was happy seeing you. Bessie gave me a black look all the way home. What if Papa had seen us?

I think you will agree with me that for the present, the correspondence had better stop. I know your good feeling will not take this unkind. By our continuing to correspond, harm may arise.

It is my earnest desire that ere lang you may be a friend of Papa's.

Sincerely,
Madeleine Smith

Two days later, by way of messenger, she received a package. Inside was a creamy-petalled flower, beginning to darken around the edges, its scent within the box almost cloying—and a note:

My dear Madeleine,

I shall endeavor to accomplish what you say. We have done no wrong. Fate will be kind. My heart tells me.

Your devoted, loving servant
Emile

The spring flew towards June, the land greening, the buds flowering around the fresh deep glacial lakes.

And Fate did bring them together. In the haberdasher's, where Madeleine had gone to get Papa a dress shirt—so close she could smell the scent on Emile's hair; at the river wall, where she had gone after marketing for fresh air, he for a smoke. They had stayed apart, leaning on the wall, looking down at the flowing waters.

"When do you come to Glasgow next?" he said.

"I don't know," she said. "Whenever Mama does. Perhaps in a fortnight."

"If you could let me know?"

"I will try," she said.

He nodded. "You had better go. Someone might see you."

"Yes." She turned to go, her knees faltering.

She was in the general store off Argyle one Monday during a downpour, sifting French roast beans through her fingers, looking at the clerks coming from the office building across the street, wishing now that she had sent Emile a note.

"Why, Miss Smith!" a voice said. "I didn't know you drank coffee."

She turned. Emile stood there, a bamboo box of tea in his hand.

"Well, actually," she said, "I was only thinking of it. They say it is good for the digestion."

She let the beans fall back into the burlap bag, wiped the oily residue off her gloves.

"Well, if you aren't going to purchase anything today," Emile said, "perhaps I could have the honor of escorting you to your carriage? I happen to have an umbrella by the door."

She nodded.

He set down the box of tea.

"But please, don't let me stop you from purchasing your tea," she said.

He grinned. "I never touch the stuff."

"I don't understand."

"I have a confession to make," he said, opening the door, stepping outside, and springing the umbrella open.

"A confession?"

"I didn't come in here for tea, *chérie*."

"Well, then, what did you come in for?"

He held the umbrella above the door, beckoned her into its shelter, and walked her to the waiting carriage. He took her hand to help her up.

"Well?" she said.

"To kiss mam'selle's hand," he said, lifting her gloved hand to his lips, his eyes meeting hers.

She stepped up into the seat, her cheeks dimpling, her bottom lip between her teeth, her skin hot under the glove.

The rain pelted down on his black umbrella, spraying like a halo around him on the sidewalk.

"I come to Helensburgh on Sunday next, to visit my friend Auguste De Mean," he said.

Her face flushed. "Sometimes, just before tea," she said, leaning out from the carriage roof, her voice becoming a whisper, "it is nice to walk on the Highland Road near the old crofter's cottage. 'Tis very quiet there."

He nodded, went to the front of the carriage, and spoke to the driver. "Drive with care."

At the corner, Madeleine looked back. Emile was lighting a little cigar, his face down, the smoke puffing up from under the dome of the umbrella.

On Friday, by means of post, a letter arrived at Huggins and Co. addressed to M. L'Angelier.

June 21—Midsummer's Day

My dear Emile,

I have a confession to make. I was not in the coffee shop by accident either.

I treasure your confession.

Monsieur Auguste De Mean knows my father. Ask him to be our friend.

Aussi avec les sentimentes très honorable, votre

Madeleine

Postscriptum: Sunday M. and P. are to be away.

TEN

Madeleine opened her eyes. The floor of the cell was a dim pearl grey: It was almost dawn.

From afar, the bugle began reveille—the garrison waking up. She reached over to the bedside table, past the stack of letters, took the glass, and sipped the negus and laudanum.

Then she lay back, watched the floor grow pink. She had been dreaming of the dell at Row—the way it looked at dusk—the same pink gold

In her dream she had been standing in the dell with Ben, looking for fairies. And the cow was there and Ben was talking to it. She thought him the cleverest boy in creation, that he could converse in a cow's native tongue, that he had seen a real fairy. And then the cow had answered back and Ben had appeared in front of her, only it was Emile's face.

In the dream she had smiled and breathed in the dell: the soft doeskin color of the cow, the gentle tinkling of the bell, the sun pink-gold and going down, the ferlies gamboling under the light, the two children in a springtime garden.

She reached again for the glass, her hand grazing the edge of the parchment. Last night she had read to Midsummer's Day. Now she remembered the Sunday after.

The Sunday after Midsummer's Day had dawned clear and sunny. Mamma and Papa had left on schedule to visit the Fergusons.

Madeleine had spent three hours on her toilette: a bath in the copper tub, an oatmeal-and-honey face pack, her hair done up in ringlets.

And then the dress: In the mirror, she smoothed the lace at her breast and turned, her white silk flounces, alternately narrow and wide, bobbing and settling.

Jack and James were in the kitchen, playing mumblety-peg.

"I'm going to collect specimens," she said.

"Who cares?" Jack said.

She went down the dark hall, adjusted her bonnet in the looking glass. Then she lifted the wide skirt, taking up three of the seven linen petticoats, curtsied. Then, humming a tocatta, she went down the stairs and along the margin of the path. Under the high, white sun, the tall elms cast patches of shade upon the walk.

She walked up the hill behind the house to where the top of the garden met the circle of fields. The heather was out, heady, mingling with the scent of her body.

She lifted her wrist to her nose, inhaled, felt the pulse beating.

At the hedgerow, she stopped and looked across the fields to the far land. Beyond the heather and rough grass growing in tussocks, a curlew called.

Then, from the far thicket, birds rose in flight.

She took a step, stopped. Emile was coming down the road. She ran to meet him, her bonnet falling back and her hair, worn long today, tumbling in curls against her neck. Her hat hung by its chocolate ribbons.

He came quickly, stopped before her, for the first time since they had met, speechless.

She smiled. "Emile, you look nice."

"I cut my hair," he said.

"Blue looks good on you."

He touched his coat. "You are simply beautiful," he said.

She looked down at her bare hands. He looked at them too. With great self-consciousness, she held her hand out. Wordlessly he took it, clasped it.

He pulled her to him. She came into his arms, her face

against his coat. She felt his member swell inside his trousers. Frightened, she pressed tightly against him.

He pulled himself away, walked a short distance, sat down on a stump.

She came and knelt beside him, her face radiant.

"Don't be sorry," she said, moving within his shadow.

He put his hand on her hair, softly, pulled her head to his chest.

"I'm going to marry you, Mimi."

"Mimi?" She smiled.

"Yes, Mimi."

She settled beside him. "Tell me about your home. Is it pretty?"

"My lodgings?"

"No, Jersey."

"Well, you would find it charming. There is the brim-full bay, stretching in a curve for many miles; there are the hills, the trees covered with ivy, even in winter. And to see the whole island, you go up to La Hougue Bie."

"La Hougue Bie?"

"The Prince's Tower."

"Why is it called the Prince's Tower?"

"Well, once upon a time, Jersey had a dragon, a man-eating one—"

"A dragon!"

"And one day, a Norman prince named De Hambie set off to slay the dragon. Which he did. . . ."

"A dragon slayer!"

"Yes. And as he slept after the fight, his manservant murdered him with his own sword, went back to France, and claimed the master's wife for his own, saying the Prince had ordered it."

"A dragon-slayer slayer!"

"Then the servant was found out and the widow built a tower to mark the spot where her husband was killed, so she could see it from her window. And that's the Prince's Tower. Haunted by the ghost of the prince."

"Oh, Emile, you left out the most important part!"

Emile rubbed his chin. "What did I leave out?"

"How!"

Emile sighed. "Mimi, *ma belle*, how what?"

"*How* the servant was found out."

Emile placed his hand gently on her chest. "Forgive me, my love, but nobody asks of a legend questions like how? or why?"

She looked down at the hand resting above the curve of her bosom. "I forgive you," she said. She took his hand and placed it by the seam of his trousers. "You really don't know how."

Emile folded his hands together and laughed. "I guess I don't," he said. "But I hope to learn."

"Is it a green one or a pink one?"

"I give up," Emile said, his clasped hands held up.

"The ghost."

"Oh, Mimi," he said, "I have much to learn, don't I?"

"After you marry me, I shall teach you," she said.

He smiled, leaned over, and kissed her cheek. Then he lay back in the flowering heather.

She picked a single sprig, placed it in his buttonhole. "What is this called, Emile?" she said, touching the tiny bell-like flower.

"I forget," he said.

"I don't believe you."

"*Calluna vulgaris*, if you must know."

"Oh," she said. "Well, a rose by any other name . . ."

Down in the valley, the cowbell rang for supper. She kissed him. Then she ran home.

June 30

My Dearest Emile,

 I am sitting by my window today looking at the hillside and thinking of my intended. You would love Row. We could take so many lovely walks. You would tell me the names of all the flowers, show me the constellations.

I smile when I think of Sunday. Papa *must* meet you. What did Auguste say?

Tell me what to read, Emile. That I may share, at least, your ideas.

Your devoted,
Mimi

P.S. If someone else were to address your letters, I think it would be safe. I would tell M. and P. that it was a friend.

Emile had a friend, Kennedy, with a feminine hand. He asked him to address the letters.

When Mama inquired after the letters, Madeleine told her that they were from Miss Parsons, an old roommate at Clapton, who was now in the nunnery in Glasgow.

In July, Aunt Tabitha invited Madeleine to go with her to the firth for holiday. She wrote Emile at once.

July 20

My Dear Emile,

We go to Bridge of Allan for a fortnight. I will be back before the new moon. If you can get away, I don't need to say that I would be delighted to see you at two on that Sunday. Wishing you were going with us.

I am your
Mimi

P.S. Do not send any more letters till I return—The Garden—2 P.M.

Her letter arrived too late. When Madeleine arrived home from the shore the first Sunday in August, an envelope waited on the silver tray. She slipped it into her bag.

At dinner, Papa, passing the turnips, remarked: "And Madeleine, what have you to say about this alleged roommate who has been corresponding with you?"

"Alleged, Papa?" she said. She swallowed a lump of turnip.

"Alleged, Madeleine."

"I don't know what you mean."

"You know exactly what I mean."

The colour drained from Madeleine's face, rose in Papa's.

She opened her mouth, closed it. She rose and walked, slowly and deliberately, from the room.

In her room, she examined her cache. All seemed in order.

Oh, why couldn't she have made some answer? Bessie had stared at her, the way she had when Madeleine had quoted Spencer, waiting for the logical explanation.

Why didn't she ask what in the world did he mean? Why couldn't she have been puzzled and affronted. What *did* he know? No, hers was the silence of the guilty. "The guilty flee when no man pursueth." How much, she wondered, did they know? She heard footsteps on the stairs, quickly put the shawls back over the letters, climbed into bed, pretended to be brushing her hair.

Mama came in the room. Madeleine turned towards the wall.

"Madeleine, I had to tell him."

"You!" She turned and looked at her mother.

"I had every right."

Madeleine held her breath.

"Miss Parsons called on Thursday. She thought it odd that I mentioned your faithful correspondence—especially the last letter."

"I'm sorry, Mama."

"Sorry's not enough, young lady."

"Did you read the letter?"

"I had no alternative."

"It isn't what you think."

"I wonder. Well, Papa sees only that you disobeyed him. But he blames the young man more than he does you."

"It's not fair, Mama."

"Nor was your lying, daughter."

"Oh, Mama, what will I do?"

"The right thing."

"The right thing? Is there a right thing?"

"Cut him off."

"But . . . I like him."

"Madeleine, you're so young. . . ." She reached out and stroked her hair. ". . . Just a child."

"I'm not, Mama."

"Oh, I know. I remember." She picked up the coverlet from the bottom of the bed, folded it.

"You don't know."

"You love him?"

"He's . . . not like anyone I've ever known."

"He's different from all the rest, is that it?"

"I guess."

"And he's handsome?"

Madeleine blushed. "Yes."

"So love strikes and you surrender to it?"

"Mama, I didn't!" She stared at her mother.

Mrs. Smith cocked her head and looked hard at Madeleine. "No, perhaps you didn't. You'd be ashamed to look me in the eye if you had."

"Mama!"

"Let me tell you something, daughter, from experience. He's exotic now, but soon he would be commonplace. Soon you'd be crying because you couldn't have a new dress, because you had to stick your hands in dishwater . . . and then, when the babies came . . . ."

"I wouldn't."

"And I'll tell you one thing more, daughter, from experience: Break with him"—her voice grew gentle—"and one day, I promise you, you will wake and the first thing you think of will *not* be him . . . and on that day, your heart will begin to mend, I promise."

"Mama, how do you . .?"

"Hush, daughter, don't pry." Mrs. Smith smiled faintly and touched Madeleine's cheek.

"Yes, Mama." Madeleine's hand covered her mother's.

"Good. Now I'll go and talk to Papa. He certainly can't expect you to go to the ball next week if he doesn't increase your allowance."

"Papa?" Madeleine said, standing in the doorway of the dark room, looking in. Papa sat with his lips pursed hard.

"Papa?"

Papa turned and stared at her. She knew he wanted her to come in, and she forced herself to enter the study. She had never liked this room, even as a child. Its dark wooded walls and glassed surfaces chilled her.

"Well," he said, "what do you have to say for yourself?"

"I . . ." she began

"And don't give me a story scabbed with lies."

"Papa, I didn't . . ."

"We trusted you."

She bit her lip, held back the tears. "Papa, may I ask . . . one thing?"

"After you have answered my questions."

"Papa, I didn't do anything wrong. Emile is an educated, honorable gentleman. I have—"

"Madeleine, I know who this Monsewer Emile L'Angelier is—and what he is."

The tears brimmed over on her cheeks.

"You listen to me, girl. This is my house and I will not suffer that its members be shamed. Especially, I will not see your mother humiliated. You dragged our good name, your sisters' names, in the mud with that ten-penny Pierre."

"He is English, Papa!"

"Enough! He is not fit for you or for anyone of your station."

"Papa, do you condemn a man for being born out of the

kingdom? For speaking two languages well? For having his fortune yet to win? Didn't you begin with nothing?"

"I began with a good name, daughter."

"Your father-in-law's," she said, her cheeks ablaze. "What virtue in that?"

He slapped her.

Later, he brought her beefsteak for her bruise. He held it against her purpled cheek while he spoke. "Madeleine, I have only one thing to say to you on the subject of this . . . young man."

She nodded.

"If I ever find out that you lied . . . that there was more to this than just the letters, I will—" He broke off.

She stared at him.

"And you are not at liberty to see him—ever. Do you understand me?"

"Or?" she said.

"I will no longer have a daughter. He may have you."

"You'd throw me out, Papa?"

"Yes, daughter," he said.

On Sunday, Madeleine ran early to the fields, a brown envelope in her pocket. She weighted it upon the old picnic table with white stones, ran home.

Sunday morning

Dearest Emile,

Many thanks for your kindness to me. I have talked to my parents and Papa will not give his consent, so I am in duty bound to obey him. It is a heavy blow to me. Our relationship must be at an end.

You have been a good friend to me. Oh, continue so. I hope and trust you may prosper in all that you do. Think my conduct not unkind. I have a father to please, and a loving father too.

Farewell, dear Emile. With much love, I bid you adieu. With the kindest love, I am your friend.

                        Mimi

On Monday, she went to Sauchiehall to buy silk stockings for the Captain's Ball. The street was bustling with shoppers. Her eyes brimmed with tears under her light veil. Near the corner by the haberdashery, she saw Emile approaching. She slowed almost to a stop, her throat dry.

As she switched her bag to her left hand to free her right hand, Emile scowled, swerved, and crossed the street.

A week passed. She lost her appetite; her head ached constantly.

When she went to Glasgow with Mama and Christine, she dreaded—and longed—to see him. As she sat in the coach, waiting for Christine to finish loading the packages, she thought she saw him. But no, the man turned and it was another. Her heart fell.

Then Christine came running up to the coach, her cheeks flushed. "Madeleine," she said, handing over an envelope.

"Who gave it to you, Christine?" she said.

Christine pointed down the street to the Tron Gate. Madeleine could just make out Emile's disappearing figure.

"A gentleman," Christine said.

"That one?"

"Aye, miss," Christine said.

When they reached home, she opened the envelope. The epistle within bore no salutation, no signature.

> In the first place, I did not deserve to be treated as you have done. How you astonish me by writing such a note without condescending to explain the reasons why your father refuses his consent. He must have reasons, and I am not allowed to clear myself of accusations.
>
> You have deceived your father and you have deceived me. You never told him how solemnly you bound yourself to

me, for if you had, for the honour of his daughter, he could not have asked you to break off our engagement. Madeleine, you have truly acted wrongly. You desire and now you are at liberty to recognise me or cut me just as you wish—I give you my word of honour, I shall act always as a Gentleman towards you.

Think what your father would say if I sent him your letters for a perusal. Do you think he could sanction your breaking your promises? No, Madeleine, I leave your conscience to speak for itself.

I flatter myself that he can accuse me only of want of fortune. But he must remember that he too began the world with his fortune yet to gain.

It is to me unbelievable that, for want of will or for want of courage, you can allow our love to perish.

She had tossed and turned in the half-tester bed all night long. Would Emile show Papa? If he did, Papa would *have* to give her away. In a month, she would be lying in Emile's marriage bed.

She slept, finally, and woke at seven to a knock on the door.

"Come in," she said.

It was Christine, looking embarrassed.

"Miss Madeleine, this cam for ye." She held out a package wrapped in white paper, tied with twine.

Madeleine sat up.

"'Twas the gentleman I pointed oot to ye in the street yisterday."

"Did he say anything?"

"Nae, Miss Madeleine, just that I gie it ye pairsonally."

The maid handed Madeleine the package, backed out.

Madeleine cut the twine, stripped off the paper: her last letters. He had kept only the first few innocent ones. He had, of course, been the perfect gentleman.

She pulled the covers back over her, spent the day in bed. Her words in that room haunted her.

By six, she was bored, restless. She pulled a book from the shelf, opened it, then threw it on the floor.

At eight, she was at her desk, Sir Walter Scott's *Marmion* open in front of her. He had been her favourite author once. At Clapton she had read *The Black Dwarf* and *The Fair Maid of Perth*. *Castle Dangerous* she had read three times. Scott, she remembered, had been Sheriff of Selkirkshire once. Imagine, a lame sheriff—amazing what a family name could do.

She felt as she had once upon coming home from Loch Lomond and passing a restless night. All night, something had smelled foul. In the morning, queasy, she had pulled the pillows from the bolsters at the foot of the bed. And there, rotting for two weeks, was what had become of the dead mouse her cat had deposited. She could still see the coils of intestines, and moving large fat white maggots crawling upon her bed.

Papa would never trust her again. She would never receive the same kind looks from her mother.

And Emile. Trusting her, believing in her. He had talked of marriage and she had listened, replied with sweet promises.

She could not stop herself. If she were to see Emile now, even now, she would have to lie: "Of course I told him I was in love with you."

A week passed, two. On a Saturday, as she was watching the Regiment Parade, a small child pulled on her sleeve.

"Miss Madeleine?"

"Yes, I am Miss Madeleine."

He pressed a smudged envelope into her hand, ran off into the crowd.

She felt faint, went beneath the canopy of nearby elms to rest. Her fingers trembled when she opened the letter.

Dearest Madeleine,

What I have said to you I could not have said. I accuse

you of lying, and I have lied so horribly to myself that I detest the sound of my voice.

Please see me.

I think of you always. I remember your voice. I remember the pain that I have caused you. I remember the pleasure that you have given me.

Please see me. Under any terms you wish. But please see me.

Emile

She held the letter, looked up through the leaves at the dappled sky. She sighed; her upper lip quivered.

She could see him standing there, his palms turned skywards, his eyes angelic. The wind blew through the leaves above, set them quaking and rustling. A lump choked in her throat.

She bit her lip, hard, thrust the letter into her pocket. She got up, dusted off her skirt, went back to stand with Bessie.

Papa would be coming along with the Regiment band soon, the kettledrum strapped to his burly frame, his straight legs white beneath his kilt. He would expect her to salute.

She was in a thicket, and wherever she turned, the thorns tore at her. She was caught between two men: afraid of both. To obey one was to disobey the other. Each considered her bound to him. She was bound to do what either wanted. What both wanted. The question was never "What does *she* want?"

A line came back to her from Scott's *Marmion*. As the bagpipe's lilting melody reached her ears, she mouthed the words:

> O what a tangled web we weave,
> When first we practise to deceive!

As if she had an alternative.

ELEVEN

It was the morning of the third day, Thursday. Moncreiff waited till the policeman had finished handing over a message to the Glasgow reporter, then rose. "The Crown calls Mr. Auguste De Mean to the stand."

De Mean, a tall, slim, debonair man, adjusted his bottle-green coat and took the stand. He had a long face with pale-blue eyes, an aristocratic nose. His English was flawless.

He placed his long gloved fingers atop the Bible, swore to tell the truth.

"Would you please the court by introducing yourself," Moncreiff said.

"I am August Vauvert De Mean, Chancellor to the French Consul at Glasgow."

"How long were you acquainted with the deceased?"

"For about three years."

Montcreiff turned to the exhibit table and picked up the photograph in the gilt frame. "Can you identify this likeness for the court?"

"It is L'Angelier."

"Is it a good likeness?"

"Yes."

"Tell us, did he bring a letter of introduction to you, or did you get acquainted with him accidentally?"

"I think accidentally—in a home in Glasgow—I don't recollect whose."

Moncreiff nodded. "Did you also know Miss Smith?"

"I did."

"And her family?"

"Yes."

"And did you know of the . . . relationship . . . between L'Angelier and Miss Smith?"

"I knew of a correspondence between them."

"How did you know?"

"L'Angelier confided in me"—De Mean paused; his hand fumbled with his white cravat—"against my wish . . . his relations with Miss Smith."

The courtroom was silent. The Lord Advocate chose not to pursue the subject.

"Tell the court please how you came to know the prisoner."

"Well, Mr. Smith had a house at Row and I had one at neighboring Helensburgh."

"Did Mr. L'Angelier ever visit you at Helensburgh?"

"Yes, he stayed a night or two with me before I was married."

"Did he ever ask for advice regarding Miss Smith?"

"On occasion. I told him then that he ought to go to Miss Smith's family and tell them of the attachment, and ask Mr. Smith's consent. I told him that was the most gentlemanly way."

"And what did he answer?"

"He said that Mr. Smith was opposed to it; that Miss Smith had spoken to her father and that he had been excessively angry and that it would be useless."

"When did this conversation take place?"

"Before my marriage, about a year ago."

"Did he confide in you after your marriage?"

"I had no intercourse with him after . . ." De Mean paused. "He did come to see me a few weeks before his death. We spoke for a few minutes only."

"What did he want?"

"He was distressed. He wanted to talk about Miss Smith."

"Did you then discuss Miss Smith?"

"I asked him not to discuss Miss Smith with me. I told him that his affections were futile, that it was now known that Miss Smith had accepted the proposal of a gentleman who was a friend of the family."

"What was his reaction?"

"He said it could not be true."

"Did he say anything else?"

"He said that if it was to come to this, he had documents in his possession that would be sufficient to prevent the banns."

"Did you see L'Angelier again?"

"Not before his death."

"But you did involve yourself with his affairs, didn't you—after his death?"

"I thought that, having often been received by Mr. Smith in his house, it was my duty to apprise him of the correspondence between L'Angelier and his daughter in order that he should take steps to protect his daughter from any untoward consequences."

"Untoward consequences? Could you be more precise?"

"I knew that the deceased had letters from Miss Smith in his possession."

"Tell us, please, about your conversation with Mr. Smith."

"On the evening of L'Angelier's death, I told Mr. Smith that L'Angelier had in his possession a number of possibly compromising letters from his daughter."

"Yes?"

"I told him that they might fall into the hands of strangers."

"By strangers, whom do you mean?"

"Bystanders."

"What did he say?"

"He was shocked. I said that I was afraid that strangers might go to L'Angelier's lodgings and read them, as his repositories were not sealed up. He then asked me if I could act as counsel for L'Angelier and have his repositories sealed."

"Did you do so?"

"I went to L'Angelier's employer, but he was not in—I requested of the two gentlemen there that the letters be signed over to me. They said they were not at liberty to give the letters without Mr. Huggins' consent. I then asked them to keep the letters sealed up till they were properly assigned."

"Assigned?"

"Sent home to his mother."

Moncreiff nodded. "Now, Monsieur De Mean, please tell us, did you go to the Smith house again that day?"

"I don't remember if it was the same day. Later I heard some rumours and I went to see Miss Smith—in the presence of her mother."

"And they received you?"

"Yes. In the drawing room."

"Tell us, Monsieur De Mean, *why* did you go?"

"I was acutely uncomfortable," De Mean said. "Nevertheless I felt it incumbent upon me to acquaint Miss Smith with the matters that had developed after L'Angelier's death."

"What matters?"

"That L'Angelier's death was rumoured to be unnatural and that it was being said that his hasty return from Bridge of Allan was at her urgent invitation."

"What connection did you make between these two matters?"

"None. None at all. Nevertheless, the unfortunate coincidence could be misconstrued by others and I thought she should be forewarned."

Madeleine closed her eyes, briefly, hearing herself say:

"Is it of your own volition that you come to tell me this, Mr. De Mean?"

"No," he had said.

Her face had frozen.

"Your father asked me to speak with you."

"Oh," she had said.

"Miss Smith, I must ask you a question."

She had nodded.

"Did you see L'Angelier the night before he died—Sunday night?"

She had stared at him. "I did not see him on Sunday."

"Then tell me something that can put me in a position to contradict the statements that are being made about your relations with L'Angelier."

"What statements are being made?"

"That L'Angelier came from Bridge of Allan to Glasgow on special invitation by you."

The room had grown a little hazy. Her voice had come out strangely. "I didn't know that Emile was at Bridge of Allan before he came to Glasgow."

"So you saw him?"

"I didn't give him an appointment for Sunday, as I wrote to him on Friday morning, giving him the appointment for the following day, Saturday."

"You expected him on Saturday, yes, I know."

"But he didn't come."

"And you didn't see him on Sunday?"

"I told you I did not see him on Sunday."

De Mean had put the question to her three times in different ways. She had denied it three times.

"Miss Smith, what am I to do then, with the conviction that he came on purpose from holiday on a special invitation by you. Will people believe that he committed suicide without knowing why you asked him to come?"

"Suicide?"

"People believe his sudden death was occasioned by poison."

"Poison?"

"Miss Smith, the case is a very grave one and the authorities are sure to make inquiries."

"I shall tell them what I have told you."

"And if someone comes forth and says that L'Angelier was in the house? A servant? A policeman? Somebody passing the house?

Don't you see, Miss Smith, a small lie could cause a very great suspicion as to the motive that could have led you to conceal the truth."

She had sprung up from her chair, her cheeks ablaze. " I swear to you, Mr. De Mean, I did not see L'Angelier, not on that Sunday only, but also not for three weeks before."

"And he was no longer your sweetheart?"

"No." She had walked to the window, looked out.

"Please tell me, then, how it was that, being engaged to be married to another gentleman, you could have written him thus—clandestinely—and proposed a secret rendezvous in your house?"

She flushed. "I don't know what you mean," she said, turning and facing him.

"Friday's letter," he said.

"Mama," she said, "could you go and ask Christine to bring us tea?"

When Mama was gone, she sat down and looked up at the man. *"I did it in order to try and get back my letters. That was the only reason."*

De Mean looked at her a long time.

"You did invite him to the house for Saturday?"

"Not to the house. He has never been in this house."

De Mean looked at her, sighed. "Madeleine . . ."

"He used to come to the corner and knock," she said.

De Mean was silent.

"He signalled me by knocking at my window with his cane, and I would open the window and talk with him."

"They say that you signed your letters appending his name to yours."

"They have read the letters?"

"As if you considered yourself his wife."

She had sighed. *"Did I, Auguste?"*

Did I? She wondered now, looking at De Mean on the stand. He had been Emile's—and her—one great hope. If he had introduced Emile to Papa . . .

Moncreiff was thanking him now for his testimony. Madeleine looked over at Inglis.

Inglis adjusted his powdered wig, rose, and walked quickly to the stand, began his cross-examination.

"Mr. De Mean, could you please tell us about L'Angelier's visit at Helensburgh before your marriage?"

"He came for a few days. We went out on the Luss Road."

"To be precise, was he ill on that occasion?"

"Why, yes, he was. He came on a Saturday, and on Sunday we went out, and afterwards, coming home, he lagged behind, saying in a feeble voice that he would be along immediately. I saw him very pale. He had been sick, vomiting."

"Did he tell you what it was?"

"He complained of being bilious."

"Did he ever talk of other illnesses?"

"He said that once he had had cholera."

"When was the attack?"

"I don't know exactly when, a year or two ago."

"Did he ever talk to you of taking medication for his illness?"

"I know that when he came to my house, he always had a bottle of laudanum in his bag."

"You mean tincture of opium?"

"I believe that that is what is in it."

"Did you ever see him use it?"

"No."

"Did you ever hear him speak of arsenic?"

"Yes, once."

"When?"

De Mean cocked his head. "I believe in the winter 1853–1854."

"Do you remember how the conversation arose?"

"I don't. . . . It lasted about a half hour."

"And what was its purport?"

"How much arsenic a person could take without being injured by it."

A murmur swept through the audience. Several members of the jury leaned forwards.

"Did he say how much?" Inglis said.

"No, only that by gradually increasing the quantity, one could take otherwise fatal amounts. The body, he said, builds up resistance."

"Did you know anything of the subject at that time?"

"I had seen something in a French text on chemistry."

"Now, tell the court, did he ever tell you anything that might have led you to believe he had contemplated suicide?"

"I don't recollect anything."

"Let me refresh your memory. Didn't he once mention to you being jilted by a rich lady, a lady from Fife?"

De Mean hesitated. "Yes. He did tell me he had been jilted and he said that on account of her deception, he was almost mad for a fortnight."

"What do you mean, mad?"

"He ran about the countryside. He lived on food farmers gave him."

"Was he of an excitable nature?"

"He was easily excited. When he had any cause of grief, he was affected very much."

"Thank you, I . . ." Young was motioning to Inglis. Inglis nodded and walked to the defence table, read from the tablet Young placed in front of him. He nodded, returned to the witness box.

"Mr. De Mean, could you explain why you ceased to have intercourse with the deceased?"

"I thought that he might be led to take some harsh steps with regard to Miss Smith. And as I had some young relatives of my wife in my house, I did not think it was proper to have the same intercourse with him as when I was a bachelor."

"Thank you," Inglis said. "No further questions."

Moncreiff stood. "What do you mean by 'harsh steps'?"

"I was afraid of an elopement."

"Then by harsh you mean rash?" Lord Hope said.

"Yes," De Mean said.

"Did you understand that Miss Smith had engaged herself to him?" Lord Hope said.

"So he said."

Lord Ivory leaned over, whispered to Lord Hope. Lord Hope nodded, turned back to the witness box. "Tell us, Mr. De Mean, was L'Angelier a steady fellow?"

"My opinion of his character was that he was a most regular young man in his conduct—religious, most exemplary in all his conduct."

Lord Hope's voice rose: "This man you feared would offend young ladies in your house?"

"'Offend' is perhaps too harsh a word."

"Or too rash a word. Did you hear objections to his conduct from others?"

"Some said he was vain and a boaster."

"And how did he boast?"

"Oh, he would speak of grand persons he knew."

"Did he ever boast of Miss Smith?"

"Well, he might say, 'I shall forbid Madeleine to do such a thing, or such another thing. She shall not dance with such a one, or such another.'"

"Did he boast of success with females?"

"Not to me."

"Did he seem jealous of Miss Smith paying attention to others?"

"No, of others paying attention to Miss Smith."

"And it was not on account of any levity in his character that you discouraged his visiting you after your marriage?" Lord Hope said.

"No, I thought that his society might be fit for a bachelor, but not for a married man."

Inglis rose partly from his seat, looked at the witness.

"Do you understand the word 'levity'?"

"Yes, lightness, irregularity."

Inglis nodded.

Lord Hope looked at his notes and spoke again. "Monsieur De Mean, when you used the expression 'I thought it was my duty to apprise Mr. Smith in order that he should take steps to protect his daughter from any untoward consequences—"

"I didn't say that, sir," De Mean interjected. "I believe I said to prevent her honour from being disparaged."

"Hmmm . . . or to prevent her honour from being disparaged . . . did you think the letters might constitute a legally binding promise of marriage?"

"I thought only that these letters were love letters, and that it would be better that they should be in Mr. Smith's hands than in the hands of strangers."

Lord Hope nodded. The courtroom was silent.

"You may step down, sir," Lord Hope said. De Mean nodded and descended the stand.

Moncreiff motioned to the policeman at the door, then approached the bench. "The Crown now calls Angus Murdoch to the stand."

Murdoch, a portly man in a grey serge coat, walked quickly up the aisle and to the witness stand.

"If it please the court," Moncreiff said, after Murdoch was sworn in, "tell us your occupation."

"I am a partner in the firm of Murdoch Brothers, Druggist, on Sauchiehall Street."

"Tell us, Mr. Murdoch, do you keep a registry book of poisons sold?"

"We do."

"Can you identify this book?" Moncreiff said, placing a large black ledger before the man.

"It is our registry book."

"What is entered here?"

"All the arsenic we sell by retail."

"Is there an entry of arsenic sold to the prisoner?"

"Yes, under the date February 21st we have an entry—

Miss Smith, 7 Blythswood Square, sixpence worth of arsenic for country house and garden—signed M. H. Smith."

"And this purchase has been initialled by you?"

"Yes."

"Mr. Murdoch, do you recollect that purchase being made?"

"I do."

"Can you identify the purchaser?"

"Yes, it is the defendant," Mr. Murdoch said, nodding towards Madeleine.

"Thank you, Mr. Murdoch." Moncreiff turned and faced the judges. "No further questions."

"Your witness," Lord Hope said to Inglis.

Inglis shook his head slowly. "No questions, Your Honour."

Moncreiff called George Carruthers Haliburton to the stand.

"Please tell us your profession, Mr. Haliburton."

"I am an assistant to Mr. Currie, chemist, Sauchiehall Street."

Moncreiff showed him the registry book for the sale of poisons. Haliburton identified it. It was admitted as No. 186 of the inventory of evidence.

"Now," Moncreiff said, "please look at the months February and March and tell me if Miss Smith made any purchases of poisons."

"I see two entries—March 5th, 1857 Miss M. H. Smith, 7 Blythswood Square—arsenic, one ounce, kill rats, and March 18th, again one ounce, to kill rats."

"Did you sign the entries?"

"Yes, and they are also signed: M. H. Smith."

"On March 5th, did you serve her personally?"

"Yes, she asked for sixpence worth, and I said, 'What for?' She said it was to kill rats. I told her we were not fond of selling arsenic for that purpose."

"Why?"

"Because it is so dangerous. I recommended phosphorous paste."

"What did she say?"

"She said she had used it, but it had failed."

"Did she say where the rats were?"

"In the house at Blythswood Square."

"Was there anyone with her on this occasion?"

"Yes, a young lady."

"Did you give Miss Smith the arsenic?"

"Yes, she told me the family were going from home the next day and that she would be careful to see it put down herself."

"Was the arsenic mixed with soot?"

"No, with indigo."

"Now, on March 18th, you also served Miss Smith, did you not?"

"Yes, sir."

"Do you recollect that occasion?"

"Yes. She asked for another sixpence worth, and said the first was so effectual—she having found eight or nine large rats lying dead—that she had come back to get the dose renewed."

"Was Mr. Currie in?"

"Yes. He said to me that he never sold it except to parties of responsibility, and he was about to refuse it when I told him that I had given her it on a former occasion."

"Was anyone with her on this occasion?"

"Yes, a young lady—I suppose her sister."

"Have you ever heard of arsenic being used as a cosmetic?"

Haliburton rubbed his chin. "A preparation is used as a depilatory for taking hairs off the face; it is yellow sulphuret of arsenic."

"Thank you," Moncreiff said.

Haliburton nodded, his Adam's apple jerking in his throat. Moncreiff took his seat.

Inglis stood, smoothed his robe, then approached the stand.

"Tell me, Mr. Haliburton, were both purchases made openly?"

"Quite openly."

"Did you know the lady who accompanied Miss Smith on the first occasion?"

"No."

"Or on the second occasion?"

"No."

"Did you overhear any of their conversation?"

"Well, the second time, the young lady accompanying Miss Smith remarked that she thought arsenic was white and I said we had to colour it according to the Act of Parliament."

"Did you mix in the colouring matter?"

"I did. I put in the proper quantity ordered by law."

Inglis nodded. "Thank you, no further questions."

The witness started to rise, but Lord Hope waved him down.

"Tell us, is yellow sulphuret similar to white arsenic?"

"No," Haliburton answered, "it is quite a different thing."

"Do you also sell Fowler's Solution in your shop?"

"We do."

"For what purpose?"

"For various ills—indigestion, angina."

"Is it covered by the Act of Parliament?"

"Yes."

"How much arsenic does the solution contain?"

"Fowler's preparation is four grains of arsenic to an ounce of fluid."

"Thank you. You may step down."

Moncreiff then called William Campsie to the stand. He wore a shiny black coat, and his hair, slicked back, smelled of cheap brilliantine.

"You are in the service of Mr. Smith?" Moncreiff said.

"Yes, I have been in his service since 1855."

"Do you work at the Blythswood Square house or at Rowaleyn?"

"At both, sir."

"Did Miss Smith ever give you any arsenic or poison to kill rats?"

"No, sir."

"Have you ever used arsenic to kill rats—at either establishment?"

"No, sir."

"Thank you."

Campsie nodded, touched his temple

Inglis walked to the stand, nodded to the witness. "Tell me, sir, in the course of your employment in the Smith household, were you ever troubled by rats?"

"Oh, yes, very much so."

"And you used poison to kill them?"

"We used phosphorous paste or some such thing."

"Some such thing?"

"We used a commercial rat killer at times; I don't know what was in it."

"Did you find it effectual?"

"What, sir."

"Did it kill the rats?"

"Oh, we got quit of them partly, but not altogether."

"Thank you, no further questions."

Mr. Campsie touched his temple.

"You may step down, Mr. Campsie," Lord Hope said, smiling.

At half past two on the third day, Mr. Minnoch was sworn in. He did not look at the defendant.

Moncreiff walked to the witness stand, asked the tall, balding man to introduce himself.

"I am William Harper Minnoch. I am an architect in Glasgow and a partner of the firm of John Houldsworth and Company." He stood erect, staring above the heads of the audience.

"Could you tell the court how long you have been acquainted intimately with the Smith family?"

Minnoch's hands gripped the brass rail of the pulpitlike box. "Upwards of four years."

"Thank you. Now please tell us what transpired between you and Miss Smith this past winter."

"I paid my addresses to Miss Smith, and I made proposals of marriage to her in January of this year. She accepted."

"You did so personally?"

Minnoch looked incredulously at the lawyer. "Yes."

"You are sure your actions were such as to make her quite aware that you were paying your addresses to her?"

"Of course."

"You had no idea she was engaged to any other person?"

"No."

"She gave you no reason to doubt that the marriage would take place?"

"None."

"And you were aware of no attachment or peculiar intimacy between her and any other man."

Minnoch looked at the front box. Madeleine smiled faintly, "No," Minnoch said. "No."

"When was the marriage fixed for?"

"June 18th."

Moncreiff nodded. "Tell me, did you ever make Miss Smith a present of a necklace?"

"I did; it was sometime in January, before the 28th."

"Tell us, please, the occasions on which you saw Miss Smith after she returned from Bridge of Allan."

"Well, after she came home, she dined in my house with her father and mother; that was on March 20th. I met her again at dinner at Reverend Middleton's on March 25th."

"Were you aware of anything wrong at this time."

He shook his head. "No."

"When did you see her next?"

"I called at the house on Thursday morning, the 26th."

"And?"

"I was informed she had left the house."

"Yes?"

"I went with her brother to Rowaleyn to look for her. We found her on board the steamer to Row, a little after two o'clock. We went with her to Row, and then we ordered a carriage and returned to her father's house."

"When did you see her next?"

"On the Saturday following. I had by this time heard a rumour that something was wrong. I asked her and she told me that she had written a letter to someone, the object of which was to get back some letters.

"That is all she said?"

"At that time."

"You were not curious?"

"She had earlier asked me to refrain from questioning, and said she would later explain."

"And later?"

"I saw her on Monday and Tuesday. On Tuesday, she alluded to the report that L'Angelier had suffered arsenic poisoning, and she remarked that she had been in the habit of buying arsenic, as she had learned at school that it was good for the complexion."

"Why would she make so peculiar a juxtaposition?"

"I supposed that she found it an ironic coincidence."

"Had *you* heard this report or was she the first to mention it?"

"I had heard rumours to that effect."

"Did you know the deceased?"

"I did not."

"Thank you, Mr. Minnoch. I have no further questions."

Moncreiff walked back to the table, took his seat.

Minnoch took a handkerchief from his pocket, wiped his brow.

The Dean of Faculty sat for a moment, looking over his notes. Then he rose and walked to the stand.

"Mr. Minnoch, where were you the evening of February 19th?"

"I don't recollect." He pulled a date book from his pocket, opened it. "Yes, I was at the opera that night, with Miss Smith and my sister."

"What time did you get home?"

"About eleven."

"Miss Smith was with you the entire evening?"

"Yes."

"You saw her go into her house?"

"Yes, the cab stopped at her door, and she went in."

Mr. Minnoch then looked briefly at Madeleine. She met his gaze, then lowered her eyes. The cross-examination continued.

William's voice, Madeleine thought, was weak. Had he been sick? She watched him, scarcely hearing his words, her eyes on his hands, the knuckles white, gripped tightly on the brass rail. There was something childlike about him. Had she noticed it before? She tried to think when she had first met him: five years ago?

She had thought him old at first. Mr. William Minnoch, a friend of her father, an architect, well-to-do. She had expected someone formidable, and had been surprised by his homey face, his ill-fitting, baggy trousers. And yet, at Michaelmas dinner, seated, he had a certain gentle grace.

Jack had been away at boarding school and Mr. Minnoch had taken Jack's old chair, across from Madeleine.

He had smiled as Janet said the prayer:

> Some hae meat and canna eat,
> And some wad eat that want it;
> But we hae meat, and we can eat,
> And sae the Lord be thankit.

His brown eyes twinkled myopically as he explained the origin of the night's feast to Janet.

"Janet, do you know the origin of the word 'angel'?"

Janet, just nine, shook her head.

"Messenger," brother James had said, and Minnoch had turned to him and nodded.

"You see, Janet, the angel who speaks to man is but a low angel, just a messenger. He has to report to his employer."

"His employer? Is that God?"

"No, God is much further up. The angel reports to the archangel."

"Does he have wings?" Janet said.

"Huge ones."

Madeleine felt left out. She concentrated on the oval breadbasket decorated with husks and rams' heads. One hunk of white crusty bread was left. Papa hadn't said anything about Minnoch being religious. It was really rather quaint. She took the last piece of bread, spread on butter, and popped it in her mouth.

"Now, you know there are four archangels, Janet?" Minnoch said.

"Gabriel, Michael . . . and . . . ?"

"Raphael," James said.

"Good boy."

"But that's only three," Bessie said.

"James?" Minnoch turned his gentle face towards the boy.

"I dunno."

"Miss Smith?" He looked at her directly for the first time that day.

Madeleine shook her head. "Surely there are only three."

Minnoch put on a serious face. "Ah, but there *are* four, Miss Smith. The last is . . . Satan."

"Satan!"

"And do you know the other angels between the archangels and God?" He was addressing Janet again.

Oh, really, man, thought Madeleine. Must you fill her head with this religious pap? It's the nineteenth century, not the Middle Ages. She looked over at Papa. There he sat, listening like a child.

She ran her fingers over the sugar cannister embossed with leaves and scrolls between gadroon borders. She drummed her fingers on the cloth, received a chill stare from Mama. She smiled sweetly, folded her hands in her lap.

Minnoch was describing the seven classes of angels, the principalities, the powers, the dominions.

"And Satan has his messengers too, just like the other archangels."

"Really?" Janet's mouth was open.

Madeleine spoke up. "But Mr. Minnoch, they are just myths."

"But of course," he said, smiling at her. "What did you think I was talking of, religion?"

She coloured. "Oh."

"Well, can *you* name them?" He smiled at Madeleine.

"Of course: Abaddon, Appollyon, Asmodens, and Beelzebub."

"*Very* good."

Madeleine looked down the table at Papa. He was smiling at her, as if she had just won a prize in school.

Madeleine looked back at Mr. Minnoch. Was he weak chinned beneath that beard?

"Well, family," Papa said, clinking his knife against his glass. The maid came and removed the cloth, brought the drinks.

Then the rounds began. Papa stood. "'Delicate pleasures to susceptible minds.'"

Then Mama: "'May the honest heart never feel distress.'"

Bessie was next. She had been silent all through dinner. She sang forth loud and strong now: "'May the winds of adversity ne'er blow open our door.'"

Then it was James' turn; he stood up like the men: "'Here's health, wealth, wit, and meal.'"

Janet was next. She stood, then sat down, blushed, spilled out her toast as though it were one word: "'Blythe may we a' be.'"

Madeleine had been debating between two toasts, "May

the hinges of friendship never rust" or "May the wings of love never lose a feather." No, neither would do. She said: "'May the hand of charity wipe the tear from the eye of sorrow.'"

Mr. Minnoch had risen and raised his glass: "'May the pleasures of the evening bear the reflections of the morning.'" He had drunk, sat down, his teeth gleaming through his beard.

Madeleine, blinked, looked back up at Minnoch on the stand. He was not happy now.

"Tell me," Inglis was saying, "on the 26th, who suggested the possibility that Miss Smith had gone to Row?"

"I did."

"Why did you think she might have gone there?"

"Her father had a house there, in which a servant was living at the time, and I thought she might be there."

"And you found her on the steamer?"

"Yes."

"What did you say to her?"

"I asked her why she had left home, leaving her friends distressed about her; but I requested her not to reply then, as too many people were present. I renewed the inquiry at Row, and she said she felt distressed that her Papa and Mama should be so much annoyed at her."

"This was the day of L'Angelier's funeral, was it not?"

"Yes, I found that out later."

"Did her Papa say anything to you when you called that morning?"

"He told me she had left the house."

"Did you ask the reason?"

Minnoch hesitated, gritted his teeth. "He said it had been some old love affair."

"Did Miss Smith say anything about a 'love affair'?"

"I understood her to refer to that in the answer she made me."

"Did she explain?"

"No."

"Weren't you curious?"

"She asked me not to press her and said she would tell me all by and by."

"On Tuesday, March 31st, you said that she referred to the report of L'Angelier having been poisoned?"

"Yes."

"And it was she who introduced the subject?"

"Yes."

"When was this?"

"About half past nine in the morning."

"Did you go to the house to ask Miss Smith about this subject?"

"No, my meeting with Miss Smith was accidental. I called for Mrs. Smith; I had heard she was unwell."

"Let us go back for a minute to the Saturday following Miss Smith's trip to Row. She told you she had written a letter. Did she bring up the subject or did you?"

"I reminded her of the promise she had made to tell me all. She then answered."

"Had you heard the name L'Angelier at that time?"

"No."

"Did she mention him by name?"

"No."

"How did she refer to him?"

"I think she said she had written to a Frenchman to get back her letters. I did not know who the Frenchman was."

"Did she tell you what was in the letters?"

"I did not inquire." Mr. Minnoch stood erectly.

"Thank you. No further questions."

It was half past five when the tired Mr. Minnoch descended the stand.

Moncreiff stood, approached the bench. "I have several more witnesses," he said.

"Perhaps then we should recess till the morrow," Lord Hope said. Moncreiff nodded.

"Court dismissed till ten o'clock tomorrow morning," Lord Hope said, rapping his gavel.

TWELVE

Inglis arrived as the tower clock struck ten. He looked up at the dial and passed within the iron-studded door.

He was tired tonight. The prosecution had called two witnesses to his every planned one. Tomorrow it would be three.

She was fresh. It quickened his pulse.

"What did you think of my friend Billy?" she said.

"Is that what you called him?"

"Sometimes." She smiled and a wistful look came over her face.

Inglis nodded. "I thought that here was a man as tired as myself."

"You have more energy."

"Thank you."

She smiled. "I did my homework . . . but it gave me nightmares."

"Should I not have asked you?"

"I find I am shaped by many things. . . . I find things that I didn't want to remember."

"By many things—do you mean many people?"

She shook her head, her eyes lowered. Her lower lip swelled and she pressed her lips together. "By things, mostly."

"I have read the *Chambers'* article," he said.

"Yes?"

"Tell me, does the moon shape you?"

"You mean am I subject to periods of caprice, of transient unequal tempers?" Madeleine said.

"Not exactly."

"What *do* you mean?" she said.

"You said you would be direct."

"I remember."

"It talks of the lunar cycle in the article, the Styrian system of ingesting arsenic. And of a notebook," Inglis said.

"Yes."

"Madeleine, be truthful."

"You haven't asked me a question."

"I am still figuring it out. There was no moon when he died. Under the Styrian system, one begins with the largest dose in the darkness of the new moon and takes smaller and smaller doses as the moon waxes, abstaining entirely when the moon reaches fullness. Then one abstains to purge the poison from the body as the moon wanes: Then the moon is gone, and one swallows the full dose again."

"It is what the article says."

"And both times he fell sick, it was during the dark of the moon, the time, under the Styrian system, that arsenic eaters take their maximum dose. So it might have been an accidental overdose—but eighty-some grains is a large accident."

"Yes?" Madeleine said.

"I have thought of my question. Did you buy him the memorandum book?"

"I . . . d . . . how did you know?"

"I didn't," Inglis said. "The article said: 'let me urge upon all who adopt the system to make some written memorandum that they have done so, lest, in case of accident, some of their friends might be hanged in mistake.'"

"Oh, it had nothing to do with the article. That was a long time before. It was just a gift—we had both made resolutions."

"I know."

She met his eyes, her chin quivering imperceptibly.

He nodded to the matron. She brought the tea tray.

"Now," he said, "we were talking of women's caprices, weren't we? You want to tell me about your nightmares?"

103

❦

When Inglis left, Madeleine lay on her cot and watched the waxing moon. Letters had been waiting for her when she returned today. Two denounced her; a third was from a gentleman of means, requesting her hand in marriage. She smiled, slid her hand under her nightclothes, felt for wetness. Her "illness" had come while she sat in court that day, capriciously. But her flow had been light; there was only a small stain on her undergarments. She had asked Miss Aitken for a pail of water to wash them out. Now she lay back, closed her eyes.

She had been twelve years old when her childhood had ended. She was playing in the nursery at Row with Janet and James. Janet was the Queen, James the Prince of Wales, and she, being the oldest, was the Prince Consort. At the moment that Mama entered, Madeleine was parading across the floor, a magnifying glass held to her eye.

She followed Mama into the master bedroom.

"Now, Madeleine," Mama said, handing her a large book, "this being a critical period you are about to enter . . . well, I have spoken to Papa—and since your judgment is as yet unstrengthened by observation . . . Well, read this, you will understand."

It was a medical book: *A Treatise on the Diseases and Special Hygiene of Females.*

Did she have a fatal disease?

"I don't understand, Mama."

"Well, it is like this: Whereas before puberty, a young girl exists for herself alone . . . having reached this age, the . . . ah . . . springtime of her life, when all her charms are in bloom, she now belongs to the entire species which she is destined to perpetuate. . . ."

She hadn't the slightest idea what her mother was talking about, only that Mama was embarrassed.

"You read this now, Madeleine, and afterwards, well, if you have any questions . . ." She fled the room.

Madeleine opened the book to the bookmark, sure now that she had a fatal disease. And she had felt so healthy.

The general attention required by women at entering the brilliant and stormy crisis, which is terminated by the appearance of the menses . . .

Menses, was that the disease? There was a dictionary on Mama's desk. She looked it up: *Menses*: "Flow of bloody fluid from the uterus, occurring normally every four weeks."

Now she was even more confused. Occurring "normally"? She looked up *uterus*: "In the female mammal, an organ for containing and nourishing the young during the development previous to birth."

In female mammals, but what of humans? Birth? Bleeding? Was she going to have a baby? When her cat had the kittens, there had been blood . . . but every four weeks?

She read on: "The food of the young girl at puberty . . ." There was the word her mother had used, at least she thought it was.

She looked up *puberty*: "The state or quality of being able to bear offspring."

Oh, my Lord! She read on in the treatise:

. . . consists principally of vegetable substances, of preparations of milk, of tender meats. . . .

Yes, Mathilde had been serving light meals lately.
She read now with a horrible fascination.

We advise gymnastic exercises, walking and riding, the game of battledore and the hoop; flannel drawers; all cause friction about the inferior extremities, and are important for inviting the flow of the menses.

She turned the page:

If the function delays its appearance too long, we should resort to very warm hip baths and pediluvia . . .

Oh, dear, *pediluvia* . . . and it was not even in the dictionary!

and applications of cups to the thighs and leeches to the vulva.

Madeleine thought she would faint. She had learnt that word in school, didn't need to look it up. But if it had to do with that word, touted about the far corners of the schoolyard, she was no longer sure it had to do *entirely* with babies.

It was said in those corners that on her wedding night, the young Queen Victoria had received the following advice from her mother: "Lie still and think of the Empire."

Something happened, and babies came . . . and it must have to do with the bleeding . . . and something a man had and she did not. She had seen babies, of course, her own brothers, but couldn't see anything in the piddling penis that would be capable . . . And yet, somehow it was done. A man kissed a woman and nine months later, by a mysterious arrangement on the part of Providence, a baby was born—though she couldn't fathom how.

She finished the passage:

It is well to say also that if some amongst them become subject to these periods of caprices, to sadness and unequal temper, we should always bear these transient humours with indulgence, because they depend upon the action of the body upon the mind, and upon an active irritation, which is radiated from the uterus towards the other organs, especially the brain.

She closed the book, stared at the black cover. Oh, if only there were pictures!

The next day the equinoxes had been raging. A high and gusty wind had swept through the treetops. Grandpapa had hitched up the roan pony to the buckboard.

She rode down the lane, listening to the monotonous soughing of the elms, eager to see if Ben had arrived.

At the corner by his garden, she saw Ben's sisters, jumping rope.

> O, ma mammy killed me.
> Ma daddy ate ma bones.
> Ma twa sisters buried me.
> Between two marble stones. . . .

"You seen Ben?"

"Back yonder," his sister said, pointing towards the fields.

She drove up the top of the lane to where the fields spread out. At the bend, she came upon a hawk, sitting atop a rabbit carcass. It took off slowly, ungracefully, needing three sweeps of its huge wings before it was aloft.

The wind was up now, and it swept her skirts around her legs; she had to sit on them to keep them from billowing.

At the top of the hill was a saucer-shaped plateau of fields—timothy, barley, heather—a long dusty road crossing the middle. She approached a rude timber picnic table in the shade of the hedgerow.

Ben was lying on his back, a blade of grass between his lips. Scotty Bairn, his white Westy, was eating grass.

"Hey!"

"Madeleine!"

He had grown since last summer, now stood up to the pony's ears. He seemed a stranger somehow. But perhaps it was just his hair. He had cut it. Instead of curls to the shoulders, he had clipped locks.

"Want to go for a ride?"

He climbed in, looked at her. He took the reins from her, his hand brushing hers.

"I've been waiting for you."

She smiled.

"Madeleine?"

"What?"

"Never mind." He clucked to the pony and they went a few paces, then stopped by a field of running grass. He turned to her.

"You look pretty."

"Thank you."

He was silent a long time. His hands were sweating on the reins.

"I missed you."

"Did you?"

"Yes . . . you know what?"

"No."

"You look older." He reached out and put his hand on her hair.

She stiffened.

"You did up your hair."

She blushed.

He tightened his grasp on her hair, pulled her to his mouth, kissed her.

She fought him.

He stopped, his eyes angry, wounded. But she was angrier. She moved to the far end of the seat, her lip bitten, tears in her eyes.

His neck and ears were red. She stole a look over at him, felt repulsed at the soft down hairs that were sprouting on his cheeks. She looked down.

"I'm sorry," he said.

"You could have asked first!"

"Would you have said yes?"

"No!"

"All right, I should have asked."

Her lower lip trembled. If anyone knew . . . and her now in puberty! She inched further away from him on the seat.

"You don't have to treat me as if I were a cad."

"Were you not?"

"Maddy, please."

"Can we go home now?"
"You won't tell?"
"Ben! Do you think I would?"
"No."
"It was a bad thing you did."
"And now I'll have to say it in confession."
"Wouldn't you have anyway?"
"I don't know, Madeleine. I guess I wouldn't have thought it a sin if . . ." He looked at her, beseechingly.

He picked up the reins, put them in her hand. Taking his cap, climbed off the buckboard. "I think I'll walk, Maddy. You go on."

She didn't mind that. She clucked to the mare and they started off down the path. As she rode, the wind came up stronger. The sky got dark overhead and the air around her whistled. Bits of straw skirred past, and her hat blew back off her head. The first drop of rain splattered on the dust of her shoe. A circle of patent leather shone.

She slowed the mare, turned her around, went back the way she had come. At the top of the bend she saw Ben. He was by the dell near the swamp tree. She waved to him.

He shook his head.

She sat in the wagon, trying to decide what to do. She wasn't ready to absolve him, but she didn't want him to get wet. And probably you couldn't get a baby that way anyhow. Why, she had seen Uncle Jack kiss Mama and . . .

There was a green flare of light from way off and then a rumble of thunder. The rain began to come down hard now, and she picked up the reins and started to ride towards Ben.

It was not as if she had broken any of the Ten Words.

A light cracked, illuminating the entire dell, casting a halo around Ben. She shielded her eyes, cried out with surprise. Then the world crumpled with sound around her and her hair stood on end.

She heard the Westy howl before she saw the ring of black grass, Ben, prostrate. The rain made it all seem far away.

She jiggled the reins, clucked to the roan. But the pony backed up, its ears pressed close to its cropped mane. She beat it with the whip, crying. It backed farther, reared up.

She jumped down from the cart, cast the reins to the ground, and ran to the hillock, the wind lashing her skirt wetly around her legs.

She thought she saw his legs move as she approached. The smell got stronger. Burnt grass. Feces.

The Westy was whimpering, nudging his master's shoulder.

"Ben!" she cried, falling to her knees inside the ring of oily grass. "Get up, Ben!"

His face was grey; even the freckles were faded, and the rain came off his skin, into his hair. She had to cover him.

"Ben, are you all right? Ben?" She took off her jacket and put it like a tent over him.

She looked around, wildly.

"Ben, I'm going to go for help. . . ."

He lay there.

There was no blood. She leant over him, put her ear to his mouth, then to his heart.

She heard her own heart pumping. She looked up. Her tears had stopped but the water still streamed down her face.

"Ben?"

The Westy whimpered, put his head against the ground, scraped his ear.

Ben's hand was cold. The tips of his fingers were shrivelled.

The rain stopped suddenly. She heard the last drops splatter on the leaves, then nothing but her heart. The smell.

Her upper lip rose over her teeth. She looked down at her hand on the skin of his arm. Her fingers were pressed to his skin, and when she lifted them, it seemed there was a film on them.

She touched her index finger to her forehead, then took it away, looked at it.

She backed away on her knees from the body, then looked up.

The clouds swept over her head; a ray of sun came out. From somewhere off over the hemlocks, a bird began to chirp.

THIRTEEN

On Friday, the fourth day of the trial, Moncreiff walked briskly to the witness stand, bowed slightly to the plump-cheeked blonde woman in the lavender-and-black-striped dress.

"Would you please introduce yourself to the court?" Moncreiff said.

"I am Mary Arthur Perry. I live at 44 Renfrew Street."

"Were you acquainted with the deceased?"

"Yes, I became acquainted with him about the end of 1853. We attended the same chapel—St. Judes."

"Would you say you were intimately acquainted?"

"I am not sure, sir, what is meant by intimately."

"I mean, madame, did you consider him a close friend?"

"I came to be very close to him; we were friends."

"Was there something that prompted the beginning of this intimacy?"

"Yes, in the spring of 1855 he heard of his brother's death. He came to me in distress."

"Did he not also meet Miss Smith that spring?"

"Yes."

"Do you recollect the date?"

"Not precisely. It was after the ides—at the time of the vernal equinox."

"What did he tell you of their meeting?"

"Merely that they had met."

"And later?"

111

"In the early part of the summer, he told me he was engaged to Miss Smith, and I was aware from that time forward of the progress of his attachment."

"Did you ever meet Miss Smith?"

"Yes, Mr. L'Angelier brought her to call on me."

"And you corresponded with Miss Smith?"

"We exchanged several letters."

Moncreiff walked to the exhibit table, brought back a letter, and handed it to Miss Perry. "Can you identify this letter?"

"Yes, it is one that Mr. L'Angelier sent to me. It is marked Bridge of Allan, March 20th, 1857."

"See that the record indicates that Letter No. 141 has been identified as such," Moncreiff said. He turned back to Miss Perry.

"Would you please read the last paragraph?"

"It reads: 'I should have come to see someone last night, but the letter came too late, so we are both disappointed.'"

"Did you know who the someone was L'Angelier was speaking of?"

Inglis was on his feet. "Objection," he said.

Lord Hope adjusted his spectacles, nodded at Inglis.

"Your Honour," Inglis said, "the Prosecution is asking the witness for conjecture. The letter names no person."

Lord Hope shook his head. "Let us hear the witness's reply."

Moncreiff smiled. "Miss Perry, you may answer."

Miss Perry nodded. "He was speaking of Miss Smith."

"Tell me, you knew L'Angelier well, how would you describe his health?"

"Down to the beginning of February 1857, he had generally good health."

"Could you tell us your recollections of his health in February?"

"Well, he seemed not so well as formerly."

"Did he confide in you about his relations with Miss Smith during the month of February?"

"Yes. He said he had heard a report of another gentleman

paying attentions to Miss Smith. He said that Miss Smith had one time denied it and that another time she had evaded the question."

"Do you remember a specific instance when he was unwell?"

"Yes. On March 2nd, I saw him. He was looking very ill. When he came in, he said, 'Well, I never expected to see you again, I was so ill the other night.' He said he had fallen on the floor, and been unable to ring the bell."

"Did he indicate which night that had been?"

"Yes—from the circumstances, I knew it was February 19th."

"Did he say he had seen Miss Smith on that day?"

"Not in so many words, but on February 17th, which was a Tuesday, he said that he planned to see her on Thursday."

"Did he tell you what had caused this illness?"

"He spoke of being ill after taking a cup of coffee; and of being ill again after a cup of chocolate."

"Did he say who had given him the drinks?"

"Yes, Miss Smith."

"When did you see him next?"

"On March 9th."

"Did he speak of Miss Smith on this occasion?"

"Yes, he was talking about his extreme attachment to her; he spoke of it as fascination."

"Do you remember his exact words?"

"He said, 'It is a perfect fascination, my attachment to that girl. . . . If . . .'"

"Yes?"

"'If she were to poison me, I would forgive her.'"

A ripple ran through the courtroom. Moncreiff clasped his hands in front of him.

"And you said, Miss Perry?"

"I said, 'You ought not to allow such thoughts to pass through your mind; what motive could she have for giving you anything to hurt you?'"

"Yes?"

"He answered, 'I don't know; perhaps she might not be sorry to be rid of me.'"

"This was said in earnest?"

"Oh, yes, but I interpreted the expression 'to be rid of me' to mean rid of the engagement."

"Even after the statement 'If she were to poison me, I would forgive her'?"

"I took it as a jest."

"You don't think he suspected Miss Smith of giving him poison?"

"I don't think he seriously suspected her."

"When did you see him next, Miss Perry?"

"I never saw him again alive." She pulled out her handkerchief, dabbed at her eyes. "On March 23rd, I received a message from his landlady—'Monsieur L'Angelier's compliments; he is ill at Franklin Place, and he would be very glad if you would call.' I went about midday and found he was dead."

"How did you receive the news?"

"I could not believe it."

"Would you describe your state as agitated?"

"I suppose. I was very shocked when I saw the body."

Moncreiff nodded, took a sip of water. "Now, Miss Perry, tell us, did you see Miss Smith that day?"

"Yes, when I left Mrs. Jenkins', I went and called on Mrs. Smith."

"On Mrs. Smith? Not on Miss Smith."

"That is correct."

"And what was the purpose of your call?"

"I intimated Mr. L'Angelier's death to her."

"Did you see *Miss* Smith?"

"Yes, we shook hands and she invited me to come into the drawing room. She asked if I wished to see her mama."

"Did you intimate to her that L'Angelier had died?"

"No. She asked me if something was wrong. I said I wished to speak to her mother and that I would tell her mother the object of my visit."

"Had you met Mrs. Smith prior to that day?"

"No, that was the first time."

"Thank you. Now, tell me, was Monsieur L'Angelier a regular attender at church?"

"Yes," Miss Perry said.

At the defence table, Inglis' jaw dropped open. He closed it quickly. Wasn't Moncreiff going to ask her what had been said? Whether Mrs. Smith had been surprised by her call? Obviously, Moncreiff was not, but why not? Would Miss Perry reveal herself to be vindictive—and therefore prejudice her testimony before the jury? Or was Moncreiff trying to trap Inglis into asking the question that would reveal Perry's motive to be moral and compassionate—and therefore enhance her status as a witness? I won't take a chance, Inglis thought.

"What was your opinion of his character?" Moncreiff was asking now.

"I thought him a strictly moral and religious man."

"Thank you, Miss Perry. I have no further questions." Moncreiff returned to his table.

Inglis rose from his seat and walked slowly to the witness stand.

"Miss Perry, were you acquainted with Miss Smith's family?"

"No."

"Did you know that the family disapproved of L'Angelier?"

"Yes."

"And still you continued in encouraging it?"

"Mr. Inglis, I considered Mr. L'Angelier a responsible, mature man. I neither encouraged nor discouraged his actions. I simply was his friend. On one occasion, I wrote to Miss Smith advising her to mention it to her parents."

"Did L'Angelier tell you how he had made the acquaintance of Miss Smith?"

"He said he was introduced at a lady's house—at Mrs. Baird's."

"He said he had met her there?"

"Yes."

"You said, didn't you, that L'Angelier was in the habit of writing to you?"

"Yes."

"How long did this correspondence go on?"

"Perhaps two years."

"Did he reply to every letter you wrote?"

"Often my note did not require an answer. It might be asking him to come to tea."

"When you wrote each other, how did you address each other?"

"Latterly, we addressed each other by our Christian names. I addressed him by his surname and he addressed me as 'Dear Mary' or 'My Dear Mary.'"

"Never 'Dearest Mary'?"

"No, never."

"Now, you said that on March 2nd, he described his illness to you?"

"Yes."

"Did he mention to you a discontinuance of the engagement?"

"On that day?"

"On any day."

"He told me, I don't remember exactly when, that some months earlier, he had offered to break off the engagement, but she would not accept this."

"*She* would not?"

"That is correct. But later, he spoke of it again. He said that she proposed a return of the letters on both sides. He refused to do that, but he offered to give the letters to her father."

"When was this?"

"I don't know the date—sometime in February."

"Was that a threat?"

"No, I understood that to be a consent to give up the engagement, and he so represented it."

"Why surrender the letters to her father and *not* to her?"

"Perhaps because she had treated him shabbily."

"Was that his opinion?"

"Not at all. He forgave her everything."

"Did Miss Smith agree to his proposal to give the letters to her father?"

"No, she would not accede to it, and the engagement remained unbroken."

"At her request?"

"So I understood."

"Thank you,"Inglis said. "No further questions."

The prosecution then called Christine Haggart MacKenzie to the stand. She was a slim woman dressed in a blue day dress adorned with small tassels at the sleeves. She looked directly at the panel, lifted her head high, and ascended the stand.

"Is it Miss MacKenzie, or Mrs.?" Moncreiff said.

"Mrs.—I was married last March to Duncan MacKenzie, joiner."

"What was your maiden name?"

"'Twas Bruce, Christine Bruce."

"Were you, prior to your marriage, employed in the Smith household?"

"Yes, for two years."

"When did you leave their employment?"

"Last Whitsunday."

"Tell us, please, who composed the family?"

"Well," she said, lifting her gloved hand and counting off the members, "there were Mr. and Mrs. Smith. Miss Madeleine was the eldest, and there were Miss Bessie, noo nineteen, Miss Janet, aboot twelve or thirteen. The eldest son is John, or Jack; he is, I should think, aboot sixteen. The younger son is James. He is two years younger."

"Thank you. Now, tell me, did Miss Smith ever point out L'Angelier to you?"

"Well, while they lived on India Street, she pointed out a French gentleman t' me."

117

"Did she tell you his name?"

She shook her head. "She didna speak o' him by name."

"How did she characterize him?"

"As a friend of hers."

Moncreiff walked to the exhibit table, picked up the photograph.

"Is this the man?"

She studied the photo. "It is."

"Tell me, did you ever see him *in* the house at India Street?"

"Yes. I was asked one day by Miss Madeleine to let him in."

"This was during the day?"

"Yes, they were all in church. Miss Madeleine went in wi' him to the laundry and the door was shut."

"How long did they remain in there?"

She shrugged, smiled. "Maybe a half hour."

"Did he ever come at night?"

"Yes, three or four times."

"Inside the house?"

"No, he would stand at the back gate."

"Did you ever speak to him?"

"Yes, during the season we lived at India Street, I spoke to him several times. He made me a present o' a dress."

"A dress? Did he say why he gave it?"

"No."

"Did you ever post letters to L'Angelier for Miss Smith?"

"Yes, many times."

"And you received them for her as well?"

"Yes."

"You might say Miss Smith used you as a confidante?"

"What, sir?"

"You made it easier for them to correspond?"

"Yes."

"Did you at one time refuse to continue to be used in this fashion?"

"Yes."

"Why was that?"

"Mrs. Smith had found fault wi' me for doing so and had forbidden me."

"Did Miss Smith ever discuss her approaching marriage to Mr. Minnoch with you?"

"Well, shortly before her arrest, I heard she was t' be married. In consequence o' that, I asked her what she was t' do wi' her other friend."

"What did she say?"

"That she had given him up."

"Did she say anything else?"

"I asked her if she had got back her letters. She said no, and that she didn't care."

"Were you troubled by rats at Blythswood Square?"

"No, sir."

"Do you remember Sunday, March 22nd?"

"I was home visiting my mother that day; I cam home the next."

"Were you the person in charge of cleaning Miss Smith's room?"

"I was."

"Did you ever observe that the water in her basin was coloured blue or black?"

"I saw nothing o' that sort."

"Thank you." Moncreiff returned to his table.

Inglis rose and approached the witness, bowed slightly.

"Who told you of Miss Smith's engagement?"

"Her mother."

"Now, you were engaged to be married this past winter, were you not?"

"I was."

"Was your husband a frequent visitor to the house?"

"Yes, he cam several times a week."

"And you often let him out late, did you not?"

She smiled. "Sometimes."

"Tell me, the door under the stairs. Does it make any noise when you open and close it?"

Her smile widened. "It makes considerable noise."

"Thank you, that is all."

Lord Hope smiled down at the woman. "Mrs. MacKenzie, when the family went to Bridge of Allan, were the servants all at home?"

"Yes, sir."

"The morning that Miss Smith left the house, do you remember if she took any clothes with her?"

"I don't know."

"Did you see her upon her return?"

"Yes."

"Did she have any baggage?"

"She had a carpet bag."

"A large one or a small one?"

"It wasna verra small. It was such as a lady might carry her night things in."

"You said before that at one time, you had refused to accept any more letters for Miss Smith. In which house was this?"

"On Blythswood Square."

"Did you then stop receiving letters?"

"I did receive some afterwards."

"I suppose, as MacKenzie was coming to visit you without Mr. Smith's knowledge or approval, you thought it discreet to oblige the young lady?"

The witness smiled and nodded.

FOURTEEN

There were five more notes from gentlemen when she arrived back at Edinburgh Prison. Strange what a woman might do and still be thought a lady—by some, anyhow.

Tomorrow, of course, even those some would be put to rest. Moncreiff was to read her letters. Soul prints, she had once called them.

Inglis arrived at nine-thirty. She was waiting for him at the oak table.

"When do you think he will reintroduce the memorandum book?" she said, as soon as he was seated.

"Tomorrow."

"And Lord Hope, do you think he will allow it?"

"We must hope not."

They both laughed.

"It would be very bad for me if he did, wouldn't it?"

"Not so bad," Inglis said.

"Mr. Inglis, be honest."

"Bad, but not so bad."

She smiled at him. "You shall stop it. You and your fair-haired boy."

"Mr. Young?"

"Yes."

"We shall try."

"I wish you could keep out some of the letters. His at least."

"L'Angelier's."

She nodded.

"Oh," he said, stroking his chin.

"Why 'oh,' Mr. Inglis?"

"It is the first time you have brought him up."

"Is it?"

"I believe so."

She traced her finger over a scratch in the wood.

Inglis opened his briefcase. "I have some news—they have located the Guibilei girl."

"Oh," Madeleine said.

"What do you think she will say?"

She sighed. "I think she will deny it."

"You can't be sure."

"She is a baroness now. Of course she will."

"Do you remember any details of the conversations? What prompted it?"

Madeleine shook her head. "It was so long ago."

"Perhaps if you talked about Mrs. Gorton's, something would come back. How old were you when you went?"

"Almost seventeen."

"Fine. Begin there. Did your parents accompany you there on the train?"

"No, I went alone."

"What did you wear? Give me as many details as you remember."

She smiled. "Pagoda sleeves."

"What?"

"I remember the dress: green velvet trimmed with ermine, a matching pardessus coat with pagoda sleeves. I was as beautiful as Lord Hope himself."

Inglis laughed. "You must have been."

She shook her head, made a slight clucking sound. "Pagoda sleeves. But I did love it. Miss Tweedle made it."

She lifted her hand and rubbed her cheekbone. "I know I've gone dowdy lately."

"You look fine. Now, you arrived at Mrs. Gorton's in all your splendour?"

Madeleine shut her eyes. The pieces came back.

At Mrs. Gorton's she was "finished." It was not at all like the four-pounds-a-year places where one learned to wash the floors as well as to dance on them. Aside from light dusting of the *objets* on the chiffoniers, or a polishing of the ivory keys on the four pianos in the salon, her housekeeping duties were very light. In other areas, her duties were more arduous. Vespers before breakfast, then French and geography, recitation from Virgil, penmanship, a smattering of sum balancing, needlework, watercolours with the drawing master. Then supper, where Mrs. Gorton, who was a Mrs. only by virtue of her fifty years, taught them the niceties: to use the silver Albany-pattern dessert spoon when eating peas or curry, to dissect a pear with a three-pronged fork and scimitar-bladed knife.

Dinners were elegant affairs. The girls, dressed in tartans and stripes and festooned with ribbons and flowers, flanked the sides of the grand table. In the center was a six-light centerpiece mounted on a fluted triform, the base embellished with trailing vines and resting upon three scrolled feet, the chased stem a vine surrounded by three standing female figures in the classical style. Mrs. Gorton sat at the end, and a distinguished gentleman—a different one each week—would head the table. They would discuss the fashions of the Empress Eugénie and the aftermath of the revolution, and then the ladies would withdraw while the gentleman had his glass of port and pipe of tobacco, but only one of each, for he was expected by the ladies within fifteen minutes for tea and conversation.

She had learned a great deal at these dinners and teas: the relative merits of the two London productions of Purcell's *Dido and Aeneas*, the question the Sphinx asked, the belief of Quakers that girls have souls the same as boys, the origin of guano.

And afterwards, in the chambers, she had learned how to avoid the teasing and bullying that were the natural lot of the new girls. She had no true friends but she had no enemies. The older girls looked at her and measured her and then quietly passed her over, not knowing if her reserve held strength or weakness.

Once, for dinner and tea, a splendid eagle-featured, shaggy-haired man had come from Leipzig to speak of poetry, and the conversation, much to her delight, had gone off track. Mrs. Gorton had dressed that evening in her most splendid parlour gown and had done her hair up in side ringlets like untwisted bell rope. The gentleman wore a black tight-waisted redingote, a white cravat, and white trousers. Madeleine was sitting closest to him and savoring his dusty, smoky smell. As he had been to Elba, she asked him how Napoleon's reputation for eating three little boys a day had begun, and the gentleman had launched into a ribald tale which had all the girls giggling.

They talked of anthropology and legal justice and even, shockingly, the rights of women—everything but poetry. He told them of a trial that had taken place lately in Austria.

"The prisoner, Anna Alexander, was acquitted by the jury, after it was revealed that the dead man, Lieutenant Wurzel, had been a 'poison eater.' You see, it seems that in Styria, there prevails the strange habit of eating arsenic to improve the wind and to obtain a fresh and rosy complexion. This is done in private, the arsenic eater always concealing his habit. Generally speaking, it is only the confessional or the deathbed that raises the veil from the terrible secret."

Madeleine opened her eyes. Inglis was staring at her. She nodded. "I remember now. It was after his visit. Miss Guibilei and I spoke before going to bed."

Inglis lowered his chin, rubbed his hand over his brow. Then he looked at her. "I don't think I can use it."

"But wouldn't it prove . . ."

"If Moncreiff knew that you knew of the Wurzel case . . . he might use it to his advantage."

"I see. How dangerous everything is to the accused."

Inglis nodded, drew his watch from his vest pocket. "It is late," he said. "You must sleep."

"So must you," she said.

He rose, came round and pulled out her chair, escorted her to the waiting guard.

FIFTEEN

In her cell, the boarding-school memory returned: the shaggy-haired man in white trousers, the smell of his tobacco, Mrs. Gorton's eager smile.

When the chimes had sounded for bed, the poet had still not read a single poem. He shrugged, winked in Madeleine's direction, said:

> A woman is a foreign land
> Of which, though he settle young
> A man will ne'er quite understand
> The customs, politics, and tongue.

As the girls crowded round, shaking his hand, he bestowed on each of them a bit of poetry.

When it came her turn, he laid a hand on her shoulder and looked into her eyes, saying, "Let men tremble to win the hand of woman, unless they win along with it the utmost passion of her heart."

And to Mrs. Gorton, he bequeathed "'Tis strange what a man may do, and a woman yet think him an angel," which set all the girls atwitter afterwards, speculating as to the way in which Mrs. Gorton might have known the good gentleman.

Madeleine had lain in bed that night and pondered her prospects. Mrs. Gorton said, as a positive truth, that a woman with fair opportunities, and without a positive hump, might marry whom she liked.

She had learned to be amiable, inoffensive, always ready to give pleasure and to be pleased. She was a model of piety, purity, submissiveness, and domesticity. She did not lace too tightly, for she wanted a straight spine and a sweet breath and to be a fit wife and mother. She was at all times agreeable and a good listener, understanding that the object of conversation was amusement and entertainment, and that, while one might state her opinions, one never argued. She never lost her temper, and she never let on that she noticed a slight, and she was never so vulgar or annoying that she called people by their given names when addressing them. She didn't hum, whistle, or talk to herself when in the company of gentlemen, and she endeavored at all times to have a calm and natural countenance, for, as Mrs. Gorton always said, a scowl begets wrinkles.

A prize pupil deserved a prize. And surely the man who saw and appreciated all that she had become would be a prince. She imagined him, tall and well-bred, in a clean Dutch linen shirt and grey trousers, tipping his silk hat to her.

She had lain in bed that night for hours, with one agonizing question: What if she chose the wrong man?

Ruskin, she had read, as a baby had grasped a hot urn and seared himself. The nurse had rushed to apply cold butter. The mother had forbidden her to apply the unguent to the burn.

"But why, madame?"

"To teach him the nature of liberty."

Now, she reached over for the packet of letters, read them in the flickering oil light.

It was her answer. "Please see me," he had written. "Under any terms you wish. But please see me."

August 27, 1855

Beloved Emile,

I have just received your note. I shall meet you. I do not care though I bring disgrace upon myself. Between us there can be no thought of terms.

I think it will be safe. By the Garden Gate at ten o'clock this Sunday night. Do not write. Send me Saturday's paper and I will know you are coming.

Wait for me.

Mimi

On Wednesday, she had received an off-white scented envelope. It was addressed in a flowery feminine hand. Puzzled, she opened it.

August 29, 1855

Madeleine,

I am a cad. You are too good for such a man. If I loved you, I would cut you loose. Instead, I ask you to betray your family. I wish sometimes that I had never been born. I shall go to Jersey, bid my mother farewell. I will go to Lima. I cannot ask you to make such sacrifices.

Godspeed,
Emile

She answered at once.

August 30, 1855

My Sweet Emile,

Emile, you desire to be happy. You are young, you ought to desire life. Oh, Emile, if you ever loved me, desire to live and succeed in this life.

Please don't go to Lima. I promise to convince Papa. I promise to find a way for us. I love you.

I think it will be safe.
Sunday night.
Ten o'clock.
The Garden Gate.

In Sunday morning's mail, she found a newspaper, folded to the Shipping Schedule.
One column was circled with red grease pen.

S.S. HOMERIC: Bound to Jersey
Dept: Saturday, 4 o'clock

Inside was a slip of paper: his mother's name and address.

SIXTEEN

It was already hot when the court met at ten on Saturday, July 4th. Madeleine's face was veiled.

Lady Anne Guibilei Walcott, a tall and slender woman with an expensive toilette, a large diamond ring, and an expressionless face, ascended the stand.

"Tell us, milady," Moncreiff said, "how you came to know the prisoner."

"I was a pupil teacher at Mrs. Gorton's Academy in Clapton Terrace. Miss Smith attended there in the year 1854."

"Did you ever advise her to use arsenic as a cosmetic?"

"No."

"You never told her to apply it to her face, neck, or arms, mixed with water, nor to use it in any way?"

"No."

"You had no conversation with her about arsenic?"

"Not that I can recollect."

"No further questions."

"No questions," Inglis said.

The Crown then recalled Dr. Christian.

"Tell me, doctor," Moncreiff asked, "would you say it was very unsafe to use arsenic as a cosmetic?"

"I would not like to try it. I should expect inflammation."
"Have you ever heard of it being so used?"
"Never."
"Thank you, doctor." Moncreiff took his seat.

Inglis rose to cross-examine.
"The common arsenic of the shops could be said to be an insoluble solid, could it not?"
"It is not absolutely insoluble."
"What if you mixed it with cold water?"
"Without agitation?"
"Yes."
"The water would dissolve one five-hundredth part. It is, of course, the worst medium to hold arsenic in suspension."
"Then if arsenic were put in cold water, the greater part of it would fall to the bottom?"
Christian paused. He scratched his whiskers, pulled at his earlobe.
"Most of it would fall rapidly down. Not much would remain in solution without agitation."
Inglis smiled. "Supposing that the water were used to wash the face or hands without stirring up the arsenic from the bottom?"
"Little would be in suspension, but I can only say that I should not like to use it myself."
"I think," Inglis said, "that you should not like to use *any* cosmetic."
The audience laughed.
"I think," Christian said, "any person who would do so would do a very imprudent thing." But Inglis had already turned his back to receive a document from Young.
"Doctor, I believe you made some experiments personally with two other scientific gentlemen as to the taste of arsenic?"
"Yes."
"Did you taste the arsenic yourself?"
"We all tasted it, and we held it only as far back along the tongue as we could with safety, so as to enable us to spit it out

afterwards. We each then spat it out and rinsed our mouths carefully."

"How did it taste?"

He screwed up his face.

"Acrid?"

"Not exactly."

"Did it have a distinctive taste?"

"Not really."

"Could you conceive of ingesting it without detecting a taste of some sort?"

"I don't know."

"Yet you made a face when I asked about the taste?"

"Did I?"

"No further questions."

Lord Hope lifted his ermine-cuffed sleeve, and wiped his forehead. Then he leaned forwards over the bench and spoke.

"Doctor, is it not so that there is arsenic naturally in the bones of the human body?"

"Orfilla renders that opinion."

"Orfilla is a very high authority in the chemical world?"

"Undoubtedly."

"None higher, I suppose?"

"In medico-legal chemistry, none."

"Thank you, doctor, you may step down."

Dr. Christian descended the stand.

Lord Hope conferred a moment with Lord Ivory and then recessed the court for lunch.

Moncreiff had his meal brought to his chambers.

Inglis took a walk.

He went up the Royal Mile, seeing his shoes grow dusty as he walked up the granite-block street, past the offices, the tenements, the chop houses. Towards Castle Rock. It was a hot, sultry day, with distant rumblings of thunder.

He was puffing when he reached the top. He stopped, drawing in his breath, looking down on the long line of Princes

Street. There, the Scott monument—and there, the Scottish Academy, its Greek pillars glowing whitely.

He looked north, towards the shore of the Kingdom of Fife—and beyond to the Lomond Hills. At night, you could see the lights twinkling in the kingdom below. Fife, shaped like the head of a wee Scottie dog. Aye, and the Lady of Fife, even now listening, dreading exposure.

He nodded. Of the two, she had less to lose. If he thought it would help him, he would name her a hundred times over. But it wouldn't.

No, he must stand on the defensive, occupy the high ground and let the charge come.

So far, it had gone half and half. Moncreiff had established the incredible dose that had killed him. This was the biggest lot of evidence against her: the large fraction of the ounce.

But it had not been without its small triumph. No indigo had been detected. And indigo had indeed been in the poison that Miss Smith had so openly purchased. In the end, that could go either way. She had not tried to hide a murder, only a vanity. Would not any other woman do the same?

Moncreiff had established that the deceased was in Glasgow the night before he died. He had said that a letter from the prisoner might have brought him there. But "might" was easily turned into reasonable doubt.

Moncreiff had revealed the state of the deceased—his anger, his mistrust, his suspicions—but these, too, showed a mercurial man, a vengeful man, a man capable of self-destruction.

Yes, it was a two-edged sword.

So far, the dates of L'Angelier's illnesses were not firmly fixed. The dates of the three purchases of poison were, regrettably, set. But had she seen him on those dates? The letters seemed harmful to Miss Smith's case, but even there, matters were doubtful. Dates were missing; postmarks were blurred; letters were in wrong envelopes.

But the memorandum book: If that were added, Moncreiff might well have a foundation.

Well, he would know by nightfall.

Inglis shook his head, looked again at the view.

"'Still on the spot Lord Marmion stay'd,'" he said in his soft burred voice, "'For fairer scene he ne'er survey'd.'"

He walked down the hill, back towards the marble pillars of the law court.

At the stone gate of a tavern, he paused, looked down on the granite stone. A small toad sat, bulging eyes, dry as dust skin.

Inglis chuckled. "Ye did tolerably gude, I'll no deny it, but, eh, mon, that's naething compared wi' what I am gon t' do."

The toad blinked. Inglis laughed, went on, his steps light. Moncreiff was building himself a sturdy house. He would drive the letters in like ten-penny nails.

It wud tak' the De'il's ain fingers to draw them oot again, he heard a voice in his head say. It was his father's smooth burly voice. He looked at his hands.

Inside the courtroom, the pit was filling up. The audience had been in their places for some time. The clerks entered, and it was beginning again.

Lord Hope came in, followed by Ivory and Handyside. They took their places.

"Your Honours," Moncreiff said. "I now propose to give in the deceased's memorandum book and to have the entries read. I feel we have now laid a sufficient foundation for these memoranda. We have proved that various circumstances did occur on the days under date of which they are entered in the book. I therefore submit that these entries are statements by L'Angelier himself and that the book should be received."

Inglis was already on his feet. He shook his head violently. "Your Honour, we can prove that occurrences listed in the memorandum book did *not* occur on those dates—and may not have occurred at all. For such evidence to be admitted as valid testimony by the deceased, there would have to be *no* known departure from fact."

Moncreiff threw up his hands, addressed Inglis. "I cannot conceive on what principles of law this book could be rejected.

True, it is secondary evidence, but where you have not the man himself alive, you must take every scrap of writing that can be found."

Inglis faced the bench. "Even had the book been regularly kept," he said, "it would be necessary to be cautious in introducing such a precedent. But it was not a regular journal. L'Angelier lived eighty or eighty-one days in 1857, and though the book began of January 1st, there were just twenty-six entries in all. That was not a regular journal. When the fancy struck him, he made an entry, but when it did not, he made no entry. Our honourable friend argued that it is good secondary evidence. But there is a manifest and important distinction. In the one case we have the security of an oath. Here we have no oath."

Lord Hope nodded, conferred with the other judges. After several whispered exchanges, he leaned forwards.

"Gentlemen, we will give our decision on this matter Monday morning. We wish to have an opportunity to consult the statutes."

Moncreiff bit his lip, nodded. He shuffled some papers on his desk and then rose. He walked slowly, almost reluctantly, to the bench.

"Your Honours, I now propose that the letters be read."

Lord Hope nodded. The clerk adjusted his collar and stepped forwards, handed the sheaf of copied letters to Moncreiff. Then the clerk took his seat, leaned forwards. He had spent four days in an office overlooking the Royal Mile, reading and deciphering the script. The first letters, penned in a neat hand, had gone swiftly.

But as he progressed, he had left the office with great weariness. Miss Smith's script had degenerated in places to a scrawl; it became more and more tedious to understand.

Moncreiff walked to the center of the floor, turned, and faced the jurors. He began with the spring of 1855:

My dear Emile,

I do not feel as if I were writing you for the first time.

though our intercourse has been short, yet we have become as familiar friends. . . .

Madeleine looked straight ahead as the letters were read. Her hands tightened imperceptibly in her lap as Moncreiff laid down the fifth letter, picked up the sixth. She was glad of the veil.

"'Dearest Emile,'" Moncreiff read.

Many thanks for your kindness to me. I have talked to my parents and Papa will not give his consent, so I am in duty bound to obey him. It is a heavy blow to me. Our relationship must be at an end.

You have been a good friend to me. Oh, continue so. I hope and trust you may prosper in all that you do. Think my conduct not unkind. I have a father to please, and a loving father too.

Farewell, dear Emile. With much love, I bid you adieu. With the kindest love, I am your friend.

Mimi

Moncreiff laid the copy down, picked up a sheet of foolscap from the exhibit table, and walked to the judges' bench. "If it please the court," he said, "I now offer into evidence a letter, or a writing, or a copy of a letter or writing, identified as production No. 7 of the inventory."

Inglis rose slowly from his seat. "Your Lordships," he said to the bench, "is the worthy prosecutor offering a letter—or a litter of kittens?"

The audience laughed.

"It is a letter," the Lord Advocate said, stiffly.

"If it is a letter," Inglis said, "was it sent?"

"No," Moncreiff said.

"Then how," Inglis said wearily, "does the Lord Advocate know that the writing is a letter?"

134

"Whether it was ever sent or not we cannot tell, as we have no counterpart, but can it not be said to be material to an inquiry into the death of the deceased that such a document was found in his repositories?"

Inglis turned to the bench. "Your Honours, the question is not whether the writing is a document, but whether it is a letter."

Moncreiff spoke: "I am content to identify the writing as a document. All I say is that the document is material in an inquiry into the death of the deceased."

"I don't understand," Inglis said drily, "what is meant by 'an inquiry into the death of the deceased.' This is a trial for murder."

"Hear, hear," a voice in the back of the gallery said. The audience tittered.

Inglis spoke. "Your Lordships, I object to the introduction of this paper into evidence. It is immaterial and irrelevant."

Lord Hope looked over his silver-rimmed spectacles at the audience, scowled. Then he conferred with Ivory and Handyside.

"This document," he said slowly, "appears to be a draft of what was intended to be addressed to the defendant. But it is incomplete and parts are scored out. In what light, then, can it be tendered? It may have been merely the outpouring of momentary exasperation. On thinking more, the writer may have thought it unjust and groundless and may have withdrawn the next moment what he had written in a hasty fit of passion."

Lord Hope looked over at Lord Ivory, nodded to him.

"I cannot say that I differ," Lord Ivory said, "although I have some hesitation. Had the writing been nearer in time to the *res gestae*, my opinion might be otherwise."

Lord Handyside nodded. "I agree," he said.

Lord Hope adjusted his spectacles. "It is not a proper narrative and ought not to be admitted in evidence. Objection sustained."

Moncreiff's brow furrowed; he made a slight shrugging motion. Inglis smiled, looked over at Madeleine. Her head was bowed, her eyes closed.

Seventy-seven letters. It took until dusk to read them all. Madeleine sat unmoving as the dry voice of the clerk recited the sentences she had composed.

For the first time since the trial began, the oil lamps were lit. Not a single spectator went home to dinner.

SEVENTEEN

Inglis was waiting for her Sunday night when she returned from the prison chapel.

"You look tired," he said, leading the way to the room off the matron's station.

"No, I am fine." She took her seat at the oak refectory table. "Thank you for yesterday."

"The two alleged letters?" he said.

"It made it all easier."

"I knew Ivory would wait for the *res gestae*. . . ." He took his seat, moving the chair back in between the heavy bulbous legs of the table.

"It worked well," she said.

"And now it's our wicket."

She smiled.

"Is there anything you need?" he said.

"No, I am fine. I miss walking, though. You could take me out; we could stroll."

"I very much wish I could."

"I know."

Inglis drummed his fingers on the triple-plank top. "I have heard from your father."

"I'm glad."

"Miss Madeleine, the letters have been read. Could we not call your father now?"

"And put him to public shame? No, he's done all he can. He could only see me on the scaffold now."

"But, certainly . . ."

"He is an honest man." She laid both her hands on the table, palms down.

"I think I understand."

"How many more days?" she said.

He shrugged. "Two, maybe three . . . you know our Lord Advocate."

"I've grown rather fond of the little toad."

Inglis laughed. He would never be able to see Moncreiff again free of her description.

Madeleine smiled, rose from her seat. "Come, I want to show you something."

She led the way to the matron's door, knocked softly. She opened the door, went in, came out with a large cardboard box. Inglis took it, placed it on the table.

She lifted the lid. Inside were letters, dozens of them, written in different inks and scripts, many with still unopened crested seals.

Inglis shook his head, looked up at her.

She laughed. "Admirers, well-wishers, sympathizers."

"It is a good sign," he said.

"All from gentlemen."

When Inglis had gone, she lay abed in the dark.

Through the bars came the scent of rain, of pavement. It felt like spring, she thought. Outside, people would be walking beneath their umbrellas, getting their shoes and stockings wet. Three months. It had been a long time.

She sat up and rubbed her wrists—how slender she had become. Then she stood, grasped the bars, and squeezed till her knuckles whitened. If they did not believe her, would she panic? Would her legs buckle under as they led her to the scaffold? Would she lose all control at the end?

She took deep breaths until her heart stopped racing. Then she lay back on the cot, lit the lantern.

In court, she had closed her mind to the drone of the letters. The words in black and white brought everything back.

P. Emile L'Angelier
Mrs. C. L'Angelier
P.O.
Lion's Head, St. Helier
Jersey

September 15, 1855

My Dearest Emile,

How I long to see you. You have been gone so long. Will you be able to come down on Sunday after you return?

I hope you have given up all ideas of going to Lima. I will never be allowed to go with you . . . perhaps you want to be quit of me.

Emile, please don't go. I feel very nervous today. My hand shakes. I try to appear cheerful before my family, but it is not easy.

I have dreamt all night of you.

There is to be a full-dress ball on the 13th and I think Papa would like me to go. If I thought you were to be there I would. Though I could not speak to you, yet I would see you—you would try to get an introduction that evening. Papa would be sure to be in good temper.

If yes on Sunday, write me. I have enlisted Christine's help. Write: Miss Bruce, P.O. Row. She will pick up the letter.

If yes, the Garden Gate: 3 P.M.—please wait.

Believe me, yours,

Madeleine

There had been a red sky that Saturday night, and the Sunday had dawned blue. By noon the air was so clear, the countryside was visible for miles without a shimmer. Madeleine proposed a walk after the large midday meal. Only James accepted. She took him as far as the front veranda.

"James, you must put on your boots," she said, crossly.

"Won't," he said.

"I shall wait for you."

"No."

"Very well," she had said, turned, and smiling, walked away.

She went to the barn, looked back, then passed through the dark center aisle, past the stalls, and out the back door. She went down the path, approached the green gate, pulled down the handle, went within.

The gazebo was hidden by a stand of birch. She went within, sat upon the old parlor settee, waited. Once, when she had been sitting here at dusk, a red deer had come within touching distance, stood, looked directly at her. Then she had breathed, and he had turned white tail and was gone.

When Emile came, he sat on the caned beechwood divan, across from her, his hat in his hand, his coat draped over the scallop-shell carved back. He seemed like a bird perched, ready to leave on a moment's notice.

Her hands flitted against the squab cushions. "You look pale," she said.

"I've been ill."

"I'm sorry. Was it serious?"

"My mother thought I would die."

"What was it?"

"A bilious derangement. I got over it." He took off his gloves, sucked his finger. "I've cut it . . . a nasty paper cut."

She came and sat beside him, lifted his hand, bent to kiss the finger.

"You have changed your hair," he said, taking his hand away.

"Just trimmed," she said, folding her hands across her chest.

"You should have saved me a lock."

"That's bad luck—'he who keeps hair keeps care.'"

"Superstition."

"Yes. I don't whistle on the Lord's Day either," she said.

He twisted the end of his mustache. "Why not?"

"It makes the angels cry."

"Well, let them." He began to cough.

"Don't be angry with me," she said, leaning closer.

"I'm not," he said.

She rose and pulled a leaf from the hanging plant above the daybed. "Emile," she said. "You made life simple for me when you refused to greet me or talk to me on the street."

He massaged his finger with the other hand, his head bent.

She touched his blond hair. "And painful."

He raised his head. "It would be better if I were able to stay away, wouldn't it?"

"Simpler," she said. "Not better."

"I do love you," he said.

"So does my father."

"Why say things like that?" he said. He crushed the crown of his hat. "Is a father a lover? You aren't a child. You're a woman."

"I know," she said. "I know."

He rose and put his hands on her shoulders. "I know what I am doing to you. But I need you"—he turned her face up to his—"and you need me." He placed his lips softly on hers.

She moved her head and said, "I do." Her hand trailed down his arm. "Emile, I do."

"Then you must talk to your mother, enlist her help."

"I shall, Emile. I promise you."

October 13th was the dress ball, the last of the summer. The Auxiliary would be hosting a group of young cavalry. She and Bessie were to wear special women's corsages.

She would wear the silky moiré with the moon-blue eyelets, the skirt gathered in coiled flowers. It shimmered into starbursts when she twirled.

Did Emile dance? P. Emile L'Angelier. Emile and Mimi. Mimi L'Angelier. Mrs. P. E. L'Angelier. What did the P stand for, she wondered? Paul? Mrs. Paul E. L'Angelier.

She rubbed glycerine and rosewater upon her legs, her arms, her breasts. At seven, the corset was laced, her wasp waist reduced another inch. The hoop was fitted round her, and covered with embroidered batiste slips from out of the copper-banded cedar chest.

At eight, she did her hair, swept up and back, the bun secured with a dozen tiny tortoise two-forked combs.

Papa ordered the carriage brought around.

"I expect Jed to have you home by midnight, girls."

"Oh, Papa," Bessie said, "they don't play 'Goan Home' before half past."

"You be home by twelve just the same."

"But *you'll* be staying till the end, Papa. Please."

"One more word, Miss Smith, and it will be eleven." His face was stern.

The ball was crowded. They went down the receiving line, stood drinking a cup of punch. The Fergusons' carriage arrived and Mama and Papa came in, hung up their cloaks.

She danced by Papa, waved at him. He nodded, turned back to escorting Mama around the floor. One-two, one-two.

When she danced with Captain McDowell, she closed her eyes and imagined it was Emile, dressed in a scarlet coat, the medals all blue and purple and green upon his chest, the gold gleaming.

Sam had ruddy cheeks, and when he was a boy, he had carved her initials one day into a tree:

S.M. + M.S.

Sammy and Maddy. He had been older and a bit of a wild Indian, but she had followed him faithfully all one summer, while the older girls raised eyebrows at her. But when it came

141

the first dance of the season, he had gone with an older girl, alone in her father's carriage.

Now he signed four blocks of her dance card.

Then the lanky Major McCleod had cut in, swept her around the floor. He *danced.* She forgot Emile for a moment, inhaled the bay-rum scent about the red jacket.

He claimed the Captain's Dance, too.

"Do you ladies have an escort home?" he asked as the set ended.

"No."

"Would you allow me the honour?"

"The honour would be ours," she said.

Papa came up behind her. "Having a good time?"

"I was saying," McCleod said, "that I would be happy to escort your daughters home."

Papa put his hand on McCleod's shoulder. "No hurry, man, have a dance."

Madeleine shook her head, swirled off in McCleod's arms. Papas.

On Wednesday, a letter from Emile arrived.

Madeleine,

> I was happy Sunday—truly happy. Today I dined with De Mean. He mentioned the ball. He said you were lovely.

> Now I am in an agony of doubt. You say you love me and then you dance all night in the arms of a red-coated major.

> I wish this moment that I were dead. I swear I must break away and leave this place. South America, Africa—somewhere, but before too long, you will be quit of me. I shall bother you no longer.

> Go to your major. You *can* tell your father about him.

> I know my folly—I shall not repeat it.

Your devoted Emile

But autumn came and he had still not gone. They returned to Glasgow the day after Michaelmas, opened up the India Street house. In her father's Glasgow house, she was required to make herself constantly available. What had they done before she came home to do the marketing, plan the menus?

She was expected to assess the men, select suitors, choose a husband. But she loved Emile.

And Emile. He expected her to behave as a wife. What might he not do if he heard of her going to more balls? Oh, if only he knew how much she loved him.

On the day after Samhain, she was on Sauchiehall Street. She saw him coming out of the tobacco store; he stopped to light a small cigar. She crossed the street boldly, stopped in front of the wooden Indian, nodded to Emile.

He looked around. The street was almost deserted. He came over to her, smiling, took her hand. She watched his eyes as he lifted her hand to his lips, kissed it lightly.

"I was on my way shopping," she said gaily. "I need a new pair of gloves for the Artillery Ball."

"Well, I shan't keep you, then." He touched his hat.

She did not see him for almost a week after that, and when she did, his hair was unkempt, his eyes were red. And he snubbed her. Or at least she thought he did. True, he had been coming with the sun in his eyes, and perhaps his eyesight was not as keen as hers.

On Friday, she was positive. He was not ten feet away and he turned his head, quite deliberately, and walked away. But why?

She saw him next the Tuesday after Martinmas outside the tobacco store. She stopped, lifted her hand in greeting. He lifted his head, his eyes averted. Then he turned towards the street, awaited the passage of a horse-drawn cart.

"You could walk down to the corner if you're in such a hurry to get away," she said.

"I am aware of the alternatives, mademoiselle," he said frostily. The cart passed; he crossed over without so much as a backwards glance.

She went home, took out her stationery, and began a letter soon tear-streaked.

Dearest Emile,

When you treat me as though I do not exist, I am invisible.

She tore it up, began again:

Dear Emile,

So, darling, now you hate me. Pray tell me, is it something I said, something I did? Or is it just my very being?

She tore that page up too, took a new sheet:

Dear, dear Emile,

I fear our being enemies. I would rather not see you again than have you be so cruel to me. . . .

She went to bed, the letter undone. Perhaps in the morning, she would know what to say.

She slept deeply that night, dreamed of Emile. He was coming towards her on the street and she steeled herself for his hateful eyes. But no, he was smiling. His old smile—he still loved her.

She woke, burned the started letter.

A week later, as she was trying on a feathered scoop bonnet in McCall's, Emile poked his head from around the glove counter.

"Hello," he said, his voice gruff.

She beamed. "Emile, you spoke to me!"

"Well, you don't deserve it," he said, scowling.

"I know, I know," she said, lowering her head, the smile spreading wide across her face.

When she looked up, he had gone.

She was still beaming as she purchased her hat; still beaming as she walked home. Emile still loved her. More, he loved her enough to hate her . . . and forgive her—anything.

Of course, he was right. If she loved him, she would have told Mama. Hadn't she promised him?

She went home to her bed room, lay in her half-tester bed, read poetry as penance: Sir John Suckling.

> Why so pale and wan, fond lover?
> Prithee, why so pale?
> Will, when looking well can't move her,
> Looking ill prevail?
> Prithee, why so pale?
>
> Why so dull and mute, young sinner?
> Prithee, why so mute?
> Will, when speaking well can't win her,
> Saying nothing do 't?
> Prithee, why so mute?
>
> Quit, quit, for shame! This will not move;
> This cannot take her.
> If of herself she will not love,
> Nothing can make her:
> The devil take her!

It would serve her right if Emile left her. She really was a coward. She sat down that night and wrote him a note:

My Dearest Emile,

    You made me happy, very happy today. I am to blame for everything, but it shall not happen again. I love you, I think only of you. I long for the day when we shall be together, never to be parted. Tonight, I talked to Mama and she has promised to help me find a way with Papa. Please be patient and look kindly upon me when you see me in the street. It is fearful never to see you, and your smile is my only solace. I hope ere long to have a sweet interview with you. Much much love,

Your adoring Mimi

She put down the letter, blotted the signature. It was only a small lie, and she would be sure to make it true before she saw Emile next. She slipped the letter into the envelope, sealed it with fancy wax.

The next Monday, Christine had a new blue dress and Madeleine had a letter—both from Emile.

On Thursday, an invitation arrived in a regal blue hand.

My Dear Miss Smith,

    I am having friends in for tea on Friday. I would be honoured if you would join us.

Sincerely,
Mary Perry

RSVP—44 Renfrew

Miss Perry? Mary? Emile had mentioned a Mary. A matronly sort, he had said. She put the note in her pocket, went to find Mama.

"Mama?"

Her mother was putting a hem in Janet's smock.

"Mama, one of the Auxiliary ladies, a Miss Perry, has invited me for tea. I believe several of the younger professors' wives will be there."

"Oh, Madeleine, could you go fetch me a spool of blue thread? I've run out."

"Yes, Mama."

"What were you saying, dear?"

"That I was going out for tea tomorrow."

"That's nice dear. Why don't you wear the new silk?"

And so it was arranged.

Emile was at Miss Perry's on Friday. The three of them sat in her drawing room and talked of Macaulay. Miss Perry was reading the latest volume in his *The History of England* and promised to lend it to Madeleine when she finished it.

Miss Perry, Madeleine noted, was not in the *least* matronly. If Emile hadn't been sitting by Madeleine's side, smiling only at her, she might have been jealous.

When Miss Perry went into the kitchen to instruct her maid as to the arrangements for tea, Emile took her hand.

"How have you been?" she said.

"Better, much better."

"Did you see a doctor?"

He shook his head. "Madeleine, we must talk—make plans."

"I know." She leaned down, whispered, "If we set a time, you could give a letter to Christine. I could have one for you."

"Would it be safe?"

"If it were late enough. Maybe ten o'clock."

"Shall we make it once a week—say every Saturday?"

"No, make it twice," she said.

"I fear we will have to elope."

"Shhh . . . Mary might hear."

"And I must talk to Mr. Huggins. I will have to have at least a small raise."

When the winter balls began, Madeleine went, faithfully telling Emile about each one, marvelling to him that she had ever been drawn to such frivolous men. Still, never was a block of her dance card unfilled. If she could not have Emile, she would have the next best thing—a man in her arms.

Let Papa think whatever he pleased as long as he did not think she still cared for Emile.

In the spring, they would proclaim the banns. She would be Mrs. L'Angelier.

Perhaps she carried it too far. It was not that she was flirting exactly, but it was her nature not to displease. It was hard to be cold.

Tonight she was reading "Young Goodman Brown," sitting in the brocade open-arm easy chair by the window.

"Dearest heart," whispered she, softly and rather sadly, when her lips were close to his ear, "prithee put off your journey until sunrise and sleep in your own bed tonight."

Papa came in. "Oh, you're reading it," he said, his voice strained.
"Yes, you didn't ask me to read to you."
"It has come to where I must ask?"
"Papa."
"I shall read it to myself. Leave it on my desk when you are through."
"No," she said, getting up. "I will be glad to do it."
He nodded, grumbled.
"What, Papa?"
". . . trouble . . ." he said, walking out. "I'll be in the drawing room," he called back.
"Yes, Papa." She went downstairs.
Papa was sitting in his favourite chair, the oak with the carved-chimera-head arms. Madeleine took the white-painted and gilded chair with serpentine seat. She opened the book, began at the beginning:

Young Goodman Brown came forth at sunset into the street at Salem village; put his head back, after crossing the threshold, to exchange a parting kiss with his young wife. . . .

By ten-thirty, Papa was nodding. She lowered her voice, read on:

By the sympathy of your human hearts for sin ye shall scent out all the places—whether in church, bed-chamber, street, field, or forest—where crime has been committed, and shall exult to behold the whole earth one stain of guilt, one mighty blood spot. Far more than this . . .

She stopped. Papa was snoring. She put down the book and crept out, went up to her room.

The next morning, after returning from Sauchiehall Street, she opened the trunk to get out her letters. She stood staring at it. Had the mohair scarf been on top? She cocked her head. No. . . .

She moved her cache of letters. And that night, as Papa and she walked into the dance, she smiled invitingly at young McCleod, smiling behind Papa's back when she saw the worried look on Papa's face.

Two days later, Mama called her into the master bedroom after breakfast, asked Madeleine why she had *not* ordered any pads made up by the seamstress lately.

"What?" She was incredulous.

"Papa thought maybe you had been ill . . . or . . ."

"Or what, Mama?"

"You have been off your appetite."

"I don't believe my ears. Did he . . . do you . . . think?"

"Of course not . . . but you have been seeing a great deal of young McCleod lately. Papa thought that . . ."

"That what, Mama?"

"That perhaps you were lovesick."

Madeleine laughed. "Lovesick? You mean . . . that perhaps I am pregnant?"

"Madeleine!"

"Which does he mean, Mama?"

"Oh, really, Madeleine, your papa has every right to watch you after last spring."

"Every right? Mama, I have done nothing wrong."

"No one is accusing you, daughter."

She turned to the bow-front chest, touched the turned hardwood handle. "Then what are we talking about?"

"Be down for supper in fifteen minutes. And you will speak to Miss Tweedle about the pads—you shouldn't skimp on them, you know."

Madeleine's face was scarlet. Did they think she had already . . .? That she was on her *second* man? How did they think she had been raised? Or was she a fool?

She used a whole box of pads the next time, heated them for thirty minutes. She wrapped each neatly as it was changed during the day, tied it with gauze, and put it into the white china chamber pot.

After supper, she went into the parlor and played the piano. She had just finished playing "The Campbells Are Coming" when Bessie came in. They did a duet; then Bessie played "Mermaids Floating o'er the Main." Madeleine went upstairs to get her sampler. As she neared her room, she heard a sound. She slipped to the doorway, peeked in.

Papa was in her room; she could see his shoes behind the rosewood screen. She ducked back, into James' room. She looked down, flattening herself against the wall, glad that she was wearing a simple housedress without hoop. Downstairs, the playing stopped. Papa passed down the hall, into his own room, shut his door.

She counted to ten, then stepped out, tiptoed to the stairs, went down to the landing. Then, whistling loudly, she came back up, went into her room.

She ran to the cupboard, examined the thread on the shoe bag within the alligator valise. It was in place. She cocked her head, looked around. All was in order. She walked in a circle, trying to remember. A sound. A chinking, sharp sound . . . from off where she had seen him first . . . beyond the screen.

She walked behind the screen, looked up and down. Her pink Chinoise robe swayed on the porcelain hook. She looked down: The lid of the white chamber pot sat ajar. A bit of gauze trailed out.

EIGHTEEN

Monday morning at ten, Lords Hope, Handyside, and Ivory walked with solemn steps to the bench.

Lord Hope adjusted his robes and sat down. Moncreiff leaned forwards, the memorandum book clutched in his hand.

Lord Hope folded his hands. "The question before us is whether the memorandum book be legal evidence."

He tented his fingers. "A memorandum book comes under the classification of hearsay evidence; but it is not ordinary hearsay evidence, subject to witnesses' testimony. One cannot tell how many such documents could be found in the repositories of a deceased person. A man might have threatened another; he might have hatred against the other; he might be determined to revenge himself. What entries might he not make in a diary for these purposes?"

At the table for the prosecution, Moncreiff's hand slid slowly from the memorandum book.

Lord Hope shook his head. "Admission of a private journal or diary as evidence to support a criminal charge is dangerous. Were we to relax the sacred rules of evidence, we would open a Pandora's box."

He stacked the papers in front of him, placed them back in the leather case.

"The memorandum book," he said, "is not competent, admissible evidence."

Moncreiff stood up, disappointment on his face. He approached the bench slowly, looked up at Lord Hope. "The case for the Crown is closed," he said.

There was a general hubbub in the stands. Lord Hope rapped his gavel and called for silence. As the court stilled, Inglis rose and walked before the jury box.

He surveyed the fifteen men. Then he began his address, his voice solemn.

"Gentlemen," he said, "in the course of this examination, reference may be made to affairs of some little delicacy in which L'Angelier was engaged in a previous part of his life. I am extremely unwilling to drag names before the public, and I hope that my learned friend the Lord Advocate will assist me in this discretion."

Moncreiff nodded gravely.

Inglis turned to the audience. "I now call to the stand Mr. Robert Baker."

Baker was a young man, a grocer at St. Helier, Jersey.

"Could you please tell the court," Inglis said, "how you made the acquaintance of the deceased?"

"Yes. I lived in Edinburgh in 1851 and acted as a waiter in my uncle's establishment, the Rainbow Tavern. I met L'Angelier there. We shared a bed."

"Shared a bed?"

"Yes. His circumstances, like my own, were then very bad. He was living on the bounty of my Uncle Baker, waiting for a situation."

"And how would you describe his temperament at that time?"

"He was in the habit of walking up and down in the room, weeping."

"Did he explain why?"

"He had met with a disappointment in a love matter."

"He told you that?"

"No, not himself, but I heard my uncle talk of it. It was about some lady in Fife."

"You are sure it was in Fife, not in Glasgow?"

"Oh, yes it was—"

"You need not mention the names," Inglis said quickly.

He turned to the jury, smiled confidingly. "I think it will suffice to speak of her as the Lady of Fife."

The second witness was Edward Vokes McKay, joiner, an acquaintance of L'Angelier when he resided above the Rainbow Tavern.

"Tell us, Mr. McKay," Inglis said, "did L'Angelier ever talk of ladies admiring him?"

"Oh, yes, he said ladies admired him very much."

"Can you give us a specific instance?"

"Well, I remember one occasion. When he came into the tavern, I was reading the papers. He told me that he had met a lady in Prince Street and that she had remarked to her companion on what pretty little feet he had. I never believed anything he said afterwards."

Lord Hope seemed to wake from a slumber. "Am I to understand you to say that he heard the lady say what pretty feet he had?"

"Yes, sir."

Lord Hope shook his head, made a small clucking sound.

Inglis smiled. "Mr. McKay, was it a common thing for him to speak of ladies admiring him?"

"Well—" McKay began.

"I object," Moncreiff said, "to the defence characterising the conversations. He has yet to establish even the suggestion of habitual pattern, much less claim such a pattern."

"Objection sustained," Lord Hope said. "Dean of Faculty, please confine yourself to eliciting evidence."

"I'm sorry, your Lordship," Inglis said cheerfully.

William McDougal Ogilvie was called next, sworn in. Ogilvie was a thin pockmarked man with a metallic voice.

"Please, tell the court," Inglis said, "your occupation and how you came to make the acquaintance of L'Angelier."

"I am an assistant bank teller in the Dundee bank. In 1852, I was secretary to the Floral and Horticulture Society.

153

L'Angelier was a member. In this way I became acquainted with him."

"Would you say you were a close friend?"

"We became intimate over the course of the year; we frequently conversed together."

"And how would you describe his state of mind?"

"Variable, remarkably so."

"What was your general topic of conversation, Mr. Ogilvie?"

"The ladies, sir."

The audience laughed.

"I see," Inglis said. "And did he brag of them admiring him?"

"I object!" Moncreiff said. "The defence is attempting to characterise again. The question is leading."

"Objection sustained," Hope said, giving Inglis a reproachful glance.

Inglis walked a few paces from the witness box, looked at the audience, gave a slight shrug. He turned back to the witness.

"Did you ever hear of him speak of what he would do if he met with a disappointment in love?"

"Once. In the florist shop he said if a woman rejected him, he would kill himself. He took up a large knife used for cutting twine and gestured towards his heart."

"Was he speaking then of any real case?"

"No, I don't think so, just generally."

"Did he ever brag—excuse me—speak of knowing high persons in society?"

"He spoke once of having been in France. He said he was travelling with some person of distinction. He said he was in charge of all the luggage, carriages, horses—everything, in fact."

"Did he ever speak to you of arsenic?"

"Yes."

"Please go on."

"He said that on one occasion in France, the horses were very much knocked up and that he had given them arsenic."

"Knocked up?"

"Winded, tired."

"Was he speaking in English or French?"

"English. I don't know French."

"Were you acquainted with the effects of arsenic?"

"No, not at that time."

"Did L'Angelier say to you what the effects were?"

"He said it made the horses long-winded. I asked if he was not afraid of poisoning them; and he said, 'Oh, no.' In fact, he said he had taken it himself. I said I should not like to try it, and he said that the effects, contrary to my impression, were good."

"Did he specify those good effects of ingesting arsenic?"

"He said it improved the complexion. I inferred that he used it for that purpose."

"Did he say he did?"

"Not exactly."

"Did he ever complain to you of illness?"

"Yes, of pains in the back, and difficulty breathing. He said the arsenic helped these."

"Did he ever show you arsenic?"

"I rather think he did—he opened his desk and showed me a paper containing a white powder. At the same time he showed me a very fine specimen of copper ore."

"Thank you." Inglis turned to Moncreiff, bowed slightly.

"No questions," Moncreiff said drily.

Inglis walked back to the defence table, poured himself a tumbler of water, drank it down slowly. He looked at the witness section, then walked back to center stage.

"The defence calls Mr. William Pringle Laird to the stand."

Mr. Laird, a portly man in an expensive frock coat, a gold watch chain at his waist, shuffled to the stand, swore his oath.

"Please introduce yourself to the court, Mr. Laird."

"I am William Laird, nurseryman in Dundee."

"You were acquainted with the deceased?"

"I was. I knew him when he worked for Dickson in Edinburgh—about 1843."

"Wasn't he at one time an employee of yours?"

"Yes—in 1852, I took him in my own employment at Dundee. He came to me on Old Handsel Monday—he had been away in France—and he remained until the end of August."

"How would you describe him at that time?"

"He was a very sober young man, and very kind and obliging, rather excitable and changeable in his temper, sometimes very melancholy and sometimes very lively."

"Did he speak to you ever of a disappointment in love?"

"He did not tell me at first, but shortly after he came, he told me he had been crossed in love."

"How long after he came?"

"Oh, a fortnight, I guess."

"Did he tell you how this disappointment had come about?"

"He said he had learnt that the girl had married another, and that he could scarcely believe it because he did not think she could take another."

"Why not?"

"I understand that it was because she was pledged to him."

"Did he tell you who the girl was?"

"Yes, he said . . . a young woman from the Kingdom of Fife. Her name—"

Inglis cut him off. "I don't want her name."

". . . I believe she was in the middle station of society."

"Do you know Mr. William Ogilvie, the gentleman who just testified?"

"Yes, he was apprentice at that time."

"Did he tell you that L'Angelier had threatened to stab himself with a knife?"

"Yes, he did. That led me to speak to L'Angelier. I told him I was sorry to hear that he had done so."

"What did he reply?"

"Very little. He was very dull. He said he was truly miserable and that he wished he was out of the world."

"Those were his words?"

"Well, something to that effect. He was in a very moody and gloomy state after this, and rarely spoke to anyone."

"From these conversations, and all you had seen of him, do you think he had any religious principle about him to deter him from committing suicide?"

"Objection," Moncreiff said. "Counsel is asking the witness to speculate. Any answer can only be conjecture on his part."

Lord Hope pushed his spectacles up on his nose. "Objection overruled. Let us hear the witness's reply."

"He attended church regularly," Laird said, "but did not show anything particular about religion; but at the same time he was very moral, as far as I knew."

"Did he ever speak of knowing high persons on the Continent?"

"Not that I recall."

"Did he speak of the Continent in any manner?"

"He told me he had been engaged in the French Revolution: he said he was a member of their national guard."

"Did you believe him?"

"I had no reason not to at the time."

"What were his wages when he was with you?"

"I don't recollect. He came to me as an extra hand when he was out of employment. I said I would give him bed and board and something more; I think he got eight shillings a week."

"Thank you, no further questions," Inglis said. He bowed to Moncreiff.

"No questions," Moncreiff said.

Inglis than called Charles Adams, M.D. Dr. Adams took the stand, was sworn in.

Inglis consulted a moment with his assistant, then approached the stand.

"Please introduce yourself to the court."

"I am an M.D. at Coatbridge, and keep a druggist's shop."

"Coatbridge is near the line from Bridge of Allan to Glasgow, is it not?"

"It is."

"Do you remember the afternoon of Sunday, March 22nd?"

"Yes, I was in my shop."

"Do you have many customers on Sunday afternoon?"

"Very few. I keep my shutters closed. But I am in, should special occasion arise."

"Did you have any customers that Sunday afternoon?"

"Yes, one."

"Could you describe this visitor?"

"He was young, maybe thirty. He was wearing a mustache. . . ." He scratched his head. "I think he had on a dark-brownish coat and a Balmoral hat . . . yes, I am sure about the hat; my assistant commented on it."

"Did he purchase anything?"

"He asked for twenty-five drops of laudanum and a bottle of soda water. I said we had no soda water, but I would give him a soda powder, which I did. He mixed the powder and the laudanum with water and took the potion."

"Is twenty-five drops a large dose?"

"It is not a beginning dose."

"Thank you, Doctor Adams, no further questions." Inglis walked back to the table, sat down.

Moncreiff stood up, arched an ache out of his back, approached the box.

"Is that sale of laudanum in your book, doctor?"

"No, we never enter it."

"Why not?"

"Opium must be recorded, but not a tincture of opium."

"You felt no need to monitor purchases of laudanum?"

"No."

"But . . ." Moncreiff shook his head. "No further questions."

Inglis rose. "I call Master Robert Baird to the stand."

Baird rose, took the stand.

"I am Robert Baird," he said, after being sworn in. "The son of Mr. Robert Baird, owner of Baird's Emporium."

"Please, Mr. Baird, tell the court how you made the acquaintance of the deceased."

"I have an uncle in Mr. Huggins' warehouse." The lad ran his finger beneath his collar.

"Did L'Angelier ever ask you to introduce him to the defendant?"

"Yes, several times. He seemed very pressing about it."

"How old were you at that time?"

"Seventeen."

"Seventeen. And you did then introduce them?"

"Well, first I asked my uncle to introduce him, thinking it more proper."

"And?"

"My uncle declined."

"Then what did you do?"

"I asked my mother to invite Miss Smith some evening, that I might ask L'Angelier and introduce him."

"And your mother said?"

"She declined as well."

"They never met in your mother's house?"

"They certainly did not."

"And where did you finally introduce them?"

"I introduced them on the street," he said, his face sallow.

"Did you know that he told Miss Perry that he was introduced to Miss Smith by your mother in your mother's house?"

"No, I have no knowledge of that."

"Then L'Angelier lied?"

"I only know that I introduced him to Miss Smith."

Inglis nodded. "Thank you. No further questions."

"No questions," Moncreiff said. Baird swallowed, went quickly from his seat.

Next, Agnes McMillan, a former tablemaid, a mousy woman in a grey sack, was called to the stand. She met Inglis' eyes.

"Tell us, Miss McMillan, how long were you in the employment of the Smith family?"

"Two years, sir."

"And during that time, did Miss Smith ever speak of arsenic to you?"

Agnes nodded.

Lord Hope leaned over. "See that the record indicates that the question was answered in the affirmative."

Agnes blushed.

"On one occasion or on more than one occasion, Miss McMillan?"

"Once, sir," she said loudly.

"What brought on the conversation?"

"I don't recall, sir."

"Do you recall what she said?"

"Yes, I perfectly remember her saying that she believed that it was used for the complexion, or that it was good for it, I don't recollect which."

"Can you recollect anything else about the conversation?"

"No, sir."

"Thank you, Miss McMillan."

The mousy woman sat, looking expectantly at Inglis.

"No questions," Moncreiff said from his table.

"You may step down," Inglis said.

Agnes smiled vacantly, and descended from the stand.

The defence then called Dr. Robert Patterson, a physician in Leith.

"Tell us, sir," Inglis said, "how long have you practised in Leith?"

"Several years, sir, since 1852."

"And during these years have you ever seen a case of suicidal poisoning by arsenic?"

"Yes, quite a few."

"Could you describe them to the court?"

"They were chiefly young females connected with the mills and colour works."

"Had they obtained the arsenic at their places of employment?"

"In some cases; in others it was purchased."

"How many cases in all did you prescribe for?"

"About seven, all young females."

"And you were able to save them?"

He shook his head. "With one exception, they all died."

"But you did prescribe for them?"

"Yes, every remedy I could think of."

"Doctor Patterson, did any of them tell you the cause of their suffering?"

"No, not one of them disclosed it before death. I asked all whether they had taken arsenic or some poison, and they all denied it. Only autopsies and further investigations indicated their deaths to be suicides. The single girl who lived revealed her story to me."

"Thank you, doctor."

Moncreiff rose and approached the witness box.

"Doctor, were all these cases since you assumed your office in Leith?"

"Well, some of them were before."

"Over how long a period, roughly, would you say that these seven cases had occurred?" Moncreiff said.

"Roughly?" Patterson scratched his chin, shrugged. "Perhaps eighteen years."

"Did all the cases exhibit identical symptoms?" Moncreiff said.

"Nearly so. They vomited matter of various colours, depending on what had been eaten previously. The vomiting ceased in some cases an hour or two before death, but in most cases continued till death."

"You say these were all proven suicides?" Moncreiff asked, his head cocked.

"They were reported as such," Patterson said.

"And you were called at their request?"

"Well, I can't say that—others called me in most cases."

"One more thing, doctor. Tell us, from the commencement of the symptoms, what was the average time till death?"

"I can't give you an average," Patterson said.

"Well, give me the shortest and the longest times."

"Death resulted in thirty-six hours in one case, and twelve in another."

"Thank you, doctor. I have no further questions."

Robert Morris was called to the stand, sworn in.

"You are an employee of W. and R. Chambers, publishers and editors of *Chambers' Journal?*" Inglis said.

"That is correct," Morris said. He was a man in his forties with blue-black hair, a grey coat, muttonchop whiskers.

Inglis walked to the evidence table, picked up four issues of the journal, handed them to Morris. Morris looked at each, his face solemn.

"Can you identify these, Mr. Morris?"

"Yes, they are four numbers of *Chambers' Journal.*"

"These were published and circulated in the usual way?"

"Yes."

"Tell us, what is the present circulation of the journal?"

Morris smiled, said proudly, "About fifty thousand."

"Would you read the dates on these four issues?"

"Yes." He fumbled in his coat pocket, took out a narrow case, put on his horn-rimmed spectacles. "Yes . . . December 1851, June 1853, February 1856, and July 1856."

"And in each of these issues, there is an article on the use of arsenic, is there not?"

"Yes."

"Are you aware that these articles excited a considerable sensation?"

"I hoped they would interest and inform our readers."

"Thank you, Mr. Morris." Inglis nodded, stepped back to the table.

"No questions," Moncreiff said. He sat back on his chair and wrote busily on a lined tablet.

"Why this 'no questions'?" Inglis whispered to his assistant.

George Young shrugged. "I think he is waiting."

"But we shall be done before he can begin," Inglis said.

Inglis stood up, walked back in front of the audience, and called George Simpson to the stand.

Simpson, a nervous-looking thin man, approached the bench hesitantly.

"Mr. Simpson, you are employed by Blackwood and Sons, am I correct?"

"Yes."

"Did you . . ." Inglis said, stepping back towards the evidence table, and taking up the journal that lay on the corner, ". . . did your company publish this issue of *Blackwood's*: December 1855?"

"We did."

"How many copies were printed?"

"Ah . . . our circulation would have been about seven thousand at that time."

"Did you not also publish the book *The Chemistry of Common Life?*"

"Yes." He cleared his throat. "But it had been circulated before as a pamphlet: The circulation, combined, would be in the range of thirty thousand copies."

Inglis walked to the table, picked up the book. It was bound in red leather, embossed with gold letters; the paper's

163

edges were marbleised. He opened the book to the leather bookmark, handed it to Simpson. "Could you read us this chapter title and the title of the first section?"

Mr. Simpson cleared his throat again: "In Chapter 23, 'The Poisons We Select,' the first part is entitled 'The Consumption of White Arsenic.'"

"Now if you please, read us the first paragraph."

Simpson cleared his throat and read: "'Arsenic is one of the most valuable remedies in the whole list of medicines. It increases tissue change throughout the body and thus improves nutrition. It is also a powerful antiseptic.'"

"Thank you, Mr. Simpson," Inglis said. He went back to his seat, nodding.

"No questions," Moncreiff said, not even looking up.

Robert Townsend, manufacturing chemist, was called next, examined.

"Now, Mr. Townsend, I understand that your chemical firm in Glasgow uses arsenic in the chemical processes," Inglis said.

"Yes, we have always large quantities of arsenic on hand."

"What would you call a *large* quantity?"

"Oh, from one to ten hundred-pound casks."

"*Where* is this arsenic kept?"

"During the night it is locked up in a private office in the counting house."

"And during the day?"

"It stands in the open casks, like meal in a meal shop."

"Do you mean to say that the casks are kept open without lids?"

"No, not exactly. One cask only is kept open for use."

"I see. And how many people do you employ?"

"From a hundred to a hundred and forty people."

"If any of these were so inclined, might they take arsenic from the premises without being observed?"

"If any were so inclined, I have no doubt they might be able to do so."

"Have you ever encountered a case where arsenic was taken away?"

"I have never known of it happening."

"Thank you, Mr. Townsend. Thank you." Inglis took his seat, smiling.

"No questions," Moncreiff said.

Inglis rose, called Dr. James Adair Lawrie to the stand. Dr. Lawrie introduced himself as a Glasgow physician, in practice for twenty years.

"And during that time, have you had cause to study the effects of arsenic?" Inglis asked, his hands clasped behind his back.

"I have not made arsenic a particular study, but I have had my attention recently directed to its effects on the skin if it were mixed with water."

"Did you observe its effects on a patient?"

"No, I tried it myself. I put in water a quarter ounce of arsenic from Currie's shop, mixed with indigo, and washed my hands with it. I also mixed half an ounce with water and washed my face freely."

"Did you suffer disagreeable effects?"

"None."

"Was there any noticeable effect?"

"The effect of the washing was as if I had used a ball of soap with sand in it; the effect was not great, but if at all, it had a softening effect."

Inglis smiled. "One more question: What sort of container did you use to mix the arsenic with the water?"

"A common-sized hand basin."

"Thank you, doctor." Inglis turned to Moncreiff, smiled when Moncreiff rose to question the witness. Inglis returned to his seat, smiled at Young.

Moncreiff strode to the witness box, looked up at the witness.

"Tell us, in making these experiments, did you put the arsenic in first or after you had put in the water?"

"I filled a basin with water and then put in the arsenic."

"Did you stir the water?"

"Of course."

"Would you say that the arsenic was in suspension when you washed your face and hands?"

"Well, a large part, of course, fell to the bottom."

"Would you care to repeat this experiment again?"

"I would have no fear of doing so."

"Would you characterize it then as a *safe* practice?"

"I don't think one experiment would justify my saying that."

"Did you feel any smarting of the eyes?"

"No, but I didn't get any in my eyes."

"Would you consider prescribing such a treatment to a patient?"

"I might."

"Really? Can you give me a case where you might prescribe it?"

"Well . . . if there were vermin on the skin, that might be such a case."

"Have you ever in your twenty years of practice prescribed arsenic mixed with water to be used on the skin?"

"No, but I would have no fear of doing so."

"I commend your bravery," Moncreiff said. The audience laughed.

"No further questions," Moncreiff said. He wheeled, walked back to the table with clipped steps.

The last witness to take the stand was Janet Smith, age twelve, sister of Madeleine Smith.

Inglis smiled companionably at the child.

"Tell me, Miss Smith, where did you live last winter and spring?"

Janet lifted her chin. The straw bonnet framed her oval

face; she said in a soft but clear voice, "In my father's house at Blythswood Square."

"And where did you sleep?"

"Downstairs, in the same bed with Madeleine."

The audience was leaning forwards, trying to see the child who was almost hidden by the witness box. The court reporter was busy sketching: white gloves, a white appliquéd blouse under a smart bolero jacket, a skirt of blue dotted swiss.

Inglis smiled encouragingly at the child. "Did you go to bed at the same time as your sister?"

"No, generally before her." The child was warming up now. She looked around the courtroom, located her sister, smiled, and lifted one clenched hand, opened it slightly, then put it back in her lap.

"Every night?" Inglis said.

"Sir?"

"Did you go to bed before her *every* night?"

"Well, on the Sabbath, we both went to bed at the same time—as a rule."

"Tell me, Miss Smith. Do you remember Sunday, March 22nd?"

"Yes."

"Do you remember if you went to bed at the same time as your sister *that* Sunday?" Inglis said.

"We went to bed at the same time. We went downstairs together from the dining room after vespers."

"And who was in bed first?"

"I don't remember. We were both undressing at the same time. . . ." She furrowed her brow.

"Did your sister seem . . . to be in any special hurry that night?"

"No, sir."

"She didn't put off her dressing?"

"No, she got her nightclothes on just like always."

"One more question, Miss Smith, and then you shall talk to my good friend, the Lord Advocate. Tell me, who fell asleep first?"

"I don't know."
"That's fine, Miss Smith. Thank you."

Moncreiff rose, went before the box. His voice was gentle too.
"Have you ever seen your sister take cocoa?"
"Yes."
"Where did she get it?"
"From a paper on her mantle."
"Yes, well . . . do you know why she took it?"
"No, I don't. She never talked of it."
"Tell me, what time did you go to bed that Sunday night?"
"I don't know the hour; it was the same time as usual on Sunday with us."
Moncreiff gave a slight shrug. "No further questions."
"I have another, Your Honour," Inglis said, rising. He walked quickly back to the box. "Miss Smith, was your sister the only one in the house who took cocoa?"
"I think."
"Tell me, when you woke on Monday, March 23rd, where was your sister?"
"In our bed."
"And what time was that?"
"About eight."
"Thank you, Miss Smith." He held out his hand, helped her down.

The audience looked towards the door for the next witness. The door was closed. A buzz went around the room. Inglis walked slowly to the bench, stood looking up at the judges.
"Your Honours," he said, his voice grave, "this concludes the testimony for the defence."
At the prosecution table, Moncreiff raised an eyebrow.
Lord Hope looked at the clock. It was half past five. He dismissed the court till ten o'clock Tuesday morning.

NINETEEN

Inglis was quiet tonight, falling at the oddest of moments into silent depressions.

"I am always that way at the end," he said.

"Do you think it will end tomorrow?" Madeleine said.

Inglis scratched at his side whiskers. "Perhaps."

"Today went so quickly," Madeleine said.

"It is part of the strategy," Inglis said.

Madeleine looked at her hands on the wooden table. "I have run out of things to tell you. You must ask me now."

Inglis looked at her. "There is one thing I can't understand. You were in love with him, you considered yourself his bride. Why didn't you *demand* that your parents accept him?"

She scratched at the wood. "I don't know. I have asked myself that. I guess I thought it would kill Papa. Perhaps *demanding* could not occur to me."

"And if Emile had shown your father the letters, early on, what would have happened?"

"I have asked myself that, too, Mr. Inglis. I don't know. I suppose it would all have been different."

"In a court of law, you know, you would have been bound to L'Angelier, not to your father."

"I was aware of the alternatives."

Inglis pushed back his chair, stretched his long legs under the table. "Daughters do marry beneath their station."

"No daughter of his."

"What were you afraid of?"

"His rage."

"Would he have beat you?"

She laughed. "That would have been kind. No, he would simply have condemned me in his heart."

"And now?"

"And now?" she said.

"Will he take you back? Would you even want to go?"

"Are you so very confident, Mr. Inglis?"

When Inglis had gone, she sat upon her cot, looked at the moon through the bars.

When had fear of losing Emile outweighed her fear of Papa? Perhaps that wasn't even the formula.

But she knew the exact time, the exact place. It was in her room, behind the screen, knowing whose hands had disturbed the gauze within the white china pot, knowing what Papa thought of her.

She had stayed home that Sunday, feigned a headache, watched the family drive off to church in Papa's new beige coach. She had stared vacantly out the window at the smoke-grimed sunlight. But she had not gone to bed.

She stood in the center of the hallway, surveyed the familiar domesticity. She sobered at the touch of maroon plush.

She looked in the gilt-framed mirror, brushed dust off the seventh wing of the nearest angel. The sunlight hit the mirror's right half, making that side of her face bright. The other half was in shadow. By moving a fraction to one side, her nose slid into silvery darkness. It was like a daguerreotype, the effect—half negative, half positive.

She moved into the shadow, looked into her mirrored eyes until she was in the mirror, looking back at a stranger, framed not in golden seraphim, but by the oak wainscotting and red tapestry.

She blinked, came back into her own face. Then she moved away, into the dark drawing room, onto the Oriental rug. A tear ran down her cheek.

Not a fleck of sunlight penetrated the heavy red velvet drapes. If it had, Mama would have rushed to tell her to spread newspapers lest the light fade the rich dark patina of the wood.

She rubbed her eyes, blinked. In her mind's eye, she saw yesterday's guest, young John McCleod, sitting on the overstuffed ottoman, his bulk filling the giant cake slice of a cushion, his hand resting on the palm back, his foot keeping time to the piece she was playing on the piano. And over there, on the wing chair, Papa, with his wee dram.

Then, outside on the veranda, McCleod assembling his mirror-shiny pipes, filling the plaid bag with air, putting it to his mouth, filling the air with the huge release sound, then, with pained concentration, playing the high lilting melody.

Tradition, that is what life with John McCleod would be. Part of the clan, fitted together with neatly lathed threads, played with pained concentration.

She walked to the mantelpiece, touched the triptych of artificial tortoiseshell. Everything in the room seemed to be pretending to be something else. Wax bloomed into flowers under a glass-dome sky. Shiny red agate apples rested in a hobnail bowl on the bird-clawed table. Carved into the table's base were sow thistles and leaflets, tendrils of convolvulus bending over like scrolls. The limbs of the piano were skirted modestly in Grecian folds. Everything was made to look as ornamental and heavy as possible, to take up as much room as it could. Worth was judged by how much fancy carving per square inch, by how much weight per piece.

That gothic tabernacle of a footstool, its back a delicate rose window. The busily patterned wallpaper that stretched from wainscot to picture rail—encrusted with oil paintings, silhouettes, samplers.

Now that she was seeing it fresh, it repulsed her. The house was like a fat spoiled child, petulant in velvets, demanding admiration.

She had been such a good girl, dutiful, obedient. Why? To please them; to win their approval and trust. And how was she rewarded when she finally chose something of her own? With scorn, mistrust, anger. It wasn't fair!

Her mind had never seemed so clear. She recalled a Lenten prayer, said it her way:

> When I was a child, I spake as a child, I understood as a child, I thought as a child: but when I became a woman, I put away childish things. For now we see through a glass, darkly; but then face to face: now I know in part; but then shall I know even as also I am known.

She went to the piano, picked out a somber four-note tune. Then she hit the bottom keys.

They had *really* thought she might be pregnant. That she had let a man . . .

Had they raised her with such hypocrisy? Saying one thing—thinking another?

For if so, perhaps she knew nothing. She had always known that if Papa were to give his consent, she might let a man touch her . . . and she had been ashamed of that secret sinful knowledge.

But if they believed *this!*

When her parents' Thursday outings with the Fergusons became a regular thing, she wrote Emile.

My Darling,

I have a surprise for you on Thursday. Come at 7.

Mimi

On Thursday, at seven, Emile knelt at the black iron grillwork. It was dark inside and out.

"Emile?" she whispered. She could just make out his dark shape.

Emile knelt, steadied himself against the iron bars. "Yes, Mimi?"

"Christine is away."

"Yes?"

She could smell his pomade. If she reached out, she might touch the wool of his trousers. "We can sit in her room," she said. "As soon as I am able to coax Janet to sleep."

He sneezed.

"You sound terrible," she said.

"It's just a bad cold."

"Well, I shall make you a toddy, then."

"How soon?"

"Ten."

He left, his footsteps light and quick.

November 30, 1855

My own, my darling,

I hope you slept well last night and find yourself better today. I did, my love, pity you standing in the cold last night, but I could not get Janet to sleep—little stupid thing.

My beloved, I can say nothing as to our marriage, as it is not certain when M. and P. will go from home. You know I know nothing of these things. You say we will proclaim the Banns in Glasgow. I fear them. Two weeks! If I had any name other than Madeleine, it might pass. Must it be done in Church? But I do want to be married in Church. But you know better than I what must be done.

I do hope you are better today. I think you should consult our Dr. McFarlan, get him to sound you, tell you what is wrong with you. If you love me, do go, do not try to doctor yourself—be good for once.

Pet, I must stop as they will be in shortly. All are out now. I am thy own,

Mimi

TWENTY

Inglis' notebook lay open on the wooden table: *7/7/57—Summaries.* Inglis himself was hunched over the pad, making last-minute notes.

At ten o'clock, the judges filed in, took their places, the reporters stopped talking, held their quills poised.

Moncreiff was first. He stood, his wig freshly powdered, and walked before the jury. He surveyed the fifteen men, his grave face eliciting grave faces in turn.

"Gentlemen of the jury," he said, "after an investigation which for its length has proved unexampled, I believe, in the criminal annals of this country, I have now to discharge perhaps the most painful public duty that ever fell to my lot."

Someone in the audience began to cough. Moncreiff waited till the cough stopped, then cast a level glance at the nearest juror, the newspaper writer.

"I am quite sure, gentlemen, that in the discharge of that duty I shall meet with that attention that the deep importance of this case requires, and that you have paid to its details from the commencement." A juror in the back row suppressed a yawn, looked sheepish. Moncreiff raised his voice:

"It is now my duty, as fully and as clearly as I can, to draw the details of the case together, to present to you in a connected shape the links of that chain of evidence that we have been constructing this last week."

He clasped his hands together.

"Gentlemen, I would have rejoiced if the result of the initial inquiry, which it was our duty to make, had justified the Crown in resting content with the investigation into the facts, and in withdrawing our charge against the prisoner. Gentlemen, I grieve to say that so far is innocence a possible conclusion that there does not remain the possibility of escape from the net that the young lady herself has woven—every link is firmly fastened—every loophole is completely stopped."

At the table for the defence, Inglis and his assistant were relaxed, Inglis gazing through the tall dusty window, Young rubbing his chin negligently.

"In stating to you," Moncreiff was saying, "the evidence on which these charges must be found proved, I shall avoid as far as possible the almost incredible evidence it has afforded of disgrace, and sin, and degradation." He took a breath here; those in the back row were wide awake now.

"To make these matters public is my duty; to dwell upon them, however, is painful to any moral society."

Inglis cast a glance over at Madeleine. She remained calm. The colour in her cheeks did not waver. If anything, her face had grown more tender.

". . . While the prisoner is justly entitled to say that such a crime should not be lightly presumed, yet, gentlemen, as you will see from the tale I have to tell, you are trying a case of as cool, premeditated, deliberate homicide as ever justly brought its perpetrator within the compass and penalty of the law."

Moncreiff then began the lengthy history of the relationship, reviewing the testimony of the witnesses, reading portions of the letters. As he spoke, the jurors made notes. They were dressed up today. The juror Momson had on a new teal-blue redingote.

"Just listen, gentlemen," Moncreiff said, "to these early expressions of passion. Here is one: *Oh, Emile, to be in thy embrace.*

"Or this one, written in January of the first year of their relationship: *I did not expect the pleasure of seeing you last evening, of being fondled by you*—the word 'fondled,' gentlemen, is underscored—*dear, dear Emile. I trust ere long to have a long, long interview with you, sweet one of my soul. I pray we shall forever remain happy and loving. But there is no fear of that, we are sure to do so, love—are we not? Much, much love, tender kisses, long embraces, kisses, love.*

"And there are more that begin in a similar fashion. Now, gentlemen, it may well be asked, after such words as these, what else did she intend or wish than sexual intercourse? Can you be surprised, after such letters, that on May 6th, 1856, he got possession of her person?

"Then, after he *has* secured her person, on the 7th of May, she writes him, and in that letter is there the slightest appearance of grief or remorse?"

Moncreiff looked over at Madeleine, his face woeful. "None whatever." His hand fell to the papers before him.

"It is the letter of a girl rejoicing in what had passed, and alluding to it, in one passage in particular, in terms that I will not read, for perhaps such words were never previously committed to paper as having passed between a man and a woman. What passed must have passed out of doors, not in the house, and"—his voice hushed—"she talks of the act *as hers as much as his!*

"And now, gentlemen," he said, stopping and pouring himself a tumbler of water, drinking off half of it. "Now, having traced the correspondence down to this date, having proved the greatest intimacy between the parties, having proved the correspondence to be of such a nature that no eye could see it without her character being utterly blasted, we now come to the crisis."

Moncreiff paused, took a sip of water. The jury looked on solemnly. The matron, Miss Aitken, leaned forwards upon the bar. Madeleine sat upright, as she had during the entire trial.

"Gentlemen, what a labyrinth of bewilderment this unhappy girl, first by her lapse of virtue, and then by her want of truth, was driving herself into! She tells L'Angelier that her affection was withdrawn, in the hope that his indignant spirit would induce him to turn her away, when she would be free to form another engagement. But, instead, he threatens to use the correspondence against her. She is so committed that she cannot extricate herself, and yet, if not extricated, her character, her fame, her reputation, are forfeited forever! Gentlemen, the *motive.*"

His voice lowered. He stopped dead center of the jury box and surveyed the members one by one. "And gentlemen, the *opportunity*, we have demonstrated, she had in such abundance she could afford failures."

He had been talking three hours now and his voice was rough. "Now, gentlemen, listen to this portion of a letter: *I loved you, I wrote to you in my first ardent love—it was for your love I adored you. I put on paper what I should not.*"

He put the paper down, looked back at the jurors, his face woeful.

"Gentlemen, doubtless, poor creature, she *had* done that, and throughout this unhappy history of the gradual decay of an ill-regulated mind, one cannot see all this without—what I feel from the bottom of my heart—the deepest commiseration."

"Little toad," Inglis whispered. His assistant suppressed a laugh.

"Doubtless, L'Angelier had abused his opportunities in a way that no man of honor ought to have done, and had stolen into that family and destroyed their peace forever."

Young raised an eyebrow at Inglis, wrote hastily on a scrap of paper, passed it to him. Inglis nodded.

Another hour and the court adjourned for lunch. The jurors filed out, passed through the same door they would pass through when Lord Hope dismissed them.

At two o'clock, they were all back in place.

"We are coming to the very crisis of the case now," Moncreiff said. "The day was Thursday, February 19th. Be kind enough to bear that in mind. Now, remember, on Tuesday, February 17th, L'Angelier dined with Miss Perry; he told her he was to see Miss Smith on that Thursday. Thursday, the 19th.

"In the middle of the night," Moncreiff said, "L'Angelier was seized with a sudden illness. You heard it described—vomiting, purging, excessive pain—by his landlady, Mrs. Jenkins. He lay on the floor all night; he was so ill he could not call for assistance. At last he was relieved, but only after a great deal of suffering. These symptoms are consistent with the symptoms of arsenic poisoning.

"Now, I would like to read another letter. You recall from Mrs. Jenkins' testimony that on the night of February 22nd and the morning of the 23rd, L'Angelier was again stricken with vomiting, purging, and pain. There is no doubt about this date. It is the evening of Sunday and the morning of Monday about which we are speaking.

"Now, remember also Miss Perry's testimony. On March 2nd, L'Angelier told her that he had been to see the prisoner on the 19th and that he had been ill immediately after and that he had been ill again, later, the first after taking coffee and the second after chocolate.

"Now, in corroboration of that, listen to this letter found in L'Angelier's tourist bag.

"Dearest Sweet Emile—I am sorry to hear you are ill—"

Moncreiff broke off here, interjected: "This letter is headed Wednesday."

Moncreiff read the middle portion of the letter quickly, then slowed down and raised his voice.

> You did look bad Sunday night and Monday morning. I think you got sick with walking home so late—and the long want of food, so the next time we meet I shall make you a loaf of bread before you go out.

"We then have the prisoner's own testimony that she saw the deceased on the dates of his second illness. We have, through Miss Perry's testimony, proof that Miss Smith was with the deceased on the occasion of his first illness. We put forth, then, that the prisoner had the opportunity to cause these illnesses, in short, to administer poison."

Moncreiff stopped before the jurors' box:

"Now we come to the third charge: Murder. We have two unsuccessful attempts, February 19th and February 22nd. The third attempt succeeds: The murder takes place on Sunday night, the 22nd of March. The victim dies on Monday, March 23rd.

"L'Angelier had not seen the prisoner since February 22nd. Longing to arrange a meeting with her, he returns to Glasgow from a trip to Edinburgh, where, parenthetically, he felt fine. Miss Smith had informed him that her family was to return from holiday March 17th and had promised to arrange a meeting with him after that date. He stays home, in good health, but in low spirits, all the following day, March 18th, expecting a letter. Disappointed, he goes on Thursday, March 19th, to Bridge of Allan. On that very day, a missive arrives at his quarters, appointing a rendezvous for that day."

Inglis erupted. "How do you know the contents of the letter or even if such a letter exists? No letter dated March 19th has been offered in evidence. Your Honour, I object!"

Moncreiff turned to the bench. He was silent, breathing heavily.

"Your Lordships, I will, with your forbearance, establish the contents of an admittedly absent letter in the course of my narrative."

Lord Hope leaned back. "Proceed, Lord Advocate."

Moncreiff walked to the jury box, "The letter was forwarded to L'Angelier by Monsieur Thuau, as L'Angelier had asked. The letter arrived at Bridge of Allan about 9 A.M. on Friday, March 20th. Now we do not have the letter, as my colleague, the Dean of Faculty, rightfully points out. But we do have the envelope, which was found in L'Angelier's tourist bag. And we have from L'Angelier's comments—and from a subsequent letter from the prisoner herself—strong indications of the contents of the missing letter."

Moncreiff stopped in front of the jury box, surveyed the jurors' faces.

"First," Moncreiff said, "from a letter L'Angelier writes to Miss Perry. The letter is dated Friday, March 20th and postmarked Bridge of Allan. It says: I should have come to see someone last night, but the letter came too late, so we are both disappointed.

"What letter came too late? What appointment did it make? Who made the appointment?

"These questions are answered in a letter from the prisoner to the deceased, a letter clearly dated and postmarked as having been mailed Friday March 20th in Glasgow. The letter reads:

> Why, my beloved, did you not come to me? Oh, beloved, are you ill? Come to me, sweet one. I waited and waited for you, but you did not come. I shall wait again tomorrow night, same hour and arrangement. Do come, sweet love, my own dear love. Come, beloved, and clasp me to your heart. Come and we shall be happy.

Moncreiff held the paper up before the jury box. "This letter was found in the pocket of the deceased's jacket."

Moncreiff walked to the prosecution table, turned, and faced the jury.

"Gentlemen of the jury," he said, "this is the sequence of that fatal period:

"One: On Wednesday, March 18th, the prisoner buys her third packet of arsenic.

"Two: On Thursday, March 19th, she writes the deceased arranging a rendezvous with him for that day.

"Three: The letter is forwarded and arrives at Bridge of Allan the next day, Friday, March 20th, causing the deceased consternation as evidenced by his subsequent letter to Miss Perry.

"Four: A second letter is forwarded, arriving in Bridge of Allan at 9 A.M. Sunday, March 22nd. L'Angelier leaves immediately, according to his landlady there, for Glasgow. He arrives in Glasgow, according to Mrs. Jenkins, at 5 P.M. He has been called: *Why, my beloved, did you not come? . . . Come to me, sweet one. . . . Come and we shall be happy.*

"Five: At midnight, March 22nd, that same Sunday, the deceased meets the prisoner in secret rendezvous.

"Six: On Monday, March 23rd, in the early hours of the morning, in great agony, Pierre Emile L'Angelier dies of arsenic poisoning."

Moncreiff turned and put his notes on the table, his back to the jury. The courtroom was hushed.

Moncreiff took a sip of water, then turned back to the jurors, his face grave.

"Now, gentlemen, I have gone through all the case; there has been a great deal of medical evidence led, but I think I have touched upon all the important portions. Evidence was led as to the character of L'Angelier. I think we all understand perfectly well what sort of man he was. But at issue here is: 'Did the defendant murder the man?' *not* 'Did the man deserve to be murdered?'"

The jurors stopped making notes, sat watching Moncreiff.

"And now, gentlemen, having detained you so long, I leave the matter entirely in your hands. I know that the verdict you give will be consistent with your oath, and with your opinion of the case. I have a public duty to discharge. But I would not have done so if my own belief in the justice of the case had not led me to do so. If I had thought that there were any elements of doubt or disproof in the case, not a man in this court, believe me, gentlemen, would have rejoiced more than myself."

Moncreiff's voice was raspy. "I have discharged my duty. I have not in any instance strained the facts. Therefore, gentlemen, as I leave the case in your able hands, I see no outlet for this unfortunate prisoner, and when you come to the unhappy and inescapable conclusion that I have, you will find but one course open to you, and that is to return a verdict of *guilty on all charges.*"

Moncreiff nodded, turned, and walked to his table.

There was a general stirring in the audience. Several people coughed. The jurors stretched discreetly.

At the defence table, Inglis was looking at his watch. It was three. Although he disliked leaving the jurors to sleep on Moncreiff's speech, he hesitated to begin his own. The jurors were tired; it would be better to begin afresh tomorrow.

He rose and walked to the bench, conferred with the justices. After a moment, he walked back to his table.

Lord Hope made the announcement. "As requested by the Dean of Faculty, we will recess the court until ten o'clock tomorrow." He rapped his gavel. "Court dismissed."

TWENTY-ONE

Inglis stayed only a moment Tuesday night. He was on his way to his study to work on his speech, a Bible and a copy of Racine's *Phèdre* in his briefcase.

She was left alone with her memories—and the letters.

In April, three days after they had come to Row, just as she was finishing her macaroni pudding, Janet had come into the room and said sweetly:

"Maddy, the postmistress says she's got a letter returned to you. It's addressed to some Frenchman."

"Well, tell her I—"

Mama interrupted. "Janet, tell Miss Mabel to throw it out. Madeleine doesn't want it."

"Yes, Mama." She went out skipping. Madeleine waited for the barrage. It did not come.

"Mama?"

"Could you please pass the jam, Madeleine?"

She passed it, numbly. She had been prepared to do battle then, to state in no uncertain terms that she planned to marry when she came of age next spring, to argue that it was her right. She had every counterargument prepared. Oh, of course Mama and Papa would be disappointed, expecting her to marry a man with money, but wasn't her happiness more important than fortune? All her friends would forsake her, but she didn't care, as long as Emile loved her, respected her.

She had waited for Mama to accuse her of disobeying, of carrying on a clandestine affair. A fortnight passed and nothing was said. The unused arguments had withered.

She shifted on the hard prison mattress. Why hadn't they insisted? Seen what was happening? Made her see?

She had passed the days then, between rounds of company, reading Hume and Macauley and the latest issue of the *Chambers' Journal*. The article that Emile had recommended on homeopathy was not in this month's issue. Oh, well, she would look again next month.

Papa was sick again and cross as a bear.

"Well, you deserve to be ill, Papa, if you won't take care of yourself. You ride out with your friends even though your throat is raw. . . . You eat the thickest of puddings. . . ."

Papa sent her to her room for being sassy. She lay on her bed, refused to come down for dinner.

Mama came up, sat on the foot of the bed.

"He is sick enough, Maddy, without you making it worse."

"Then why doesn't he go to bed and get better instead of going off all day with company? He just makes himself miserable."

"Your papa believes in being a good host."

"To *his* friends."

"What does that mean?"

"It means . . . Mama, why didn't you tell Papa?"

"He has worries enough. And I thought perhaps you had learned your lesson."

"Mama, I don't want to learn any lesson. I want . . ."

183

"What?"

"I want Papa's consent."

"Oh, Sweet Son and Holy Father!"

"Mother!"

"Go off and be a pauper then, you and your popinjay!"

"Mama!"

Her mother turned to the gilt-wood convex mirror, straightened it on the wall.

"Would you consent?" Madeleine said.

"Never."

"Oh, Mama, but if you were to talk with him, reason with him?"

"Are you deaf, child? Oh, what am I to do with you? I'm at my wits' end."

"You want me to die an old maid?" Madeleine pulled the comforter up from the bottom of the bed, drew it up under her chin.

"Heaven forbid!"

"But it's not fair, Mama."

"Of course it's not. It's merely sensible."

"But my mind is made up."

"I believe you."

"I shall never change it."

"Oh, that's enough, Madeleine, now get busy and pack."

"Pack?"

"Yes, we are going to Edinburgh for a fortnight."

"But Mama."

"Don't 'but Mama' me. If you are going to ruin your life, you may as well enjoy a few more balls before you put on rags."

"You think I am so fickle?"

"I think you are very young—and that it is as easy to love a man of substance as to love a clerk without prospects."

Madeleine threw off the comforter. "Then why did you marry Papa?"

"Hold your tongue or I'll wash your mouth with soap, Madeleine Hamilton.

"Oh, Mama, won't you take my part?"

"That, my dear, is precisely what I am doing." She adjusted a curl in the mirror.

"Then there is no hope from you?"

"Only if you promise to give him up."

"And if I do?"

Mama looked at Madeleine for a long time, then nodded. "Then I shall never tell Papa—and we shall see what we can do to find you a suitable caller."

The fortnight in Edinburgh had been an eternity. She wrote Emile in stolen moments, posting the letters at the pillar box next to the courthouse. He would have to understand about the balls and parties. It was not her doing.

When they came home, she could not wait to run down to the kitchen. Mary and Christine were by the oven, pouring sauce over the ham. She waited till Mary had gone to the sink with the pan, cocked her head at Christine.

"Aye, Miss," Christine whispered, and motioned toward the hall.

Madeleine went out, received a wink and a dimpled smile.

"Well, Christine?"

The girl thrust her sticky hand into her apron pocket and held out a blue envelope sealed with red wax.

Madeleine took it, thanked Christine.

"Will you want to answer?" Christine said.

"Perhaps—I will let you know. You can go back and help Mary now."

"Yes, Miss."

The kitchen door swung shut behind Christine. Madeleine went to her room, opened the letter.

Dearest Madeleine,

    I think only of you. I think of you to the exclusion of my work, my friends, my health. Meanwhile you dance, you flirt. You break my heart.

If I cannot be with you, I must leave. I will be at the Garden Gate on Tuesday, May 6, at 10 P.M. If you are not there, I will no longer deceive myself.

            Emile

 Tuesday, May 6th had dawned clear, and by nine the sun was blazing. By noon it was scorching, laying siege to humans and animals.
 Janet had clung to her today, wanting to play games, crying when she lost at conundrums, making Madeleine play another round. Madeleine let her win that time.
 Now Janet was scared of the dark, and it was Madeleine's charge to soothe her to sleep. The grandfather clock struck nine-thirty. Everyone else was long asleep. Oh, Janet, you wretched child, if you make me late . . .
 She sang Janet a lullaby.
 "Now another one, Maddy."
 "Oh, Janet, be a dear now and sleep. I'll rub your back."
 Janet shut her eyes, sighed as Madeleine rubbed.
 "Now sleep," she said softly.
 "Maddy?"
 "What, Janet?"
 "Maddy, tell me why the man in the moon is?"
 "Is? It's just holes, Janet, holes in the rocks. And mountains. Only they're far away."
 "No, I see him."
 "Yes, but—"
 "There, see, that's his eye—"
 "No, Janet, that's just a dead sea: the Sea of Serenity. And over there, the left eye, it's the Sea of Rains. And his mouth, it isn't really a mouth, but the Sea of Clouds and Nectar. And there, the eyebrows, that's the Bay of Rainbows, the Lake of Dreams."
 "You're making it up."
 "No, it's science. I learned it at school."
 "You're not making it up?"

"Sure as death, Janet, it's a fact."

"Tell me again, the names."

Madeleine recited them softly: "Bay of Rainbows, Lake of Dreams, Sea of Rains, Sea of Serenity, Sea of Clouds and Nectar, Bay of Rainbows, Lake of Dreams . . ."

Janet's eyes closed; she curled up under the thin blanket.

By ten, Janet was snoring softly.

Madeleine edged out of the bed, threw off her wrapper, opened the tambour sliding door beneath the washstand and took out her clothes. She dressed in the dark: Emile's favourite dress, the white self-patterned cotton muslin with the bobbin-lace trimming at the collar and cuffs.

She let herself out the French window, ran quickly over the wet lawn to the path. The stars were out and the moonlight made the night bright. As she stepped lightly over the gravel, she heard the doves cooing in the eaves above.

She turned onto the garden path, went to the gate, thinking that her newly ironed damask shawl smelled like starch. She had taken a bath this afternoon and knew that she was still scented with glycerin and cucumber.

Emile was waiting.

She opened the gate, took him quickly within, kissed him.

"How beautiful you are." His voice was low and knotted. They were by the small man garden now. Choked with vines and weeds, it resembled a worn husk doll. Emile sat on the stone bench. She stood, holding his hands.

The night was starry, moonlit. She smelled the mild scent of his hair mingling with the smell of lilac. She leaned down and kissed the top of his head. He pulled her closer, down onto his knees, kissing her hard, his tongue against her teeth.

She pulled away, went to the end of the garden, stood looking at the night. He came up behind her, put his hands lightly on her shoulders, kissed the nape of her neck.

She moved back against him, letting him hold her, stroke her. He moaned softly.

"What is it, Emile?"

"I'm afraid to touch you."
"Don't be afraid."
"I'm afraid of what I will do."
"I am not afraid." She turned and kissed him then, parting her lips, feeling his surprise and delight as his tongue entered, probed her mouth. Her head felt light and her feet disappeared from under her; she almost fell.

He held her and lowered her gently onto the grass, kissing the hollow of her throat.

"'My spouse, my beloved,'" he said, his hands touching the hard bud of her nipple. He lowered his head and pressed his lips to the cotton. She turned her head so he could kiss the back of her neck, shuddered and shivered as his tongue lingered there.

He was unbuttoning the row of pearl buttons at her breast. She shook her head, her eyes wide.

"Yes," he said.
"No, Emile."
He rolled over, sat up, stared at the sky. She left the buttons undone.
"Emile?"
He was silent.
"I know you think me cold."
"What am I to think?"
"But you said you wouldn't."
"Oh, Mimi, you are driving me crazy."
"I'm sorry."
"It's not your fault."
"Yes, it is."
"All right, yes it is."
"Emile, if you want to . . ."
"How could I not want to?" He sighed, deeply.

She took his hand, guided it to her breast, not to the cloth but to the skin above the buttons. He sighed and stroked the skin, then moved his hand down, against the swell of her breast.

She closed her eyes, felt him unbuttoning the last buttons, felt his fingers on the hard pink nipple.

He touched her ankle, slid his hand up to her knee.
She pushed him away. "Don't, Emile."
He sat up on the grass, stared at her. "Are you a child?"
"No, Emile." She buried her head in her skirts.
No one need know. Could anything so powerful be a sin? Hadn't they pledged their love?
"It is not fair," she said at last.
Emile stared at the stars.
"I want you, too, Emile. Oh, if only there were not children to worry about," she said, her voice trailing off. She looked at him, wishing there were a magic potion one could take and not get with child.
Emile sat up, buried his face in his hands. His voice was muffled. "Mimi, you know I am not a virgin."
She nodded.
"I go to whores, Mimi."
"Because of me?"
"Yes."
"Please don't, Emile. Don't ever again."
He laughed. "Have you heard of a badruche, Mimi?"
She bit her lip, nodded. "A conjugal fraud?" she said, finally, softly.
"God forgive me, but I have one."
"I see." Her eyes blazed. It was her fault that he went to whores. Her fault that his pocket contained . . . That was the sin, not their desire.
She lay back in the grass, sighed.
Off in the woods, an owl began to hoot. She waited till it had stopped, then rolled over till she was touching him.
"Emile?"
"What?" he said roughly.
"Kiss me?"

She yielded ground in inches, her yielding almost a tyranny. His hands moved softly.
He was heavy atop her now, taking her breath away with kisses, crooning her name. His member was huge now in his

breeches, widening against her belly, insistent, and she was yielding, yielding, drawing him with her, arching against him, no longer afraid of his manhood.

He pulled at her bodice, buried his head at her breast. She felt the flowing between her legs.

She moaned.

Then his hand dipped down, past the seventh skirt, and up, across the meridian of her belly, touching her equator.

She was too far gone to see him unbuttoning his pants, slipping on the lambskin sheath. Her hips writhed beneath her and she moaned softly.

Now he was tearing past the wet silk pants, separating the wet lips with his fingers, driving inside, penetrating her.

She cried out as he entered her. Then, from her body a sweet grasslike odor arose and she began to move in his rhythm, naturally, endlessly.

He came, spurting into the condom, then falling back, rolling off her. She subsided, murmuring his name.

"Oh, Mimi, my love, my love," he whispered.

Back in her bed, there was no sleep. She rose at five, wrote:

My own, my beloved husband,

I trust to God you got home safe.

My beloved, if we did wrong last night, it was in the excitement of our love. Oh, if we could have remained, never more to have parted.

I shall consider talking again to Mama. But I don't see any hope from her—I know her mind. You, of course, cannot judge of my parents. You know them not.

I dread next winter. Only, fancy, us both being in the same town and unable to write or see each other. Why, beloved, are we so unfortunate?

I did not bleed last night—but I had a good deal of pain. Tell me, pet, were you angry at me for allowing you to do what you did—was it very bad of me? I shall always remember last night.

Tell me the names of your sisters. They shall be my sisters someday. I shall write dear Mary soon. What would she say if she knew we were so intimate—lose all her good opinions of us both—would she not?

I know you have little confidence in me. I should be only pleasant to Gentlemen, free with none. I shall endeavor to please you in this. Now, will you tell me at the end of the summer if you have heard anything about me flirting. Just you see how good your Mimi shall be.

Kindest love, fond embrace, and kisses

from thy faithful
Wife

She addressed the letter to his office, so he should not have to wait for it, then stole out of the house barefoot, went back to the garden. It was changed this morning, shimmering with dew, hushed and listening. She was changed.

She approached the bench, knelt in the wet grass. To her right the small man garden, its ravaged weed-clotted bed. Where once there had been blue gentians, sweet Williams, now there were wild grasses and weeds. A dandelion bloomed at his chest, a ragged boutonniere.

The grass to one side was pressed down. She knelt there, as if in prayer.

She wrote him again that night.

My own dear darling husband,

Tomorrow by this time I shall be in possession of your dear letter. I shall kiss it and press it to my bosom. I fear we shall spoil each other when we are married—we shall be so happy in our little room, no one to annoy us.

I have no news. Friends are staying with us, which is a great annoyance to me. I am weary of it. I did like this way of living once, but I hate it now—it makes me long for our own quiet home.

She read what she had written, checked the spelling of "bosom." Then she dipped her pen again. Papa had invited Mr. Minnoch to spend the weekend. She had best tell Emile before he heard it elsewhere.

True and constant shall I prove. Don't fear me. I shall be thine. Don't give ear to any reports you may hear. There are several going about regarding my going to get married to Mr. Minnoch. Regard them not. How could I? I *have* a husband.

I am most devotedly thy

Mimi

She reread the letter, and added a postscript:

Heaven bless you, love, with everything you might wish for. Take care of yourself. A fond dear embrace. I am thine, until death do separate us, thy wife,

Mimi

Madeleine turned the letters over on the cotton spread, shook her head, "'And they were both naked, the man and his wife, and were not ashamed,'" she murmured.

Moncreiff had almost exposed it.

"I tender the production No. 25," he had said on Saturday.

"I object," Inglis said. "I contend that this document follows the rules laid down this morning in objection to No. 7.

The document never left the repositories of the deceased. It was found there. It was never signed. There is not one whit of evidence to support its ever having been sent."

"But," Moncreiff said, "this was found in an envelope—bearing the name of the defendant." He smiled.

"All it bore was the word *Mimi*. Can you prove that it left his room?"

"Yes."

"How?"

"It refers to inquiries contained in letter No. 23. For example, in letter No. 23, Miss Smith requests the names of L'Angelier's sisters. This letter answers that request."

"That is no proof," Inglis said.

"No?"

"Is it tendered as an original, or as a copy?"

"We believe it to be a copy, and we tender it as such."

"Then the only difference between this case and the last is that this makes reference to a letter received?"

"Certainly a sufficient difference," Moncreiff said, looking up at Lord Hope.

The judges retired to their chamber to confer. They returned after twenty minutes.

Lord Hope took his seat, spreading his robes behind him. "Although there is undoubtedly a difference as to the circumstances in which this letter or scroll is tendered, a majority of the court is of the opinion that the document cannot be received." He looked over at Lord Ivory. "Lord Ivory thinks that the writing is receivable in evidence. But both Lord Handyside and I think that it cannot be received."

And so document 25 had not been admitted. But of course, there were rumors of its contents. More and more, L'Angelier's name was linked with the one word: *cad*.

The letter had been written in a heavy hand:

My dearest Mimi,

Why, why did you give way after all your promises? You

had no resolution. I am not angry at your allowing me, Mimi, but I am sad.

We should indeed have waited. Nothing except our marriage will efface it from my memory.

Mimi, dearest, you must take a bold step to be my wife. Speak to your mother again. It is your parents' fault if shame should result.

My dear Wife, I could not take you to Lima. No European woman could live there. Besides, I would live one or two thousand miles from it, far from any white people and no Drs. if you were ill or getting a baby. No, if we marry, I must stay in Glasgow until I get enough to live elsewhere.

I do not understand, my pet, your not bleeding, for every woman losing her virginity must bleed. You must have done so some other time. Try to remember if you never hurt yourself washing, etc. I am sorry you felt pain. I hope, pet, you are better. I trust, dearest, you will not be *enceinte*. Be sure and tell me immediately when you are "ill" next time, and if at your regular period.

My sisters' names are Anastasie and Elmire.

I cannot help doubting your word about flirting. You promised me the same thing before you left for Edinburgh and you did nothing else during your stay there. You cared more for your friends than for me. I do trust you will give me no cause to find fault with you again on that score, but I doubt very much the sincerity of your promise. Mimi, the least thing I hear of you doing, that day shall be the last of our tie, that I swear. You are my wife, and I have the right to expect from you the behaviour of a married woman—or else you have no honour in you; and more, you have no right to go anywhere but where a woman could go with her husband.

Burn this letter. I cannot bear the thought of the consequences if your action were known.

Your loving
Emile

TWENTY-TWO

Wednesday morning Inglis waited till the clock had finished striking; then he walked to the patch of scuffed tile before the jury box.

He brought himself up to his full height. His voice, though of only moderate compass, was clear as glass.

"Gentlemen of the jury, the charge against the prisoner is murder, and the punishment of murder is death; and that simple statement is sufficient to suggest to us the awful solemnity of the occasion that brings you and me face to face." He looked quietly at each of the fifteen jurors.

"You are invited and encouraged by the prosecutor to snap the thread of this life, and to consign to ignominious death on the scaffold one who, a few short months ago, was known only as a gentle and confiding and affectionate girl, the pride of her happy home."

Three of the jurors glanced over at Miss Smith, their expressions undeterminable.

"Gentlemen, I am going to ask you, to beg, to *demand* that quality to which every prisoner is entitled, whether she be the lowest and vilest of her sex or the maiden"—here he himself turned to Madeleine, let his gaze linger a moment on her as he finished his sentence—"whose purity is as the unsunned snow."

In the back row, a single spectator tittered.

Inglis turned back to the fifteen, raised his voice by one degree. "I ask you for justice, and if heaven grant me the patience and strength, I shall tear to tatters that web of sophistry in which the prosecutor has striven to catch this poor girl and her sad, strange story."

Inglis kept a sharp eye upon the jury, using his hands, his body, to command their attention, raising his voice when the edge seemed to drop from their attention.

"Somewhat more than two years ago, accident brought her acquainted with the deceased L'Angelier; and yet I can hardly call it accident, for it was due unfortunately in a great measure to the indiscretion of a young man you saw before you the other day. He introduced her to L'Angelier on the open street because, as shown, L'Angelier could not procure an introduction otherwise. And what was he who thus intruded himself upon this young lady? An unknown adventurer, of whom we know only that he is a native of Jersey."

Of course, Jersey was English; but in Inglis' mouth, the word seemed decidedly foreign.

"In considering the man whose history emerges from this inquiry, we are bound to form an estimate of his character, and of the principles and motives that influenced his conduct. We find him, according to all those who then observed him, most narrowly vain, conceited, pretentious, with a great opinion of his own personal attractions, and a silly expectation of admiration from the other sex.

"We have heard of one disappointment that he experienced in England with a lady from the Kingdom of Fife. The manner in which he bore his disappointment reveals the true character of the man. Depressed and melancholy beyond description, he threatened to commit suicide. He was not a person of strong health, and this, among other things, had an important effect in depressing his spirits, rendering him changeable and uncertain—now elated, now depressed—a temperament most mercurial."

Inglis' voice deepened as he spoke, taking on more resonance, the words rolling smoothly.

"Such was the person with whom the prisoner became acquainted. The progress of the acquaintance is soon told—my learned friend the Lord Advocate said to you that the correspondence must have been from the outset an improper correspondence, because it was clandestine, yet we find that the letters of the young lady at that first period of their connection breathed nothing but gentleness and propriety. The early correspondence shows that if L'Angelier had it in his mind to corrupt and seduce this poor girl, he entered that attempt with considerable ingenuity and skill."

Inglis looked over at Madeleine. She was dressed in pale blue today.

"But alas, the next scene is the most painful of all. The correspondence that begins in the spring of 1855 results by the spring of 1856 in the victory of L'Angelier: His victim is seduced. How vile his art and how great his skill are shown, most pathetically, by the altered tone and language of the unhappy prisoner's letters. She had lost not merely her virtue, but, as the Lord Advocate said, her sense of personal decency."

Inglis had been watching the jurors the past week, trying to pick the most likely choice for foreman. He had narrowed it down to three: the teacher, the writer, and the elderly farmer. He concentrated his gaze on these three, using their reactions to guide his pace.

"Gentlemen, whose fault was that? Think you that without temptation, without evil teaching, a poor girl falls into such degradation? No! Only the influence of a corrupt, calculating, and determined man can account for such a fall.

"And yet," he said, his voice growing soft, "through the whole of this frightful correspondence, she conveys a spirit of devoted affection towards the man who had destroyed her—a spirit that strikes me as most touching."

Inglis stopped here, cleared his throat, poured a tumbler of water, sipped it.

Then he straightened, walked to the jury box.

For the next two hours, Inglis traced the relationship from the spring of 1856 to the end of that year.

"But now we come to an important stage of the case. On

the 28th of January, Mr. Minnoch proposes. Now, if I understand the theory of my learned friend's case, on that day the whole character of this girl's mind and feelings changes, and she sets herself to prepare for the perpetration of what my friend has called the most foul, cool, deliberate murder ever committed. Gentlemen, if his assumption did not imperil a human life, it would be an absurdity worth our laughter."

The jury was attentive; he plunged on.

"All past experience teaches us that perfection, even in depravity, is not rapidly attained, and that it is not by such short and easy stages as the prosecutor presumes to trace that a gentle, loving girl acquires the savage grandeur of a Medea, or the appalling wickedness of a Borgia."

Some jurors, he hoped, would be familiar with, if not classics, at least history.

"What had she to gain from L'Angelier's death? Revenge? She loved him. Security? His death would expose, not conceal, their secret affair. No, L'Angelier's death by arsenic was the death of an unstable, self-centered, corrupt man who numbered among his vices the eating of arsenic. Is it strange that an eater of arsenic should die from eating arsenic? Less than strange, it follows so naturally as to be almost inevitable."

Inglis had begun to pace. With each turn, he swept his gaze from juror to juror, seeking their eyes.

"Such is the state of the evidence. The case for the Crown is a failure; the one fact indispensable to bring guilt home to the prisoner—I mean the act of administering—remains not only unproven but unreasonable."

Inglis stopped, took another sip of water, then looked over at Moncreiff, smiled. Moncreiff's face was glum.

"The Lord Advocate has suggested that it is necessary for the defence to explain how the deceased came by his death. The Lord Advocate, by that suggestion, abdicates the public duty to which he so proudly and often refers. The State cannot pluck a person from the crowd and say to that person, 'If you do not find the murderer, I will execute you for the murder.' I am shocked by the Lord Advocate's concept of what we free-born Scots depend upon: the protection of the Law.

"His Lordship the Chief Justice will tell you that a defender in this court has no further duty than to demonstrate that the case of the prosecutor is not proved. I believe that no man will or can ever tell how L'Angelier met his death."

Inglis saw a flicker of a smile cross Mr. King's face. The writer. No man, certainly.

"But whether he met his death by suicide, or whether he met his death by accident, or in what way soever he met his death, the question for you is: Is this death proved to be murder? The case the Lord Advocate presents shocks the intelligence. Did Miss Smith murder Mr. L'Angelier? Gentlemen, the question cannot even exist until a prior question is posed. And answered. Was Mr. L'Angelier's death a murder? There is not sufficient evidence to answer even that essential preliminary question. I marvel that my learned colleague convened so many to present so little. If the fact of the crime is in doubt, how can the existence of the criminal be presumed? We cannot permit a question based on an assumption yet to be proved."

Inglis clasped his hands in front of him. "I pray you to remember that you are asked to affirm as a *fact* that the arsenic that was found in this man's stomach was presented to him by the hands of the defendant."

The sun was thin in the courtroom. Inglis paused. The jurymen were tiring, beginning to shift in their chairs.

"My learned friend said that, great as was the courage the prisoner displayed when charged, such a demeanor was not inconsistent with her guilt. He said that a woman who had the nerve to commit murder would have the nerve to meet the accusation calmly. I doubt that very much."

Inglis wiped his brow.

"Gentlemen, I know of no case in which such undaunted courage has been displayed, from first to last, by a young girl, where that girl was guilty. But gentlemen, our experience does furnish us with examples of as brave a bearing in a young girl when innocent. It is the courage of the guiltless. It is faith in justice. If not man's, God's. Do you know the terrible story of Eliza Fenning?"

He stopped before the box, stared at the blank faces.

"She was a servant girl in the city of London and she was tried on the charge of poisoning her master and family by putting arsenic in the dumplings. When the charge was made, she met it with a calm but indignant denial; she maintained the same demeanor throughout the trial, and when she received the death sentence, she did not flinch. When brought to the scaffold, she seemed serene as an angel. She was hanged."

Inglis paused.

"But time brought the truth to light. The perpetrator of the murder confessed it on his deathbed—years too late. The only guilt in her case belonged to those who condemned her."

Inglis sighed audibly, nodded wearily.

"Gentlemen, you are brought here for the performance of this great duty, not because you have any particular skill in the sifting or weighing of evidence—not because you are a class set apart for the work; you are here because, as the law expresses it, you are *indifferent* men—that is, not because you are unlike other men but because you are like; not merely in that you have clear heads, but in that you have also warm and tender hearts. To rely, therefore, upon your reason only, though reason in this case is enough to reject the assertions of the Public Prosecutor, is impiously to refuse the noblest gifts that God has implanted in your breasts.

"Bring with you, then, to this service not only your clear heads, but your warm hearts—your fine moral instincts, and your guiding consciences—for thus, and only thus, will you satisfy the oath that you have taken. To determine guilt or innocence by intellect alone is the prerogative of infallibility; when man's arrogance tempts him to usurp the attribute of God, man only exposes the frailty of his own nature."

Inglis' voice was still strong when he finished. Outside the high arched windows, the July sun hung red and wobbly on the horizon. The faces of the jury were bathed in the soft light.

"Gentlemen, I cannot explain it to myself. Never have I felt so unwilling to part with a jury—never have I felt as if I must say more. I am deeply conscious of a personal interest in your verdict, for if there should be any failure of justice, this day and this prisoner would haunt me to the end of my life as a dismal and blighting spectre.

"For your verdict to be honest and just and true, it must satisfy the scruples of the severest judgment, yet leave undisturbed and unvexed the tenderest conscience among you."

Inglis stood still, his hand on the jury-box railing. There was a silence. In the last rays of sun, dust motes floated through the courtroom.

Lord Hope rose, recessed the court till the next morning.

TWENTY-THREE

Inglis had been in a hurry tonight. Madeleine went to bed depressed. It was, after all, for him just a profession. He would be defending another next month. She would pass out of his life.

They had avoided talking of court tonight. But his speech still rang in her mind. Of course, she had known what would have to be said—still, the words had been harsh.

She took out the loosely wrapped packet of copied letters, reread the draft of Emile's letter. He had changed parts, left out small parts, but the bulk of it was as it had been sent:

> Burn this letter. I cannot bear the thought of the consequences if your actions were known.

She had wept for hours after reading the letter, seared with shame. And then the anger had taken over and she had done what he asked, burned the letter.

And penned a brittle cool reply.
No salutation, no signature.

"When a man hath taken a wife, and married her, and it come to pass that she find no favour in his eyes, because he hath found some uncleanness in her: then let him write her a bill of divorcement, and give it in her hand, and send her out of his house. And when she is departed out of his house, she may go and be another man's wife."

Emile had answered in the next post: She had watched that letter burn line by line.

My dearest Mimi,

What am I that you should use the Holy Scriptures to wound me? Find no favour in my eyes? Find uncleanness in you? How could these strictures apply to us?

I love you. You are the temple of holiness to me. If I have led you to believe I could think otherwise, forgive me. Anything I ever said, however stupid, was impelled by my love for you, my need for you.

Do not give me what I deserve. Give me your forgiveness.

I love you,
Emile

Postscriptum: My darling, our agony springs from your being not in my house, but in your father's. I swear to you, beloved, that from my house you will never *wish* to depart.

Two days later, this letter was sent to Mr. P. Emile L'Angelier, Bothwell Street:

My own, my dearest, my kindest husband,

How I have reproached myself all week for writing you such unkind letters.

Whatever your lot may be, I shall be thine, and however humble your home, it shall be mine. No wealth shall ever cause me to forget that I am the wife of my own, my darling Emile. I swear to you that no man shall ever *love* me but you. Emile, if you were here, I would love you with my heart and soul.

Now, my pet, you are wrong in thinking I am not preparing. I shall leave all, sacrifice friends, relations, family, and everything for your sake, for the love I have for you.

I have not been riding. No one knows why, not even Bessie, but I shall tell you. The Wilsons and Mr. Ferguson asked to ride with me. I knew you would not like this, and it would cause people to make remarks. I don't think I shall ride this summer.

I shall read useful books—I shall not read Byron anymore. I shall do all I can to improve myself and I shall not spend my time idly.

Tell me, darling, how are you? Do you sleep better? I must say good night. With very fond love, I am thy true, thy loving, thy devoted, and repentant wife.

I am thine forever
Mimi L'———

Emile lay atop the picnic table at Row, watching the clouds. Madeleine was in the apple tree, fanning herself with her painted fan, her ankles dangling. Celibate, they were finding a new source of pleasure: conversation.

"Tell me more, Emile, what happened then?"

"Well, the mob began to charge and the French police began to shoot. A man next to me dropped. . . . I . . ." Emile paled, clutched his stomach.

"Your stomach again?"

"Yes . . . ohhhh." He ran behind the bushes, was gone a long time. He came back and lay down again on the table, his face white.

"Is it bad?"

"Not as bad as last month." He sat up, took a vial from his pocket, dropped several drops into his mouth, made a face.

"How does it taste?"

"Terrible. I usually take it with water."

"Tell me again how it works."

"Well . . ." He thought a moment. "It is like the tap of a fan, for instance. It is a blow, just as the stroke of a club is a blow, but the one gives an agreeable sensation, while the other fells the recipient to the ground. That is homeopathy in a nutshell."

"Papa took Fowler's Solution once, but the doctor prescribed it. For anemia, I believe."

Emile nodded, turned over on his stomach. "If he took it regularly, he would probably never have the problem."

"But it's poison, isn't it?"

"What have I been explaining?" He sat back up on the table. "The tap of a fan—that's all. It's a mithridate."

"A what?"

"Haven't you ever heard of Mithridates?"

"Who?"

"Mithridates the Great, the Black Sea king."

"Never."

"He ate poison to avoid being poisoned—kind of a universal antidote."

Madeleine closed the fan, climbed down from the apple tree, sat on the bench in front of the open magazine, read: "

> Arsenic increases tissue change throughout the body and thus improves nutrition. One grain will protect nearly seven thousand times its weight of tissue from degenerative or putrefactive changes.

She closed the magazine. "The article does make it sound quite beneficial—all flushed cheeks and healthiness."

"I think Hahnemann said it well: 'Small doses kindle;

moderate doses ignite; massive doses kill.' It's really very scientific."

"Still, I'd feel better if a doctor had prescribed the solution."

"There you go with your doctors again. The tonic might be just the thing you need. . . ." He leaned over, poked a finger against her ribs. "It would help you put on weight."

"Am I so skinny?"

"No, but you could stand a little more flesh. And what about your stomach? Does that trouble you much? Laudanum is good for that."

"My stomach never bothers me."

"What does bother you?"

"My heart."

"Be serious."

"Well, when I am 'ill' I sometimes have cramps."

"Hmm. And you are a trifle pale. Though I think that is just from the parasol."

She giggled. "I hate the silly thing."

"You hate it? I've never seen any woman twirl a parasol with more delight."

"Do I?"

"You know you do."

"Well, I don't know. Perhaps I should take the solution. But I shouldn't like the taste."

"It's not too bad in water."

"I hate medicine. When I had the nirls . . ."

"The nirls? My God, what's that?"

"You know . . . the spots . . . what do you call them . . . measles."

"And you an eddicated lady!"

"Well, that's what they're called."

"Yes, I know. The nirls, and the blabs, and the kinkhost, and the branks."

"Well, if you knew, why did you ask?"

"Personally, I'm fond of branks. It sounds so mumpish."

"Now you're being crude."

"No, I'm being very discreet. You want to go through life sounding like Glasgow?"

"And how does Glasgow sound?"

"Like a gob of treacle dropped on a rainy sidewalk, followed by a thud of books dropped atop the mess."

"I don't find you at all enterteening."

"I, on the contrary, find you most amusing."

"You think I am stupid."

"I think you are your father's child."

She turned her back, watched a cast of hawks swoop through the clouds.

"Mimi?"

"Hmmmmph." She opened her fan, moved it back and forth before her face.

"I think you shall be my tonic, Mimi. You are what ails me. And only you can cure me."

She turned round. He was lying on the table, his hands cradling his head. The fan stilled in her hand. She leaned over, kissed him with the mildest of lips.

"Ah, Mimi, read to me some more," he said.

She snapped the painted fan closed, drew the magazine nearer to her:

> If any of your readers, concludes Dr. Inman, still feels disposed to try the effects of arsenic, let me give them the following cautions: to use only a preparation whose real strength they know, such as Fowler's Solution. It is well to remember the Styrian rule, and invariably suspend use of the solution every alternate fortnight. The dose cannot be increased indefinitely or with impunity. When once the full dose is ascertained, it is better to begin with that, and go on diminishing it to the end of the fortnight, than to begin with a small dose, and go on increasing it daily . . .

Madeleine looked up from the magazine, made a face. "How can you ascertain the full dose which can be borne, if you're supposed to *start* with the full dose? Guess? If you guessed wrong, you'd be dead! That's silly." She picked up her fan, closed the book.

Emile looked up at her, spit out the blade of grass he had been chewing. "The Fowler's Solution bottle has the maximum dose on it, my love. Don't flare so."

Madeleine smiled, tapped him with her fan.

"Don't be coy," he said.

She smiled, rested the fan against her chin.

He reached out, touched her hair. She bowed her head till her cheek touched the wide wale of his cord breeches.

Strange, strange, she thought, bringing her hand up beneath her hot cheek. That his smooth skin lay just beneath.

When he had gone, she wandered around the farm, tending the chickens, petting her new donkey. She was, for the moment, happy. She even read to Papa for an hour that night without being asked.

And the next day, as she set the table for breakfast, she slipped a few drops of Papa's old Fowler's into her water glass, drank it down in the kitchen. It took her appetite away and gave her insomnia that night. She felt anxious the next day, and she took a smaller dose. That night, she stood in front of the mirror a long time. She did look rosier.

The next day she went walking over the hill to Loch Lomond with Papa and Jack. Emile had been right: Her wind was much improved. They walked the seven miles as if they were two, arriving at the Queen of Lakes without a rest. Oh, it was so beautiful, the water a sheet of glass, more a picture than a reality.

The summer dragged on. It was fearful never to see her husband. But, of course, there was always the constant whirl of guests, parties, teas, and dinners.

She was reading the life of Sydney Smith now and almost enjoying it. Emile would be quite proud of her.

Papa had given her a small Skye terrier with silken hair. And the coachman had given her an English terrier named Albion. She took them both with her on walks. Both dogs took great delight in killing rats, and she was happy to provide them the opportunity.

Twice a week, she wrote Emile; and twice a week, Christine arrived at her door with a letter from him.

June 3, 1856

Beloved, dearly beloved husband,

I was "ill" the beginning of this week, so if I should have the happiness to see you next Tuesday night I shall be better.

I feel better this week—I cannot eat. I have not taken any breakfast for about a fortnight—not even a cup of tea. I don't sleep much. I wonder that my looks are not changed, but I look as well as if I ate and slept well. I don't think I am any stouter, but you can judge when you next see me.

Would to God you were here. I think I would be wishing you to *love* me—and I don't suppose you would refuse me. For I know you *will* like to *love* your Mimi. I am thine own true

Mimi L'Angelier

July 15, 1856

Dearest and Beloved Emile,

We are to have friends on Friday. Minnoch was here today. *Only* left on Saturday and back again today. He was here for four hours. I think he might have a little better feeling than to come so soon knowing that everyone down here has heard the report regarding myself and him. P. and M. were very much displeased at him—they said nothing, but M. said it was enough to make people think there was something in the report.

My love burns for you. Oh, to be with you this night.

But I fear I would ask you to *love* me, and that would not do. It is hard to restrain one's passions.

I must close now as they will be in soon. Your wife,

Mimi

July 21, 1856

My own beloved Emile,

Your likeness is such a comfort to me. I never saw such a good likeness, I love it. I shall try and get mine for you soon. Tell me, beloved, if there is anything I can do to please you. B. told me she saw you. And on Sunday one of the ladies in Mama's carriage saw you and fancied she fell in love with your appearance. I feel quite proud of having such a nice-looking husband, but it is not only your appearance that makes me feel proud—but your superior mind, and ways of thinking different from other men. I look upon "fast" young men now with horror.

I feel ill, really ill, today with cold. I got my feet wet crossing a stream and had to drive for 15 miles without getting them dried. I was very glad I was not "ill" or I might have been very unwell—but that won't be for another few days.

I shall expect a letter from you soon. May God bless you is my earnest prayer. Your devoted

Mimi

July 30, 1856

Dearest,

I do love you for telling me all you think of me. Emile, I am sorry you are ill. For the love of Heaven, take care of yourself.

I shall not see you till the nights are a little darker. Now, Emile, I shall keep all my promises. I shall do all you want me to. Trust me, keep yourself easy. I know what awaits me if I do what you disapprove of. Off you go. That shall always be in my mind—go, never to return. The day that occurs I hope I may die.

Emile, our *loving* was not criminal! Darling, never repeat that again to me.

Minnoch left this morning. He said nothing out of place, but I was not a moment by myself with him. I did not wish to be alone with him.

We have an old gentleman of 86 years in the house, and he is trying, as he says, to make love to me. Poor old man, he has taken a lot of your kisses from me. But you would not mind if you saw the poor old man. His name is Mr. Bald.

May God grant you better health. I am thy wife, thy own,

Mimi L'Angelier

August 14, 1856

Beloved and ever dear Emile,

Your visit of last night is over. You did look cross at first, but thank Heaven you looked yourself ere you left—your old smile.

I spoke in jest of your going last night. Would you leave me to end my days in misery? For I can never be the wife of another. Emile, you were not pleased with me because I would not let you *love* me last night. But on your last visit, *you* said you would not do it until we are married. What am I to do? You hate me if I do not enter into full embrace, and you despise me if I do. Last night, I said to myself, well, I shall not let Emile do this. It was a punishment to myself to be deprived of your *loving* me, for it is a pleasure, no one can deny that. It is but human nature. Is not everyone who *loves* of the same mind? Yes, I did feel so ashamed after you left of having allowed you to see my (any name you please to insert) but as you said at the time, I am your wife.

Forgive me—and be what we once were. I shall not wear Crinoline as you don't like it. It is off today. No one heard you last night.

Do, beloved, stay near me, my only love. You, and you only, are the only being I love on this earth. You could not live in a far country, you would die. Stay with me.

Someday we may love without fear or trick—we shall then be happy.

I must stop now as my candle is going out. Adieu, sweet husband,

I am thy
Mimi

September came, the autumnal equinox. Summer became winter, winter summer. No matter what she wore, in an hour the choice was wrong.

September 29, 1856

My Dear Emile,

I don't think I can see you this week. But I think next Monday night, as P. and M. are to be in Edinburgh, but my only thought is Janet—what shall I do with her? I shall have to wait till she is asleep. But you may be sure I shall do it as soon as I can. As a favour, do not refer to what is past. I shall be kind and good, my husband.

What cold weather we have had. Mr. Minnoch has been here since Friday—and P. being so fond of him, I am sure he shall ask him in often. I hope to hear from you soon. I can write no more at present, so with very kind love and kisses, believe me, ever yours,

Mimi

She had spent the rest of the day reading, except when William Minnoch came and claimed her for a walk. But it was too cold; they had come back after only half an hour.

And that night, the wind howled on and on. There were two things she disliked most in the world: the noise of wind and that of water. But Emile might like those very things. Didn't she love melon and he hate it? How many other things did she not know about him? He had said he was once frightened of a noise he heard—a sound of rats running behind him. Well, he and she would have years and years to find out all.

She took a scrap of paper, wrote down a chant she had learned as a child to rid oneself of rats.

> Ratton and moose
> Awa' frae the hoose
> Awa' ower tae the mill
> An' there tak yer fill.

She had spent the rest of the next day with her books. She had finished the life of Leonardo da Vinci and now she began the life of Andrea del Sarto. It made her quite melancholy. Del Sarto's life had been constant unhappiness. He died deserted by all, even by his wife, the one who above all should have stayed by him.

The cottons of summer began to give place to fabrics more substantial. *Godey's Lady's Book* wrote that the Byzantine style formed the appropriate link between the seasons. Madeleine ordered a new outfit. It was daring—Emile wouldn't approve. She had it made up in Napoleon-blue gros d'Ottoman, with black velvet bands, and appliqued Oriental figures. She wrapped her tasseled cloak around her, swirled. It would be warm at the concert, and the lowcut gown would be perfect. She would arrive à la Chinoise, by William's side.

She wrapped the cloak tighter. It was so cold and Emile's letters were depressing again. Couldn't he understand that she was unhappy too? That she missed him as much as he missed her? Couldn't he understand about William? A grey thought crossed her mind. She would have to tell him soon about the house. William had sold Papa a house he had designed and built on Blythswood Square. He had given Papa a most reasonable price. Of course, it was only business—still, Emile would wonder.

She would do it when she saw him. For now, she wrote a short note; she didn't want to be late for the concert.

> Fie, fie, dear Emile, you must no more say that you mar my amusements and that you are a bore to me. I do what I must do, to be and seem dutiful and to prepare my parents to accept you. . . .

The letters were all they seemed to have left now. They blended, one into another, as the nights grew shorter and colder.

October 31, 1857.

Madeleine sat at her writing desk. They were all out riding but she. Mama had given her a strange look when she left, but had said nothing.

The twelve lines of diary lay before her. But what to write? The day was cold—I did *not* go out. But should she tell the cause? That *Emile forbids me*. There are men present. A woman cannot—a married woman cannot—go out with other men. They might flirt with her. And poor little pet of a child, she might flirt back. So what if she did? What harm in it was there?

She took out a sheet of writing paper, dipped her quill in the open well, wrote a line: "Emile, you are not reasonable."

His letter yesterday had been strange. As if he did not love her or trust her at all. As if, because she had *loved* him, she was an immoral woman.

If they could be together, all would be right. But she was not with him. She was in her father's house. Any minute now, Christine would ring the gong and she would know it was time to put away her cache, to contemplate, as she had done a thousand times, whether or not she was a fool not to burn the stack.

But she couldn't. If she lost him, she would have the letters. She tore up her first page, took a clean sheet of paper.

My very dear Emile,

This has been a long wet nasty day. I hope you are quite well. I have been so stupid today, it would only have been you that could have made me feel alive.

I think we shall leave for town in about three weeks. James is liking school very much—only poor boy, he complains of not getting enough sugar or butter, fancy, he pays £80 for his board alone—it is far too much for a little boy.

I am to have a pony next summer. I told a horse jockey man to look out for one. I think P. means to drive a pair next summer. Anything for more expense. Sweet love, I have thought more of you for this last fortnight than ever I did—Emile is the only name ever on my lips.

Did you go to the concert? I went with Jack and B. and looked at everyone but could not see my husband. Mr. M. was there with his horrid old sister—I only bowed to them. I shall send you my likeness sometime soon. I am sure you won't like it. I am looking as cross as I did *that* night.

I have a new bonnet. It is fawn. B. has a pink one, and M. wanted me to have pink, but I knew you would think pink vulgar. Dear love, when I am your wife, I shall require you to tell me what I am to wear, as I have no idea of dress myself. Emile, my love, if you were here now, I am sure I would allow you to *love* me. . . . I could not resist, my love. I have been ordered by the Dr. to take a fearful thing called Piece Meal to help me put on weight—such a nasty thing. I would rather take cocoa.

Your Loving and Affect. Wife,
Mimi L'Angelier

She had scrawled the letter quickly, with large strokes. Now she folded it, put it in the envelope, sealed it with brown wax.

She knew it would wound him and she wanted to.

Eighty pounds for board alone—well, it was almost true . . . it was the fee for *two* years; for Emile, whose pay was ten shillings a week, the figure would be in the stars.

And the pony—the plans for next summer. Papa had promised her one if she would go riding. Not a pony, actually, but an Irish jumper bred for six-foot fences.

Even the bonnet. She had got a new one. But of course, Emile had forbidden her to promenade such items, so no one would see it.

She had been perfectly wifely, she thought . . . even down to the "I could not resist, my love. I have been ordered by the Dr. to take a fearful thing called Piece Meal to help me put on weight—such a nasty thing."

A truthful letter, on the whole. Only a few small insignificant things. She walked to the kitchen, gave the letter to Christine.

A smile spread over her face as she prepared the cocoa. She unwrapped the Cadbury's folder on the mantle, scooped two tablespoons of the cocoa powder into the pot, carried the pot back to the kitchen.

She added the sugar and the milk, took the wooden spoon, beat at the soggy lumps that crumbled to dry powder, beat at the dry powder, mixed the liquid.

She poured the steaming liquid into the orange and flowered Spode cup, set the fiddle-pattern spoon on the saucer, carried the cocoa back to her room, locked the door. From the toe of the shoe at the bottom of the closet, she took out another packet, opened it. There was a blue-flecked white powder within. She set the open paper on the tray, picked up with the spoon a white crystal the size of a lentil. She held it gingerly, dropped it into the cup, stirred.

She sipped the liquid, waiting for an effect that would be hours coming if the powder was like the Fowler's.

Really, it had been a most truthful letter. Only small, insignificant lies.

When she had drunk down the cup, she walked to the hat

stand, took down her cloak and bonnet, unlocked the door, went up the hall and up the stairs, into the grand hall. The three chandeliers hung at spaced intervals down the fifty feet, gleaming softly in the lacquered floor. She passed by the giant black, gold-scrolled doors that led to her father's study.

She stood in front of the hall mirror, fastened the amber buttons of her tangerine cloak. She would go to the bookstore. That was not yet forbidden by Emile. She smiled at herself, cocked her head. Her hair fell across her face. She reached up, undid the pins, fastened her hair back up again. Then, untying the tangerine bow, she placed the pink bonnet on her head, pinned it in place.

TWENTY-FOUR

Madeleine woke before the bugler Thursday morning. She lay on her cot, waiting. It might happen today.

When reveille sounded, she sat up, brushed her hair a hundred strokes. In court yesterday, the artist had sketched her likeness. She wondered if it would appear in the papers. She had worn the same cameo that she had worn in the daguerreotype that she had given Emile. She wondered, when it was done, what would become of the exhibits. Would they give her back Emile's likeness? Would they give her back her own?

She smiled.

At seven, she got up and dressed, then lay back on her cot. There was still an hour before breakfast.

She had sat quietly in the photographer's mahogany balloon-back chair, waiting for the sun. She had passed the time reading a copy of *Godey's*, or rather, reading the advertisements. With their striking woodcuts, they were much more interesting than the articles.

Logan's Lotion: A long-haired Grecian blonde beauty

draped in clinging gossamer, one arm propped languorously behind her head, a bare-breasted black Nubian fanning her with feathers. In the clouds above, four cherubim, two black and two white, held the amphora of precious ointment over her body, while in fine script: "It keeps the hands in beautiful condition—as soft as velvet."

She skipped several pages, came upon a full-page advertisement for Pear's. A black child was sitting in a tub of soap and water, scrubbing off his blackness with Pear's soap. Already, his arms and torso shone white as the result of his ministrations.

Yes, she would purchase it. A pity all the dusky-skinned people couldn't. It wasn't fair, of course, but she would buy it anyhow, as she didn't see how she could help the poor dark creatures by *not*, just as she could never understand when it was an issue of mutton left on her plate and the children starving in Calcutta.

She passed over the advertisements for cutaneous visitations, chillicoat, headaches, insomnia, and ringing noises in the head. Thank God her constitution was formidable.

The advertisement for Cadbury's flesh enhancer was quite scientific. She approved almost before she had read the copy. She trusted the doctor in the picture, his spectacles resting upon the bridge of his nose, his fingers, beringed, making a steeple at the bob of his Adam's apple. The woman beside him sat straight in her curved-back chair, looking admiringly at the box of chocolate in front of the microscope.

And then the list of flesh-forming ingredients:

34¼	Cadbury's cocoa essence
11	Best French chocolates
13	Best homeopathic cocoa
23	Cocoa nibs
35	Dried milk

And the good doctor saying: "Of absolute purity and freedom from alkali, Cadbury's Cocoa may be prescribed without hesitation with the certainty of obtaining uniform and gratifying results." And there was the royal seal of approval itself.

The sun came out and Mr. Pinkins motioned her to a

chair by the skylight. She would have to sit posed for two minutes while the daguerreotype plates took. She could have had a photograph and been done in a minute. But she wanted this one-of-a-kind likeness.

She had focused on the small table to her side. It was rosewood with an inlaid top and a turned underframe. On the mother-of-pearl surface was centered a lace doily, and on the doily was a Staffordshire figure of Rabbie Burns in yellow stockings. Aunt Tabitha had the companion piece of Sir Walter on her mantelpiece.

Burns was resting against a post, reading a book. Quite the dandy in his blue coat and plaid, his pink breeches.

Madeleine blinked and unfocused, wished she could rub her eyes. Not that the sunlight was intense. There wasn't even a glare, the blue skylight acting as a shield. She wondered what Mr. Pinkins did on rainy days, what he was thinking under the black hood, whether he was watching her. A coolness crawled up her spine; it was a bit like seduction, this process. He there in shadow; she giving herself up to him.

Madeleine was sure it must have been five minutes. She felt a statue now; her painted fan and small bottines belonged to porcelain hands and feet.

"I count only the sunny hours, I count only the sunny hours," she echoed in her mind, the words coming from the sundial at Row.

Oh, pshaw, Madeleine, you do go on, don't you? Could it have been two minutes yet? Or had a cloud passed over the sun? She dare not look at anything but this bonny china man.

She recalled the camera obscura Papa had given her on her tenth birthday and the color pictures she had captured, creations of the moment, destined to fade away. *Points de Vue*, Papa had called them. Mama had called them heliographs, drawings from the sun. Madeleine had called them fairy pictures. They belonged to the bottomless well of childhood, those caught images. She was surprised to find them recurring to her.

Another thought came to her from the well. When she

was three, Papa had taken her on a train to London while Bessie was recuperating from the yellow fever and they had gone to Mr. Daguerre's "Original Diorama." It was just paint and canvas, but now it came back to her as the only real thing out of her childhood. Daguerre hadn't been famous then, he hadn't yet created the first picture of a human being, hadn't been endowed by the French government for life. He was a poor struggling artist, trying to make a sou. He had the idea that light affects matter, but hadn't yet discovered the matter that light could affect quickly enough. He could project images onto matter, but the matter didn't remember, didn't trap the picture.

The Diorama was 350 feet long and 50 feet high. From outside, atop her father's shoulders, it looked like a circus tent. The name of the show, *The Beginning of the Deluge*, was painted in large red letters above the entrance.

Once she entered, all resemblance to a circus ceased. All around, water was rolling towards her. Water to the right of her, water to the left, waves forming and rolling and houses and cattle and trees being picked up, coming and hurtling towards her. The spray spit angrily and the wind howled; the lightning and thunder crashed. Above, a vault of grey, rolling clouds.

She began to scream.

Papa had to carry her out while all the grown-ups smiled.

Outside, Papa knelt and pointed to the top of the tent.

"See, Madeleine, 'tis only make-believe. The man has painted giant pictures with transparent and opaque paints. Light passes through and creates effects. And there are oil lamps held by men above. Come, I'll show you." And he led the way to the side of the tent, where she saw the small lamps and shutters.

But when he tried to bring her inside again, the light began to move and she gasped. Papa, his face angry, had swooped her up and carried her outside. After she apologized, he promised to bring her back to see the next week's show, *The Interior of Chartres Cathedral*. Only there had been no show the next week. The Diorama had burned down on Friday and poor Mr.

Daguerre had been forced to come up with a new invention.

"Okay, I think we have it, Miss Smith," Mr. Pinkins was saying, rising from the black cloth and stretching the stoop from his back.

Madeleine blinked and rotated her shoulders, stood up,

A day later, she came back for the likeness. Mr. Pinkins opened his walnut writing desk and handed her a parcel wrapped in white paper.

In the privacy of her room, she unwrapped it. Her face was an oval within an oval, covered with two layers of glass. The whole affair was set into a red-leather case.

With a flick of her wrist, she turned the likeness, letting the light reverse her. Negative, positive, back to negative.

Her body in the likeness was muted, passive. The tulle of the off-the-shoulder dress was so still it seemed painted on. The short hairs around her ears and forehead feathered out, creating a soft halo around her face.

She sat for some time looking at this picture drawn by the sun. Then she closed the case, wrapped it again in the white paper. She hoped Emile would not hate it.

After that, it all started falling apart.

"Miss Madeleine?" Christine had said, peeking her head in the doorway.

Madeleine had jumped up.

Christine shook her head. "I've got no letter, Miss Madeleine."

"What's wrong, Christine?"

"I . . . I . . ."

"Is it the Monsieur?"

Christine shook her head quickly. Her eyes were brimming.

"Yer mother, she said I must tell ye . . ."

"What, Christine?"

"That I am nae . . . nae t'be . . . yer . . . go-between."
"You told her you *had* been?"
"Miss . . . ss . . . Madeleine, I didna."
"But you admitted it?"
"I . . . I didna ken what else t' do."
"You could have come to me. I could have told you."
"Miss Madeleine?"
"Yes, Christine?"
"May I speak frank wi' ye a moment?"
"Of course you may."
"I regret verra much if I ha' broken a trust. But 'tisna ye who pay me wages. . . . I . . . I'm sorry, Miss Madeleine. Please dinna be angry wi' me."
Madeleine nodded. "Of course I am not. You must look out for yourself. I will manage without you."
"Miss Madeleine. . . ?"
"No, it's all right. Go now, please."
"Aye, ma'am." Christine turned, her shoulders sloped, walked to the door, closed it as Madeleine liked, softly.

"We shall be home on Sundays, too, from now on. The Fergusons will be coming here," Mama had said, the first day in the new parlor at Blythswood Square. The rug still smelled of glue, and Madeleine could not get over the effect of the room with the very modern wall-to-wall carpeting.

She sat down in front of the big bay window, looked through the curtains at the public square. And after Mama left, she opened the curtains, because there was no wood to fade, let the sunshine pour in. For a moment, she imagined the room as she and Emile would furnish it—sparsely.

A bed there . . .

At the dinner table, Papa sat like stone. He had not spoken or looked at her directly since Christine had told them. She had trusted the girl, and now Mama and Papa knew that Madeleine had let Emile into the house at India Street. Now she began to understand why the India Street house had been sold. And that wasn't all. Papa had begun to talk of selling Row.

She would have to see Emile, talk to him, tell him. They had been able to slip into the India Street house, within its spaces and privacies. But this house. This house built by Minnoch. And the Murdoch sisters across the way, the town criers of Glasgow, the gimlet-eyed, sap-dried, see-all spinsters. Sitting at their windows this very moment.

She would have to tell him.

November 14, 1856

My darling,

There is for you no access to this new "home" in which my parents now safeguard their child. *Every* entrance is in full, lighted view. Every entrance is under surveillance by two harpies standing watch across the street.

Dear love, write me. Put your letters in a brown envelope—less conspicuous—pause on the paving at the second window from the corner—that is my bedroom (how I pleaded and contrived!)—feign to be tying your shoelace, and drop the envelope into the well of the window.

I love you.

Mimi L'Angelier

Postscriptum: If I am (to be) Mrs. P. Emile L'Angelier, should I not know for what the P stands?

This morning she had been tired. She had not got to bed till two and her feet were swollen. William Minnoch had monopolized her all evening.

But the sun was out. And she had errands. She dressed for shopping—her new promenade costume, a green, black, and white tartan taffeta with tight-fitting corsage and lie-down linen collar. Despite her sore feet, she still felt happy; she went out humming a tune from last night.

The pigeons huddled under the barn eaves and the chickens clustered in small groups round the stall doors, but she walked briskly. She passed the frost-bitten pumpkin vines, the dried hollyhocks, their heads dipped to the wind, turned down Mains Street.

It was crowded out this morning. The sidewalks were full; some men walked in the street. She came to the Tron corner, looked down the street at the Old Tower of the Tolbooth, the statue of horse and rider. Above the tea store, pink curtains fluttered in the window of the second-floor walkup. A geranium sat in a green pot upon the windowsill.

A furnished room. She saw herself, sitting at the window, looking down on the street, watching the crowd come and go through the Tron Gate.

And then, Emile, coming home. That was as far as she got each time. It seemed the perfect picture.

Her breakfast tea purchased, she paused a moment on the street, looked over her left shoulder. It was too nice to go home.

She had promised Emile not to go to Sauchiehall Street till market day, or rather Emile had forbidden her, but she had to go sometimes and it was not fair that the time she went should also be the time Emile was there. Her humming broke off as she saw him approaching. She smiled, started to bow. He looked at her coldly, walked silently by.

She went home, collapsed in tears. What did he want? Now he was angry at her again. Oh, it wasn't fair. All she had done was to amuse herself and now he would be so hateful. She took out pen and paper.

Dear Emile,

You are cool when I am bad and then I try to drown my sad thoughts in being careless. When you are cool to me, I feel as if I did not care what I do or where I go. Now, I must tell you something you might have heard. I was at the Theatre, and people, my love, may tell you that Minnoch was there too. Well, love, he was there, but he did not know of my going. He was in the Club Box, and I did not even bow to him. Yesterday, when Bessie and Mama and I were walking, M. joined us, and he was most civil and kind. I have been candid with you. . . . A kiss, sweet love . . . I often wish you were beside me—I think I would even ask you to *love* me. I often fear you will yet get so cool to me that you won't have me for your wife. . . . For however much I adore you, if you were cool, I would not be your wife.

Adieu sweet love, I do adore you,

Mimi L'Angelier

Papa and Mama were going to Edinburgh this Sunday and staying over to shop for Christmas presents. She had considered telling Emile but had not—what if they came back early? What if someone saw him? What if Jack or James came downstairs to raid the pantry?

At eight, he was to drop his letter in the well. Her letters to him would be waiting there.

Just before vespers, she went back to her room, locked it. She doused the candle she had carried and went to the window, pulled open the drapes, looked out past the dark bars to the dimly lit street.

At the corner of the Square, the streetlamp had been lit, but in the shadow of the building, the pavement was dark.

Emile approached, knelt down, tied his shoe. She saw him look at her, then stand up, his hands on his waist.

"What is it, Emile?" she whispered.

"What is it?" he said, not softly.

"Shhhhh. . . . Emile!"

"What is it, Mimi? Will your mother come running? Will your sister wake up?"

"Emile, you know it's not safe."

"Safe?" He laughed. "Oh, Mimi, just tell me; I am an annoyance to you, no?"

She sighed exasperatedly. "Emile . . ." She motioned towards the service door. "Come in, Emile. . . . You know they're not home."

When she opened the service door, he was standing there, waiting.

"Come in," she said. She motioned to Christine's room.

"No, not there . . . not this time." He stepped just inside the door.

She could just make out his face. He was scowling.

"I am going to clear the whole matter up, once and for all."

"Which matter?"

"Minnoch."

"I don't know what you're talking about."

"Minnoch. He built this house. You didn't think I'd find out? Minnoch. He took you to the concert. You had no chaperone. Mimi, do you think I am a fool?" He banged his fist against the wall.

"Emile, calm down. . . . There is nothing, absolutely nothing, between Minnoch and myself. If you don't believe me . . . I . . ."

"I don't. But I am going to clear it all up. As I said."

"As you said? What are you going to do? Ask my father?"

"No. Minnoch."

"Minnoch!" She laughed; the laugh echoed down the dark hall.

"You find it funny?"

"How are you going to talk with him? You don't know him. You don't move in the same circles. Are you going to accost him like a footpad in the street?"

"Mimi!" His voice was low, shocked.

"The only thing you would accomplish is to make yourself absurd and our situation even more impossible."

"You really can't stop yourself, can you?" he said.

"Why should I? But how many times can I tell you I love you? How many times can I ask you to trust me? I long for your letters. When you are low, and I am the cause, I pain with you. . . . I know sometimes you wish you had never met me. . . . I am doing all I can to please you."

"You *were* with Minnoch at the concert. Stevenson saw you."

"Who is Stevenson?"

"A friend."

"You send your friends to spy on me?"

"No, Mimi, but my friends are not blind; they are not deaf—as I am."

She looked up at him.

"Well?" he said.

She smiled. "Emile, if you don't trust me, leave me. How could anything you say to Minnoch make me trustworthy?"

His face paled. "Oh, Mimi, I trust you. You simply don't understand the consequences of your actions."

"Do *you?*"

"Do I what?"

"Emile, I want you to consider carefully the consequences of *your* actions. I do not expect my father to know my state, but I do expect from you sympathy and understanding. Between you and my father, I am a rag to be torn."

He bit his lip. "Madeleine," he said. He loosened the knot of his cravat. "I am . . ."

Madeleine said, "Tell me next time, Emile," and walked into her bedroom, closing the door behind her.

It was three days now and Emile had not written. She smiled. She was supposed to be beside herself with worry and doubt. How many times did he think she would react to the same old stale device? Besides, who had insulted whom?

She loved him, but he did do some things too often.

She sat down at the kneehole desk to compose an answer to the letter which would sooner or later arrive.

She found his letter in the well when she woke on the fifth day. She took her time answering.

December 20, 1856

My own darling beloved husband,

    I am sorry to hear you have a sore hand. I am glad you are sound. I had a fear you were not. I am very well (but "ill"). My sweet love, I shall contrive to see you some night soon for a short while. Mr. M. dined with us tonight. Do you know, I think if you knew him you would like him, he is most kind. I like him very much better than I used to. I am engaged every night this week. I am yours,

Mimi

    It was New Year's Day and Madeleine was in the dining room, setting out plates of cookies, pouring more whiskey into the athole brose. She heard steps, then a knock at the door.

    She went to the door. Of course it would be Minnoch. And he was the perfect "first footer," his arms laden with food.

    "Come in, William, come in. . . ."

    "I shall if you find the foot acceptable." He came in, handed her the bowl.

    "What is it?"

    "It's a pudding."

    "Mmmm, I smell marmalade," Madeleine said.

    "Yes, dear, it's a Clootie dumpling. I made it myself. There's even trinkets in it for the childer." He touched her hair. "You like childer?"

    She smiled up at him. "Would I be a woman if I didn't?"

    On January 6th, Epiphany, she woke from a dream of bandits. The bandit leader, a dark-haired tall man named Rao, had been tying her hands. He had had a knife.

    She forced open her eyes, focused. The cat was "rao"ing at the door. She smiled at herself, jumped up, and let him in, then crawled back under the warm covers. It was Little Christmas Day, the day of the Wise Men, and she was going to dinner that night with William.

    Footsteps sounded in the hall. It must be seven, she

thought, time to rise. She stretched luxuriously, yawned.

There was a knock on the door.

"Come in."

It was Bessie. She curled up at the end of the bed under the comforter.

"I think it will be sunny," Bessie said. "Will you still wear the taffeta?"

"I haven't decided."

"I couldn't sleep all night. Do you think Papa has bought us the cart?"

"I don't know."

"It would be nice," Bessie said.

"Well, Papa is nice."

"What did you get him, Maddy?"

"Cigars. A box of Little"—she stopped, her eyes widened—"Vics," she said.

"Maddy, what's wrong? You look like you've seen a ghostie."

"Oh, I just swallowed the wrong way." It had happened. What Mama had said would happen. She had wakened, thought of the cat, thought of the day, Little Christmas—Epiphany!—and of many things—and not until this moment of Emile.

She sat down before Vespers to write to Emile and to think about him as lovingly and as long as she could.

She wore the rich russet to Vespers. Papa had invited Minnoch. He stood a head above her, and in his new redingote, he looked very handsome.

They offered the collect in unison, their voices a gentle harmony:

> O, Lord, we beseech thee mercifully to receive the prayers of thy people who call upon thee; and grant that they may both perceive and know what things they ought to do, and also may have grace and power faithfully to fulfill the same, through Jesus Christ our Lord.
>
> AMEN

That night just as she was drifting off, she turned, and the necklace William had given her pressed sharply at her breast.

She shouldn't have accepted it, she knew, but it was so beautiful and he had been so humble about it, calling her homemade scarf a masterpiece of thoughtfulness. She had been touched and it had made him so happy to clasp it around her neck.

She had grown used to William being around, having him at Vespers, going to concerts. Poor Emile, the holiday season was such a trial. She was so busy. She had no spare moments.

The next night, the whole family, William's sisters included, gathered round in the drawing room, surrounded by the patriarchal oak panelling, sang and played: "Mermaids Floating o'er the Main"; "Scotland's A-Burning"; "Bonnets of Bonnie Dundee"; "The Campbells Are Coming."

She hoped Emile was with friends.

She still loved Emile. But she saw with astonishment that the path ahead forked. There were two paths.

January 16, 1857

My very dear Emile,

> I ought ere this to have written you. Well, my dear you did look cross at your Mimi the other day. Why, my pet, you cannot expect I am never to go to Sauchiehall Street. Sometimes I must. It is not quite fair of you. . . . When I saw you, my little pet, coming, I felt frightened even to bow to you. . . .

January 19, 1857

My sweet beloved,

> I could not get this posted for you today. . . .

January 21, 1857

My dearest Emile,

> I was so very sorry that I could not see you tonight. . . .

January 23, 1857

My dear Emile,

    I have just five minutes to spare. . . .

    One night she lay in bed, thinking of the two of them. Minnoch would tower over Emile. But it was Emile she loved, despite his always finding fault, threatening, mistrusting—why, really, he was much like Papa.
    And then there was William—pleasant, rich, easy to look at, admiring, blind to all her faults.

    The 25th was Rabbie Burns' birthday. She made William a cake to celebrate his favourite author. He escorted her to the Gentleman's Ball.
    She found herself thinking often of Emile's size now. She had never considered him short, really. "He thinks he's big," she found herself thinking, "but a wee coat fits him."
    And she no longer thought William old; no longer thought him homely. She was comfortable with him. He *liked* women. He liked *her*. When she was with him, she felt light and pure and happy. And he was so healthy, apt to live a long life. Whereas Emile . . .
    She thought of her future.

    At the end of January, she found herself listening to William's proposal that they consider joining lives.
    She was seated on the rosewood piano stool, her fingers resting on the keys. William had been pacing back and forth for several minutes now. He came to a stop next to the mahogany banjo barometer, stood studying the silvered dial. Then he turned to her.
    "You, know, Madeleine, I have always preferred the company of women to that of men. And I prefer your company to that of any other woman."
    She turned to him. "William, I am flattered."

"I feel I could make you happy, Madeleine."

"Oh, William . . ."

"I'm not a bad man."

"You're a very good man."

"I try to live a Christian life," he said, running his finger over the convex mirror front. His fingernails were square, carefully buffed. "You would never want for anything. . . ."

"William, I . . ." But she couldn't bear to say anything. She lowered her head, looked at her hands.

"Don't say anything now," he said. "I just wanted you to know how I . . ."

"I know," she said.

"We will talk about it again. Now, would you give me the pleasure of hearing you play?"

He moved to the satinwood davenport, sat on the center cushion. She turned the sheet music on the stand. With William, it was like family. She really was genuinely fond of him.

She finished the tune. He applauded.

He sat erect. "Madeleine, what did you think of me at first? Be honest."

Madeleine smiled tenderly, thinking how her first word for him had been *homey*. Old like Row.

"I thought you would enjoy Row," she said, and believed herself to be telling the truth.

"I thought you were like music," he said.

"Did you? Which piece?"

"An opera."

"Yes? Who was I?"

"You were Frigg, wife of Woden. Sort of an earth goddess . . ." His voice lowered. "A goddess of Love."

"Like Venus?"

"Exactly, exactly." He sat, looking at her, wonderingly. "I know. I shall take you to see it. You'd like that, wouldn't you?"

"The opera?"

"Yes, I hold a box."

"I'd love to go."

"Friday then, Frigg's Day?"
"Yes."

Only after he had gone did she remember that she had made Friday the time to receive Emile's letter.

When she arrived home at midnight on Friday, there were two notes. She was ashamed, then angry.

Saturday morning

My very dearest Emile,

Your note last night pained me. I was sorry if you were put to any inconvenience by returning at 10 to see if your letter remained there. My husband, do you for an instant suppose that your wife would forget that you mentioned that you would drop a note?

The tone of your letter was so different from the last. I wept for hours. It was Minnoch that I was at the Opera with. You see I would not hide that from you. . . .

On Saturday, she accepted Minnoch's invitation for a walk on Sauchiehall Street. Let him see them. She even wore the necklace Minnoch had given her. William wore a black cashmere coat tapered in front.

Near the florist's, she saw Emile. And he saw them. He hesitated, then started towards them. If she had not turned William into the glove shop at the last moment, there would have been an ugly scene. How dare he?

On Monday, Candlemas, she went to church still seething, watched as the Virgin Mary presented the Baby Jesus to the temple fathers.

When she came home, there was a letter in the well. Inside was her Saturday letter. Opened and returned, unanswered.

Monday February 2

Dear Emile,

 I felt truly astonished to have my last letter returned to me. But it will be the last time you shall have an opportunity. When you are not pleased with the letter I send you, then our correspondence shall be at an end, and as there is coolness on both sides, our engagement had better be broken. Also you annoyed me much on Sauchiehall Street by your conduct in coming so near me. Altogether I think owing to coolness and indifference (nothing else) that we had better for the future consider ourselves as strangers. I trust to your honour as a Gentleman that you will not reveal anything that may have passed between us. I shall feel obliged by your bringing me my letters and likeness on Thursday evening at 7—be at the area gate and Christine will take the parcel from you. On Friday night I shall send you all your letters, likeness, etc. I trust you may yet be happy and get one more worthy of you than I. On Thursday at 7—

I am

             Mimi

 It was too late for the post. She put the letter at the back of the desk. At four, she unsealed it, added a postscript:

Postscriptum: You may be astonished at this sudden change—but for some time back you must have noticed a coolness in my notes. My love for you has ceased, and that is why I was cool. I did love you once, but for some time back I have lost much of that love. There is no other reason for my conduct, and I think it but fair to let you know. My conduct you will condemn, but I did at one time love you with heart and soul. It has cost me many sleepless nights, but I must tell you. If you remain in Glasgow or go away, I hope you succeed in your endeavors. I know you will never injure the character of one you so fondly loved. I know you have honour and are a Gentleman. What has passed you will not mention. I know when I ask you that you will comply.

Adieu

Thursday the 5th, came and went. Madeleine waited. He was sick, that would explain it. She wrote again, appointing the next Thursday.
No response.
But surely he would be a gentleman.

On Septuagesima Sunday, she went to Church, prayed.

O, God, who knowest us to be set in the midst of so many and great dangers, that by reason of frailty of our nature we cannot always stand upright; grant to us such strength and protection, as may support us in all dangers, and carry us through all temptation, through Jesus Christ our Lord.

AMEN

After church, she went home, climbed into bed, a chill upon her. The letter she feared arrived in Monday's morning post. He would not release her. *Never. Never. Never.*

Monday, February 9

Emile,

I have just had your note. Emile, for the love you once had me, do not bring your once-loved Mimi to open shame. Emile, write to no one, to Papa or any other. I will see you on Wednesday night at Midnight. I shall open my shutter, then you come to the service door.

Emile, do not drive me to death.

I did fondly truly love you. Oh, Emile, do nothing . . . for the love of God. . . .

Mimi

Emile's reply came the next morning. Yes, he would meet her. But he promised nothing.

Madeleine went into Papa's study, picked up the cut-glass decanter with *Brandy* inscribed within the octagonal cartouche, carried it to her room, locked the door. She drank a goblet full, shuddering. Then the burning stopped and she felt better except for the wobbliness.

Tuesday, February 10

Dear Emile,

When you have found fault with me, I cooled—it was not love for another. My love has all been given to you. My heart is empty, cold. Now you can know my state of mind. I have suffered much for you, lost my father's confidence. And my mother has never given me the same kind look.

Emile, for the love you once had for me, do not denounce me. If P. should read my letters to you—he will put me from him, he will hate me as a guilty wretch. I loved you, I wrote to you in my first ardent love—it was for your love I adored you. I put on paper what I should not. I was free, because I loved you with my heart. If he or any other one saw those fond letters to you, what would not be said of me. On bended knees I write you, and ask you as you hope for mercy at the Judgment Day do not inform on me—do not make me a public shame. Emile, my life has been one of bitter disappointment. You and only you can make the rest of my life peaceful. My own conscience will be a punishment that I shall carry to my grave. I have deceived the best of men.

You may forgive me, but God never will—for God's love forgive me.

Mimi

Postscriptum: Wednesday—Midnight.

TWENTY-FIVE

The court met on Thursday at ten o'clock. Lord Justice Hope arranged the collar of his gown and leant forwards, one ermine-cuffed arm resting on the table.

"Gentlemen of the jury," he said. "The contest of evidence and argument is now closed. You must now deliberate and decide. To discharge that duty aright and justly, you must remember that the case is to be tried and decided *solely on the evidence*.

"You are not to give the slightest weight to any personal opinion of the prisoner's guilt, as expressed, for instance, by the Lord Advocate. Nor to any personal opinion of the prisoner's innocence, as expressed, for instance, by the prisoner's counsel. I think on both sides such expressions of opinion by counsel ought never be brought before a jury. Neither of them is so good a judge of the truth as all of you are."

"In short, you are to judge the guilt or the innocence of the prisoner from the evidence, and not from the speeches of the counsel, however eloquent they are."

He leaned back in his chair and tented his fingers.

"Gentlemen, in a case of poisoning, which is almost always an offence secretly perpetrated, it seldom occurs that anybody has seen the mixture and preparation of the poison, or seen it put into the fluid or substance in which it is administered.

"Poisoning usually must be proved by circumstantial evidence, as the defence counsel very fairly and properly admits.

But that body of evidence must be strong enough to rule out either a conclusion of innocence or the possibility of a mysterious occurrence.

"A great misfortune attending the administration of poison is that, if the party is not immediately detected in some way as to leave no doubt of actual guilt, the person who last gave the deceased a cup of coffee, or a glass of water, or a glass of wine—the person who made the last appointment with him—is exposed to strong suspicions, and may be subjected even to false and groundless charges.

"You must therefore keep in view that, although on the one hand such a crime is committed in secret, and no one has seen the parties at the time, or what passed—on the other hand you must not allow positive evidence to be supplied by suspicion, and still less by loose presumption."

The Lord Justice-Clerk sighed. "The duty I have in aiding you to come to a decision is very different from that of either counsel. I have simply to go over the evidence in detail, and to make such observations as the evidence suggests is fitting and proper for your assistance.

"I wish to impress upon you that flaws in the prisoner's defence are not sufficient for a presumption of guilt. You must have evidence against her, satisfying and convincing in your minds, evidence in which you find no conjectures, but only irresistible and just inferences.

"You may not be satisfied with any of the theories that have been propounded on behalf of the prisoner—you may not be inclined to adopt the notion either that L'Angelier was the man taking laudanum in the course of the journey to Glasgow, or that he took arsenic himself, or believe Miss Smith's statement of the use for which she got the arsenic—still, though all these matters may fail in her defence, the case for the prosecution may be radically defective or inadequate in evidence."

Lord Hope shook his head. "I own there are things introduced into evidence on the part of the prisoner which I think cannot aid the prisoner in any degree. . . .

"Now, gentlemen, we move to the three charges of the indictment. The first charge is that she administered poison on the 19th or 20th of February 1857. But she was not proved to have had arsenic or any other poison in her possession, and there is no medical testimony, by analysis of the matter vomited, that that illness did proceed from administration of arsenic.

"I have no hesitation in telling you that that charge has failed. I think it is my duty to tell you, as a judge, that on that charge you should find her not guilty.

"But we are in a very different situation as to the illness of the 22nd and 23rd of February. The evidence that connects the prisoner with that is much stronger. Still, if you should think to acquit her of the first, why, then, you will observe how much that weakens all the theories that may be raised about the alleged poisoning.

"If L'Angelier was sick three times in rapid succession, each time of arsenic poisoning, the third time unto death, and no link can be established between the prisoner and the first illness, then linking her with the second and third illnesses leaves unanswered the question, 'By whose hand did the deceased receive arsenic at the first illness?' A reasonable presumption is that the second and the third illnesses were caused by that same hand. Otherwise, we have a series of unexplained coincidences, or the unlikely possibility of *two* persons administering poison to the same victim.

"Now, as to the specifics of the third charge: Murder. The point for you to consider—surrounded as the defendant is with grave suspicion, with everything that seems to militate against the notion of innocence—is this: Are you prepared to say that you find an interview with the deceased, on the night of March 22nd, proved against her?

"She had arsenic, but you must keep in mind that the poison could be administered by her *only if an interview took place,* and that interview, though it may be the result of an inference that may satisfy you morally that it did take place, still rests upon inference alone; and that inference is to be the very ground, and must be the ground, on which a verdict of guilt is to rest.

"Gentlemen, you will see, therefore, the necessity of great caution in dealing with inference. You may be perfectly satisfied that L'Angelier did not commit suicide, and, of course, it is necessary for you to be satisfied of that before you could find that anybody administered arsenic to him. Probably none of you will think for a moment that he went out that night and, without seeing her, without knowing what she wanted to see him about if they had met, that he swallowed over eighty grains of arsenic on the street." Lord Hope waved his hand; the jurymen sat erect.

"Probably you will discard that altogether; yet on the other hand, keep in view that such a conclusion will not of itself establish that the prisoner administered the arsenic.

"The matter may remain most mysterious—wholly unexplained; you may not be able to account for it on any other supposition; but still that supposition or inference may not be a ground on which you can safely and satisfactorily rest your verdict against the defendant."

Lord Hope laid his hands flat on the papers in front of him, looked levelly at the jurors. "Now, the great and invaluable use of a jury, after they direct their minds seriously to the case, is to separate firmly—firmly and clearly in their own minds—suspicion from evidence."

His voice was solemn, his face austere, as he gave his final charge.

"I am quite satisfied that whatever verdict you may reach, after the attention that you have bestowed upon this case, will be the best approximation to truth at which we could arrive. Let me say, as I said at the outset, that of the evidence you are the best judges, not only in point of law, but in point of fact; and you may be perfectly confident that, if you return a verdict satisfactory to yourselves against the prisoner, you need not fear any consequences from any future, or imagined, or fancied discovery that time may uncover.

"You will have done your duty under your oaths, under

God, and to your country, and may feel satisfied that there cannot be, and will not be, any necessity for remorse."

Lord Justice-Clerk Hope looked at the ceiling, pushed back his wig. He nodded, once.

"Gentlemen, consider your verdict."

The jury filed out the side door. The court waited.

At half past six, having deliberated for almost five hours without reaching a verdict—with none in sight—the jurors were conveyed to their hotel. Lord Hope dismissed the court till ten the next morning.

TWENTY-SIX

At dusk, Madeleine listened to the drums and bugles rallying in the garrison. The last flourish melted away into the darkness.

She closed her eyes, rested, but there was no sleep. Her fate, to be denied or to be given liberty, was in their hands.

She had an east-facing cell. When the sparrows began to sing outside, she opened her eyes, watched the cell fill up with light. From off down the corridor she heard a woman coughing a dry-as-dust cough. Keys rattled and the smell of porridge drifted. The sun poured between the bars onto the floor.

It would be time soon. Miss Aitken would come with her dress, the chocolate silk, the one she had worn the first day. The matron would stand and watch her as she dressed.

But there was time still. She closed her eyes, her hands folded over her breast, listened to the birds.

There had been bars on the windows of Blythswood Square, too.

The *Farmer's Almanac* had lain on the kneehole writing desk, open to February and March. She had scanned down the February numbers: 9, Monday, Pigeon lays; 11, Wednesday, Partridges pair; 12, Thursday, Red dead nettle flowers.

She must be sure William would bring her home early. A headache perhaps. She had wondered what it would be like for William to touch her. Not so very awful. Her mind was a muddle—she had no idea what she would say to Emile.

This could not be happening.

She looked down at the almanac, in the left column. The tiny circle was one quarter shaded. The moon would rise at nine past eight and not set till morning; the moon would be waning.

At midnight, she had been watching the window. Janet was asleep, snoring lightly. Madeleine took a deep breath.

Moonlight was faint in the square. The streetlamp threw a round circle. She saw a man coming across the square, recognized Emile only by his walk. At the corner post, he stopped, lit a match. And then a policeman was stopping. She saw Emile nod, reach into his smoke pocket, put something in the officer's hand. He tipped his hat; the policeman nodded, walked past him down the block.

He was coming now, his cigar like the red taillight of a carriage. She waited, biting her lip.

He was bending down now to tie the lace.

"Mimi?"

"The service door."

She listened to his shoes clicking away, ran for the door. She took him by the sleeve, led him quickly into the kitchen, closed the door. She had left one oil lamp burning. It cast huge shadows on the wall.

Dropping his hand, she stood, facing him, her eyes meeting his.

"Well, Mimi?" he said, his hands on his waist.

"Emile, you can't . . ." She shook her head.

"What, Mimi?"

"When a man finds some uncleanness in his wife . . ."

"A woman may go and take another man—is that it?" He leaned back against the wooden icebox.

"There is no other man."

"Your Billy."

She shook her head silently.

"Then why, Madeleine, why?"

"I told you."

"A coolness?"

"On both our parts, Emile."

He stared at her, his hand fretting at his mustache.

"You can't deny that, Emile. So many annoyances—always Mimi's fault."

"We had our setbacks, I know, but—"

"Oh, Emile, be realistic, face facts."

"Facts, Mimi? Did you have me come to recite facts? I'll tell you a fact. You lie to me."

"Yes."

"Did you ever ask your parents? Does your father even know I exist? Sometimes I wonder. You're ashamed of me, admit it."

His face was shadowed in the weak light of the lamp.

"Admit it, *chérie*."

She was silent.

"Mimi, you can't marry someone else."

She looked at him, sighed. "And I can't marry *you*, Emile. You have driven out everything I felt for you."

"Mimi, I love you." His shadow loomed, trembling, on the wall.

"You're a fool, Emile."

"You don't know what you're saying, Mimi."

"And my name is Madeleine."

"I still won't let you marry him—or anyone else."

"You would deny me any chance of happiness?"

"You would deny me?"

"Emile, it would be kinder to us both. I thought . . . I truly thought at one time I could beat them all—bend them to my way—and please you too. But I can't fight anymore. And I'm not going to betray them."

Emile laughed. "So that's what all this has been leading up to."

"*What* has 'all this been leading up to'?"

"Billy."

"That again?"

"What shall we talk of, then?"

"Your future."

"*Merde.*"

"Emile!"

"We shall talk about something else—the necklace."

"What necklace?" she said.

"You tell me. It's an opal, I believe."

"Papa gave it to me."

"Mimi?" He put his hand out, touched her sleeve.

"Yes?"

"You're a bitch," he said, tightening his grasp, pulling her to him.

"Emile, don't make me . . ." She stiffened in his arms.

He held her at arms' length. "You know what they are saying, don't you?"

"They?"

"De Mean and Kennedy."

"No, I don't know."

"That I'm a fool."

"You are."

"Mimi!" His hand tightened on her flesh.

"Let me go!"

"You are my wife, for better or worse."

"No, Emile, you know I'm not." She pushed his hands away, went and sat at the kitchen table, her arms folded. "No, Emile, I'm not."

His voice softened. "Mimi." He came to the table, put his hands on her shoulders, gently, raised her up, "I'm sorry, *chérie*," he said.

"You won't release me?" she asked.

"Never, Madeleine," he said, his voice calm.

She was silent.

"You are my wife, Madeleine."

She looked vacantly at him, past him, her eyes unfocused.

"Madeleine?"

She sighed. "Yes, Emile, I am." She reached out her hand, let it fall to her side. "But my husband won't touch me."

"You say it as though it is *I* . . ."

She took a step towards him, lifted his arms and placed them around her. She pressed against his coat.

He held her stiffly in place. They were silent a long moment.

She began to cry, deeply, her breath coming in gasps.

He held her then, tightly. "Don't cry, darling. Mimi, don't."

"You don't understand," she said.

"Shhh," he said.

"You never will. . . ."

"Shhhh, shhhhh."

"I'm afraid, Emile."

"No, darling, they can't hurt us. It will all work out, Mimi."

"What about Papa?"

"You will tell him, you promised."

She sniffed back her tears, looked up at him through reddened eyes. "And the letters?"

"I told you," he said.

"Oh, Emile, let us burn all our bridges."

He laughed. "I don't trust you that much."

"But . . ." She nestled against him, said in a small voice, "What if you were to get sick, die . . . the letters might be . . ."

"Hush," he said. "My friends would destroy them."

She looked up at him. "Your friends?"

"I trust them."

"You mean you told them—about us?"

"Don't be naïve."
"Miss Perry?"
"Yes."
"How would she know what do to? Have you given her instructions?"
"Perhaps."
"I don't trust her."
"*Chérie*, she has been a good friend to us."
"She never liked me."
"On the contrary, she finds you . . ."
"Much improved, weren't those her words?"
"Mimi, let's not start that again. You know she cares for you—for us."
"She would destroy them?"
"Of course, but—"
"And you do love me?"
"Of course, Mimi."
"Say it, then, Emile. Say you do."
"I do love you, Mimi."

She smiled a tremulous smile, lifted her chin, closed her eyes.

He kissed the salt from her mouth, then kissed her again, his tongue insistent inside her mouth, one hand caressing the small of her back. With his free hand, he unbuttoned his trousers.

Friday the 13th had dawned dull and cloudy. She had sat all day by the fire, her bones cold. The flame held her, led her from thought to thought. She had gained time, that was all. She must still break with him.

And when she did, he would show Papa the letters. That was as far as she got each time.

She examined another course: Convince him to leave.

She had torn up three letters so far. When he came to the window tonight she must have a letter—she had promised.

She looked out the glazed window at the dark sky. At last, she took up her sewing scissors and pressed the point to her index finger, till the skin grew white. She pressed harder.

When she took the scissors away, a globule of blood appeared. She let it drop on the paper, picked up her pen, wrote:

My dear Emile,

    I have got my finger cut and cannot write. I want, the first time we meet, that you bring me all my cool letters back—the four I mentioned to you. They are not true. I hope to see you very soon. Excuse me, just now it hurts to write, so with kindest love, ever believe me, yours with love and affection—

She started to sign her name, hesitated. Mimi? Madeleine? What wasn't a lie now? She put down the quill, sucked at the prick on her finger, drawing up blood. Then she dipped her pen, signed:

                                                                        M

At eight, before the moon rose, Emile stopped by the window. She handed up her letter, took his. His shoe tied, he went on.

On Sexagesima Sunday, the weather still had been bad. She woke early. The wind was rustling through the treetops and Madeleine felt leaden. She lay in bed, followed her thoughts. She had found out from Robert's uncle what the P stood for. Pierre. She said it like a spell, over and over . . . till it seemed not a lie. Pierrot, the marionnette, dancing in his loose white clothes.

If only it were warm. She got up, put pine on the hearth. The wood was green still; it began to smoke. Finally the wood caught, sending up a white flame.

She watched the fire reflect in the brass heads of the old

iron fire dogs, brought her clothes in, and dressed by the hearth. Then she went to church, prayed.

She left church, looking for a sign, a marker, something to steer her. Old Man Cobb had his tumblers out for the first time that spring and the young pigeons were testing their wings, going into hesitant spins, while the oldsters made wide swooping circles. Old Man Cobb nodded to her as she passed, his fowling piece across his yellow knee breeches.

"Is it for hawks?" she asked.

"Yes, but no need t'kill 'em; I just blast t'sky wi' noise."

Madeleine stood a moment, watching the tumblers circling and spinning. The moon was still in the sky, a milky wafer. One bird began to twirl towards earth, faster and faster. Behind her, she heard Cobb draw in his breath. The pigeon hit the ground dully.

"Damned bird!" Cobb said, going and taking up the pigeon, which was struggling to rise, its wing askew.

"Can you save it?" Madeleine said.

"Nae, it'd roon the breed, you have t'kill 'em when they do that," he said, twisting the bird's neck.

"Oh," she said.

"Sorry, miss," he said, touching his cap.

She went home, consulted the almanac. The moon would be but a thin yellow wedge tonight. It would not rise till past midnight. On Thursday the 19th, it would rise, a quarter crescent, at twenty-four minutes past four. And then, later and later each night.

She took out Emile's likeness, buried it facedown at the bottom of the steamer trunk, then went to Mama's bathroom, locked the door. She went quickly to the medicine chest, began looking through the bottles and vials: laudanum, Godfrey's Cordial, Carter's Pills, paragoric, Fowler's. She opened the last bottle, turned it over—it was dry.

On Tuesday the 17th, at six, just as the dusk was fading

into blackness, Emile's cane stroked against the iron stanchions.

She doused her light, ran to the bars. "Emile?"

"Yes."

"Thursday night I can see you."

"What time?"

"Ten."

"They will be away?"

"Yes. Edinburgh. For the weekend."

He squeezed his hand through the stanchion; she reached out. He grasped her hand.

"How are you?" she said.

"A little under the weather."

"I'm sorry," she said. "Your stomach again?"

He nodded. "I am taking something."

"Thursday, then," she said, taking back her hand.

"Thursday."

Thursday, February 19, 1857.

She had sat at her kneehole desk, stared at the page in front of her. She had shaken her head, crumpled the paper.

There was the sound of a door closing, then light footsteps.

"Rob?" she called. The footsteps stopped before her door.

She got up, opened the door. The new servant lad stood there.

"Rob, I'd like you to run an errand for me to the apothecary's."

"Yes'm."

"Here, I'll give you a line." She turned to her desk, wrote a few words upon a slip of paper.

"It says I would like a vial of prussic acid," she said, pressing the paper into the lad's hand.

"Yes, mum."

"You hurry back."

"Yes, mum."

"And take care with the vial—it is poison."

When he had left she paced the floor. She had read somewhere that prussic acid could be made from bracken. Dried bracken.

Where was the boy? But it had been only minutes. The nearest shop was on Cambridge Street; he would be back soon.

The lad came back puffing, empty-handed. He had the slip of paper in his moist hands. He shook his head. "Wouldna gie it t' me, lady."

"Did he say anything?"

"Yes, mum, that it was rank poison."

"Oh." She shrugged. "Very well, never mind."

He left, closing the door carefully.

That night at nine thirty, she had excused herself from the game of whist she had been playing with Bessie, gone to her room. Bessie had pooh-poohed her for spoiling their fun. With Mama and Papa away, they might stay up all night and sleep till noon.

Janet was sound asleep, her arm around her stuffed dog.

At ten, Madeleine was at the bars, waiting.

Emile knelt.

"Emile?" she said.

"The service door?"

"No . . . it's not safe."

"Didn't they go?"

"No, not till tomorrow. Mama is ill."

"Tomorrow?"

"Yes, dear. I'm sorry, but it can't be helped. Come at midnight, tomorrow."

"Midnight? Yes," he said, rose, and walked off down the block.

Friday night, they had sat in the drawing room. The children were asleep.

"You sure your parents won't be back till Monday?" Emile said.

"Yes."

249

"Can we go below?"

"No, Christine is in."

"I feel strange." He looked up at the long-case clock, sighed, lingeringly, the way he did each time. He was giving her the cue. Wasn't this, every time, the way they proved their love: by *loving*?

"Emile, it is that time of month."

"The curse?"

She nodded.

"Just as well." The colour was drained from his face and his hands twitched upon the horsehair.

"I'll fix you coffee."

She went down, brought back two of the underglaze-blue cups. They drank in silence, then sat, each waiting.

She spoke first. "Are you still doctoring yourself?"

"Yes."

"What causes your distress?"

"I don't know. Hot liquids seem to ease the constriction."

"Here, drink my coffee too. It keeps me awake."

Emile drank down half of the other cup.

After an hour, his stomach began to churn noisily. He had to go, use her chamber pot. When he came back, he lay down, put his head in her lap.

She ran her hand through his hair, massaged his temples.

"You don't do that anymore," he said. "You used to do that all the time."

"Perhaps it's the Fowler's itself," she said.

"Fowler's?"

"You said you were doctoring yourself. Might it be a side effect?"

"I haven't begun yet. Not till the dark of the moon."

"Will it help your stomach?"

"It might."

"Then I shall get you some of Papa's."

"No, but I'll take some laudanum if you'll get me some water. You don't have soda water, do you?"

"No, does that make it better?" She went out, brought back a glass of plain water, offered it to him.

He took out a vial, squeezed out twenty drops. He drank it standing up.

"Do you want more coffee?" she said.

"No, I think it disagrees with me."

"Sunday night I'll fix you cocoa."

"I've never had it," he said. "I may find it soothing."

Madeleine stood on Sauchiehall, looking across the street at the gold letters: MURDOCH AND BROTHERS, DRUGGISTS. She had walked the four blocks too quickly; she was still breathing hard. She took a deep gulp of air, lifted her skirt, and walked slowly across the street.

The bell rang as she opened the door. The shop was empty. She stood behind the white marble counter, looked at the rows of bottles and vials. A clerk came from the packing room.

"Yes, Miss?"

"Is Mr. Murdoch available?"

"I'm sorry, he's engaged. I am Mr. Simpson—might I help you?"

"Well, I'd like to purchase sixpennyworth of arsenic."

"Well, ah . . ." His Adam's apple bobbed. "Excuse me, will you?" He backed down the hall.

A few moments passed and the clerk returned, followed by Mr. Murdoch.

"Mr. Murdoch," she said, bowing.

"Miss Smith."

"Pleasant day, isn't it?"

"Not bad, for a change."

"I'd like to place an order. We're getting ready to leave for the summer house."

Mr. Murdoch pulled out the pad.

"I need sixpence worth of arsenic for the summer house."

Mr. Murdoch set down his pad. "There's a government

form you must sign. You must tell me the purpose so I can write it down." He turned round to the clerk. "Dickie, see that one ounce of arsenic is put up."

Murdoch reached up on the first shelf, pulled down a black ledger. He opened the book, dipped his quill, and penned: "For the garden and country house." He turned the ledger round, pointed to the next line, handed Madeleine the quill.

Behind the counter, the boy had taken down a large glass jar, uncorked it, and measured out a quantity of black-speckled white powder.

Madeleine signed. Mr. Murdoch took the quill and book, initialed Madeleine's signature, and closed the book. Behind him, the boy was wrapping the white packet in a second paper. He tied it with string and handed it to her. She put it in her purse.

"Dickie, that will be a charge," Mr. Murdoch said.

"And I would also like two dozen soda water," Madeleine said.

The boy nodded, wrote on a small green slip of paper:

> Saturday, February 21, 1857:
> 6d arsenic
> 2 doz. soda water

He tallied the slip, marked it *charge*, wrote *send* beside the soda water, and placed the slip upside down on the sharp nail.

"Good day, sirs," Madeleine said.

"Good day," Mr. Murdoch said. The clerk bobbed his head.

Sunday the 22nd of February was the dark of the moon. That morning, the last Sunday before the Lenten season, she went to church, prayed for strength.

In St. Andrews Parish Church, the white Corinthian pillars glowed dimly in the lights of the three-section stained-glass window.

Madeleine watched Rev. Middleton mount the stairs to the carved mahogany pulpit, looked past him up to the vaulted ceiling.

Reverend Middleton opened his prayer book, began to read.

When I was a child, I spake as a child, I understood as a child, I thought as a child: but when I became a man, I put away childish things. For now we see through a glass, darkly; but then face to face: now I know in part; but then I shall know even as also I am known.

I'll never become a man, Madeleine thought.

She did not stay in the churchyard afterwards, when the men lit their pipes and the children and the collies romped. She went home.

That night, they sat again in the drawing room.

"I promise, Emile, I will tell Papa—on my birthday. I swear it to you on my Bible."

"Where's your Bible?" he said.

"It won't be long." She moved closer to him on the horsehair sofa.

He nodded.

"Well," she said, "I have made you the cocoa—it is Cadbury's."

"The Queen's own." He smiled.

She brought it in the blue cups, set the tray down on the oval gateleg table, handed him the nearest cup.

She watched him drink.

"It's so sweet," he said.

"What did you expect?"

"I don't know. I thought it would be stronger—more like coffee."

"Do you like it?"

"I don't know. It's different."

"It's good for you. Drink it up and I'll fix you some more."

"No, one cup is enough." He set it down. "You are still. . . ?"
"Yes."
"Oh."
"We could play at conundrums," she said.

On Monday, she stayed in bed. Her head ached.
On Shrove Tuesday, "Jolly Tuesday," she sat up and took tea and toast.
At five, she got up, dressed, called the carriage, and went to church. Jack accompanied her as far as the door, then took off for a Fastern's Eve cock fight. Madeleine shook her head: He was becoming a wild young man.
She went into the church, was shriven of her sins.

The next morning, at seven thirty, the new moon rose, translucent in the dawning sky. She dressed and went again to church, received the wafer, closed her eyes as the ash was rubbed on her forehead.
Her voice was weak as she read the collect:

Almighty and Everlasting God, who hatest nothing that
Thou hast made, and dost forgive the sins of all those who
are penitent . . .

When Mr. Middleton announced the hymn for the day, she took it as a sign, sang out joyously.

Blessed is he whose unrighteousness is forgiven and whose sin
is covered.

Blessed is the man unto whom the Lord imputeth no sin, and
in whose spirit there is no guile.

I will confess my wickedness, and be sorry for my sin, Haste
thee to help me, O Lord God of my salvation.

When she arrived home, Christine handed her a letter. She responded at once:

Wednesday

Dearest Sweet Emile,

I am so sorry to hear you are ill. I hope to God you will soon be better. Do not go to the office this week—just stay at home till Monday. I have not felt very well these last two days—sick and a headache. Everyone is complaining: It must be something in the air.

I cannot see you Friday as M. and P. are not away—but I think Sunday they will be away and I might see you, I think, but I shall let you know. Do not come and walk about and become ill again.

You did look bad Sunday night and Monday morning. I think you got sick with walking home so late—and the long want of food, so the next time we meet I shall make you a loaf of bread before you go out. I am longing to meet again, love. We shall be so happy.

I have a bad pen—excuse this scrawl. And Bessie is near me. I cannot write at night now. My head aches so, and I am taking something to bring back the colour. Put up with short notes for a little time. When I feel stronger you shall have long ones.

Ever with love,

Yours
Mimi

On Friday, she wrote again. She knew of nothing else to do.

Friday

My Dear,

I cannot see you this week, and I can fix no time to meet you. I do hope you are better. I am a little better, but have got a bad cold. I hope we may meet soon. We go, I think, to Stirling and Bridge of Allan about the 10th of March for a fortnight.

Excuse this short note. Ever believe me to be yours,

Mimi

On Sunday, she went to church, trembled as the minister cried out, *"Get thee hence, Satan!"*

She wrote again on Tuesday, received a letter from Emile. He was better.

The house was so cold, her fingers could barely hold the pen. She wrote in gloves.

Tuesday

My dearest Emile,

I hope by this time you are quite well, and able to be out. I saw you at your window, but I could not tell how you looked. On Friday we go to Bridge of Allan for a fortnight. I am so sorry, my pet, I cannot see you ere we go.

Will you, sweet one, write me for Thursday night (6 o'clock) and I shall get it before I go—which will be a comfort to me—as I shall not hear from you till I come home again. I will write you, but sweet pet, it may only be once a week. Mama and Papa have fixed a busy schedule.

If you would take my advice, you would go to the south of England for ten days; it would do you much good. In fact, it would make you quite well. Do try and do this. I hope you won't come to Bridge of Allan while we are there as P. and M. would say it was I brought you there, and it would make me very unhappy. Stirling you need not go to as it is a nasty dirty little town. Go to Isle of Wight.

The first thing I do on my return is to see you. I must stop as it is post time.

Yours, ever,

Mimi

During the night, she thought she heard his cane scrape against the bars. When she woke before dawn, she looked in the well: a letter.

My dear, sweet pet Mimi,

Your cold, indifferent letters, so reserved, so short, without a particle of love in them, and the manner in which you *evaded* answering the questions I put you in my last letter, fully convince me that there is a foundation in your marriage with another. Besides, the way you put off our union till summer without a just reason is very suspicious.

No, Mimi. You often go to Mr. Minnoch's house, and common sense would lead anyone to believe that if you were not on the footing reports say you are, you would avoid going anywhere near there. Mimi, place yourself in my position and tell me I am wrong in believing what I hear. I was happy the last time we met—yes, very happy. I was forgetting all the past, but now all begins again.

Mimi, if not answered this time in a satisfactory manner, you must not expect I shall again write to you or meet you. I shall do what you have forced me to do. I do not wish you to answer this at random. I shall wait a day or so if you require it. I know you cannot write me from Bridge of Allan, as the time you have to write is occupied in doing so to others. Once you would have found plenty of time.

Answer me this, Mimi. Who gave you the necklace you display? Is it true it was Minnoch? Tell me, are you directly or indirectly engaged to him, or to any other?

The doctor says I must go to Bridge of Allan. I cannot travel 500 miles to the Isle of Wight and 500 back. What is your object in wishing me so very much to go south? I shall not go to Bridge of Allan till you return. I shall refrain for your sake. I hope, dear, nothing will happen to check the happiness we were again enjoying.

May God bless you and with many fond and tender embraces, believe me with kind love, your ever affectionate husband,

Emile L'Angelier

P.S. I must see you before you go. Thursday night—midnight? Mimi, do not turn me aside with excuses.

She had folded the letter carefully, answered immediately.

Wednesday morning

My sweet dear Pet,

I am sorry that you should be vexed—believe nothing, sweet one, till I tell you myself—it is a report I am sorry about—but it has been six months bruited about. There is a rumour of the same kind about Bessie. Believe nothing till I tell you, sweet one of my heart. I love you, and you only.

Mrs. Baird asked me if it was Mama gave me the trinket you saw—and I told her no. Had she said Papa, I would have said yes.

My sweet love, I love you. We shall speak of our union when we meet. We shall be home about the 17th from Bridge of Allan. I wish, love, you could manage to remain in town till we come there. Could you, sweet, not wait for my sake? You might go the 20th or so. I would be so pleased if you can do this little thing to please me, my own beloved.

I have quarrelled with Christine so I cannot see you on Thursday night. I do not seek excuses; my desire to see you is great.

Please be patient, my dear Emile. I shall write you next week. Neither Minnoch nor his sisters go with us—only M., B., J., J., J., and I—P. on Sunday.

I have only been in Minnoch's house once and that was this week. I delivered a message because Mama could not go herself.

I will answer you all questions when we meet.

Believe me to be your own fond dear and loving

Mimi

P.S. Drop a note in the well Thursday night. I shall have a going-away note for you.

Thursday morning, Mary Jane Buchannon came to call, and Madeleine asked her to go for a walk. The two girls talked the whole way to Sauchiehall.

"Well, I promised you that you would be the first to know, didn't I?"

"Oh, Madeleine, congratulations. I had heard rumours. It is Mr. Minnoch, isn't it?"

"Yes."

"Is he very rich?"

Madeleine smiled. "He's a very fine architect."

"Like your Papa. How nice."

"Yes, and they get on so well. Oh, here is Currie's." She stopped in front of the apothecary. "I have to order some things. I won't be a minute—come in with me, will you?"

They entered and Madeleine went to the counter. The clerk came forwards. "What can I do for you, miss?"

"I wish some arsenic to kill rats."

"We recommend phosphorus paste for that."

"Oh, I tried that and it didn't work."

"Well, I'd rather give you something besides arsenic."

"Well, I would prefer arsenic. There would be no danger, as the family is going away and the townhouse will be quite empty."

"Except for the rats," Mary Jane said.

The clerk laughed. "You'd have to sign the scroll book and state your purpose. It's the law."

"I have no objection."

The clerk got out the book.

"What is the usual dose?" Madeleine said. "Would sixpence worth be sufficient?"

The clerk laughed. "Sixpence worth would kill a great many people."

Madeleine laughed. "I want to kill only a great many rats."

He made up sixpence worth: one ounce. He turned aside and wrote it in the government scroll book: *For rats*. Madeleine signed the entry log and he initialed it.

"Would you put it on our account, please?"

He nodded, handed her the package.

They left, laughing.

That night, she dropped her missive into the window well.

Dearest Emile,

I have just time to give you a line. I saw you at your window today, but you did not see me. We leave tomorrow before dawn.

God bless you and keep you,

Mimi

That Sunday, she had lain abed in the guest house at Bridge of Allan, listening to the wind and waves. Strange, she did not hate it now. It was almost soothing.

William came that afternoon from Glasgow, brought her a gold brooch in the shape of a rose. They took a long walk, over the hill to Dunblane.

When he departed, she sat down and wrote two letters.

Monday, March 9

Dearest Emile,

I hope you are well. I am very well, but it is such a cold

place—far colder than town. I have never been warm since I came here. I think we shall be home on Tuesday, the 17th, so I shall let you know, my own beloved pet, when we shall have a dear sweet interview.

I hope you will enjoy your visit here more than I am enjoying mine. You will find it so dull, no one here we know, and I don't fancy you will find any friends, as they are all strangers, and don't appear nice people.

I am longing to see you, my only dear love. I know your kindness will forgive me if I do not write you a longer letter, but we are just going to the train to meet friends from the north, so I shall conclude.

Ever with love, yours

Mimi

The second letter was to William:

Monday, March 9

My dearest William,

It is but fair, after your kindness to me, that I should write you a note. The day I part from friends I always feel sad. But to part from one I love as I do you makes me feel truly sad and dull. I do so wish you were here today. Our walk to Dunblane I shall ever remember with pleasure. That walk fixed a day on which we are to begin a new life—a life which I hope may be of happiness and duration to us both.

My aim through life shall be to please you and study you.

Accept my warmest kindest love and ever believe me to be yours with affection,

Madeleine

She lay in the dark that night, listening to the waves crashing against the rocky sea wall. In her mind, she saw the preacher standing with his black book, his red face, his picture of Hell. She closed her eyes, peered closer: The Black Book in which everything yet to happen was written. If only she could make out the words.

She fell asleep, dreaming of the flaming floor; the suit of burning clothes. She heard the flames crackling and roaring, saw the writhing, screaming child: Where was Father?

On Tuesday, March 17th, Madeleine arrived back in Glasgow. She wrote Emile, appointing Thursday night, the 19th—midnight.

On Wednesday, the 18th, she mailed the letter, went to Currie's, bought arsenic again and a bottle of frangipani, the "eternal perfume." She charged it all to the household account.

Normally, the post in Glasgow took one day—sometimes two. Her letter arrived at Emile's lodgings in two—just after he boarded the train for Bridge of Allan. It was forwarded the same afternoon by his fellow lodger, M. Thuau, a Frenchman, as Emile had arranged.

Madeleine spent Thursday, the 19th, sewing on a sampler for her hope chest. She felt poorly and Mama made her a bowl of milk toast. But she couldn't eat. She went back to her needlework, sang a nursery song:

> M is for Mignonette, sweet-scented weed
> Which Mary has raised in her garden from seed.
>
> N for Nemophilia, lovely of hue
> Like the sweet summer sky in its delicate blue. . . .

She waited that Thursday till the last wedge of the moon rose at nine past three. Emile did not come.

She sat at her desk with the chamber candle and wrote again.

> Why, my beloved, did you not come to me? Oh, beloved, are you ill? Come to me, sweet one. I waited and

waited for you, but you did not come. I shall wait again tomorrow night, same hour and arrangement. Do come, sweet love, my own dear love. Come, beloved, and clasp me to your heart. Come and we shall be happy.

Mimi

She marked the envelope *Immediate Delivery*, posted it as soon as the sun came up.

The letter was delivered at Mrs. Jenkins', 11 Franklin Place, at one thirty. It was forwarded to Bridge of Allan.

Saturday night, she climbed into bed when Janet did. Christine built up the fire. She and Janet sat up, watching the flames. Her little terrier, Albion, curled up on the hearth, watched the fire too.

Janet slept.

"Come to me, dog," she said, but the terrier turned his head away.

"So be it," she said.

When all was quiet above, she got up, took the packet of cocoa from the mantelpiece, went to the kitchen, got out a pot. As she scalded the milk, she dropped the powder into the pot, stirred vigorously. Then she put the pot on the back warming burner, went back to her room.

When the moon rose just past three thirty, she got up, took the pot from the stove, tilted it over the sink and let the brown liquid pour out.

On Sunday, there was no moon. Christine was home visiting her mother, armed with a small simmel cake pudding.

Madeleine went to Vespers at nine, prayed solemnly.

> . . . For if the blood of bulls and of goats and the ashes of an heifer sprinkling the unclean, sanctifieth to the purifying of the flesh: How much more shall the blood of Christ, who through the eternal Spirit offered himself without spot to

God, purge your conscience from dead works to serve the living God? . . .

After Vespers, she and Janet went downstairs. While they were putting on their nightgowns, Janet began to sing "Ring Around the Rosie."

"Don't," Madeleine said.

"Why not, Maddy?"

"It's an awful song."

"Why? I won't sleep till you tell me."

"It's a death song."

"'Ring Around the Rosie'?"

"Yes. Long ago, young children, when they first caught the plague, would have the rosiest of cheeks, and then, afterwards, when they burnt their bodies . . . those alive would press posies to their noses to hide the smell."

"Ughh."

"Yes, uggh, now come, I'll sing you 'Rock-a-Bye Baby.'"

"That's just as bad, with the baby falling. Besides, I'm too old for it."

"Then I shall sing you a church song."

"That would be nice."

"Rock of ages, cleft for me, Let me hide myself in thee. . . ."

Janet fell asleep just before ten. Madeleine waited.

As the stroke of twelve died, the cane stroked softly against the iron grill. She ran out of the room, ducked into the hall, listened for footsteps. It was pitch dark. Scarcely breathing, she tiptoed to the door, opened it a crack.

"Who's there?"

"The devil!" he whispered loudly.

"Emile!" She opened the door and pulled him in.

"Mimi, what is it?" he said.

"Shhhh . . ."

It was dark in the hall. She grasped for his hand, found it, guided it past the thin batiste of her nightdress to her breast.

He made a small noise in his throat.

"Are you well, dear?" she said.

"Oh, yes," he said. "If I wasn't before, I am now."

"I thought you'd forsaken me." She found his face, touched his lips with her fingers.

"What is it, Mimi?"

"Come, I'll tell you," she said.

"Is it safe?"

"I don't care."

"Mimi!"

"Don't be shocked."

He laughed. "Nothing you do shall ever shock me."

She tugged on his hand. "Yes, it's safe. And Christine is away."

They inched down the black hall, into Christine's room.

She woke the next morning to the smell of bacon frying. She could hear Mama's voice off down the hall. She opened her eyes.

She was in her own bed.

A dim memory of a dream lingered. She had been at Row again, a child again, and scared. A bird had got into the house, flown at her hair. Papa had flapped his long-tailed coat and the bird had hurled itself through an open window.

She blinked. The sun was already past the treetops. She had slept like a child. The day lay ahead of her, bright as a new penny.

TWENTY-SEVEN

At twelve noon on the tenth day, after seven hours of deliberation, the jury filed through the door.

Inglis held his breath, looked over at Madeleine. She tensed imperceptibly in her seat.

It was in God's hands now.

The usher closed the door of the jury box. The clerk walked to center stage, addressed the fifteen.

"Gentlemen, have you reached a verdict in this trial of solemn procedure?"

Lord Hope leant forwards.

"We have," the foreman said. Inglis noted that it was Mr. King, the writer.

"And what is your verdict?" the clerk said.

A vein on the foreman's head swelled. He swallowed and said, "We find the defendant of the first charge Not Guilty."

A murmur ran round the court. Inglis still held his breath.

The foreman looked across at the defence table, met Inglis's eyes briefly. "We find the defendant of the second charge Not Proven." He put his paper down on the rail, looked up at the high bench, almost smiled.

"And we find the defendant of the third and last charge: Not Proven."

The audience broke into a cheer. The jurors smiled. Madeleine began to tremble, but she remained poised, the one calm person in the room. Reporters were running to the hall.

Lord Hope rapped his gavel. "Will the prisoner stand?"

Madeleine rose gracefully, her hands folded before her.

"The jury has rendered its verdict," Lord Hope said. "You have been absolved of all charges. You are free to go."

Madeleine bowed.

She was led below, where she changed her dress of rich silk, put on a dark-grey travelling dress and a heavy veil.

Jack was waiting for her at the side door with a rented hackney coach. He whipped the horses to the train.

The train brought them to the station nearest Helensburgh, where their trap was waiting to take them to Row.

TWENTY-EIGHT

The trap had come between the grey rock posts, its paraffin lantern illuminating the moss. She watched the house loom up as the horses trotted up the drive beneath the canopy of elms. A dim light shone in the upstairs sitting room.

They emerged from the canopy, into the circular drive. Above, the night was starry.

"We're home," Jack said, taking up her bag.

She nodded, let him help her down.

She watched him walk off towards the barn, his strides long and sure. Then she turned the brass knob and pushed open the door.

Except for the moonlight reflecting on the pine floors, the hall was dark. She looked towards the stairs. The cut-glass prism drops of the chandeliers glowed dimly.

She set her bag down, stood waiting.

Footsteps sounded upstairs. A light flickered over the bannister. It was Papa.

He came down the stairs slowly, looked at her.

"So they sent you home?" His voice was flat.

"They chose to."

He nodded. "No one here is fooled." He came down the last step, past her, lifted the glass globe of the oil lamp, turned the key, held the chamber candle over.

She looked at him in the flickering light. "Papa, would you have rather they hanged me?"

"There might have been salvation that way. . . ."

"Only if I had repented."

"Yes. Repented."

"I asked God for freedom and he granted it."

"You asked the Devil."

"He, too, is a Prince of God . . . a messenger . . . an angel. . . ."

Her father lifted his hand to slap her. Her strong arm reached up, grabbed his hand.

"Madeleine, I'm . . ."

"No, Papa." She shook her head, smiled at him. "Don't you know that . . ."

"Know what?"

"If I did it, I did it for you, Papa."

"No!"

"I did what you wanted."

"No!" he said, his voice rising.

"Yes, Papa. You said he was not good enough for me. You said I must cast him out."

She saw the pain she had spread on his face. "Where's Mama?" she said softly.

"Sick . . . sick waiting to hear . . . sick when Jack went. . . ."

"You mean you did not send him?"

He shook his head.

Madeleine walked to the hall chest, lifted the star-etched lid. Inside, past toy soldiers and miniature doll people, past the cloth reader and the grey castle, she picked up the toy whip.

"He is in the barn, Papa," she said, handing him the whip. She walked past him, up the wide staircase, her bare hand on the mahogany bannister. She smelled the panada and catnip.

"Mama?" she whispered.

It was all right then. Mama would forgive.

"Maddy?" Mama said in a small voice. The room was dark, vaporous.

Madeleine made her way in the dark to the bed. Her

mother put out her hand. Madeleine held it. Her mother turned Madeleine's hand to her cheek, moved the hand.

"Mama, are you all right?"

"Yes, now. Did Jack get there in time?"

"You sent him, didn't you?"

"I sent him. But he wanted to."

Madeleine smiled. "Thank you, Mama."

They were silent.

"He will come round," her mother said, softly, after a moment.

Madeleine nodded in the dark. Yes, now, she supposed, he would. They were at liberty now—all of them—to do or to be anything. Except to be what they were before.

"Light the lamp, read to me?" her mother said, breaking the silence. Madeleine turned to the bedstand, fumbled for the matches, lit the wick.

"I have left my Bible . . ."

"Mine is under the pillow."

Madeleine reached down, pulled the black-covered book from beneath the scented pillow.

"What shall I read, Mama?"

"I have it marked, dear."

Madeleine opened to the crimson ribbon, nodded. She sat back in the rocking chair, began to read: *"Let us hear the conclusion of the whole matter: Fear God, and keep his commandments: for this is the whole duty of man. For God shall bring every work into judgment, with every secret thing, whether it be good, or whether it be evil."*

"Not that, dear." She reached over, touched Madeleine's hand, stroked it lightly. "Not that, dear, I meant the next book."

"Oh," Madeleine said, smiling.

Her mother lay back in her bed, closed her eyes.

"The Song of Solomon," Madeleine said. *"The song of songs, which is Solomon's. Let him kiss me with the kisses of his mouth: for thy love is better than wine. . . ."*

AFTERWORD

In Mount Hope, New York, seventy years later, Madeleine Smith, now Lena Wardle Sheehy, leaned forward in her chair.

"Do you ever think of Mr. L'Angelier, Mrs. Sheehy?" The young reporter sat on the porch bannister.

The old lady smiled. "No," she murmured.

"The newspapers of that day were unkind," the young man said. "They called you heartless. But you went on, you married, you raised a—"

"They were right," Mrs. Sheehy said in a still-strong voice.

"Right?" The young man shifted on the bannister.

"My heart is dead," the old lady said. "It has been stone-cold ever since I gave all the warmth in it to a scoundrel."